S. F. BARDAUS

MockingBard Press

Written by S. F. Bardaus. Cover Illustration by Alex McVey.
Cover design by A. W. Bardaus.

ISBN-13: 978-0-9967563-1-0   ISBN-10: 0-9967563-1-0

First Printing, 2015

Rose's warning to the reader

Old folk I know. I've seen my share. Though, none stirred me up as bad as the man whose story I'm about to put down on paper. He's in my care and I know I should respect him, but as I watch him every morning sleeping with his head under the pillow, snoring as loud as the walls can take it, I feel I might hate him more than I fear Judgment Day. Sooner or later, I'm afraid, I'm gonna do something to undo all my prayers and Sundays spent at church. Seeing as now I know what hell looks like, only the fear I might meet him again, or maybe even spend eternity together (for you can be sure that he won't go anywhere else after his death), prevents me from doing anything.

He calls himself a pirate, you see, and that wouldn't be a great deal, except he is crazier than ten of them put together.

He arrived out of the darkness on a stormy night a few years back. I was on then, the night shift, and I can see him even now: bottle of something in one hand, long, gnarled stick in the other, water raining from that white thatch of drenched hair. He blew open the doors, cracked a tile with his stick and declared solemnly that he needed "to drop anchor here for some time." Tired of riding the seas, he was, but not because he was old, no, no—he slapped poor Mary's, our night receptionist, behind to prove it—but because he needed to feel some hard dirt under his feet, to taste the dry wind, and befriend some curvaceous damsels – such as myself, he dared to add.

If it weren't for our rules and the rain, I would have sent the shameless fool on his way. Or recommended him down the street to the psychiatric ward.

He is crazy. Don't you doubt it a second! I could see it in his eyes the moment he stepped inside; and I do not know how he has fooled everyone else so well for so long. Though, should he keep his word and come through with some compensation for the time I have spent recording his blabber, I will take it all back, 'cause I was brought up in decency and taught to never bite the hand that feeds you.

But I must warn you: his words are as hard as his eyes and his mouth knows no limits. Catch him on a bad day, and God forgive you, your eyes are going to be stained with some of most unpleasant talk that ever soiled my ears. Half of it is not even in our language, thank heaven!

So I wash my hands. What follows are his words just as my honest ears heard them. If you are still going to pay money for an old man's spittle, and then find yourself offended or plainly insulted, don't say I didn't warn you—because I did.

Rose

Before I begin, a word with you

Many of the stories you have read in your life are stories about great men—men whose lives deserved to be set on paper. A great number of these stories have been written by simple people; people whose boldest adventure was to close their eyes and imagine themselves the main character, the nub of their pencil the most exotic thing they ever put in their mouth. Well, this is not one of those. For, yet being the same which I was born, I am not the one that I was, and far more than I should've become. And I can only thank Providence, for I don't like the taste of wood unless smoke runs through it, and when I close my eyes, I don't imagine. I remember.

I never intended to write. My words were, for the better part of my life, feared and made to be obeyed. If I ever put something on paper it was to bethink myself of the place I'd buried it. Now, sniffing the wretched edge of this life, it would be good to know that I leave behind me, besides one or two unwanted tears and a sterile tombstone, something that carries my name. I am the last true pirate alive, and I say, the greatest of them all. I refuse to quit as if I never lived, with no trace or evidence of my glorious days—just another ship that tried to leave a trail on the face of the sea.

I have lived, as I told you, a most uncommon life. More has happened to me in one day than most of you will experience in a lifetime. I have seen the sun rise and set many times over many seas and I have seen things in between that you will not believe. If I weren't as sad as I am and as decrepit as I feel, I would pull the gods out the sky and have a talk with them. Because, you see, no matter how extraordinary my life was, no matter what incredible things I did, I will still suffer the same ignoble fate as any of the world's nameless creatures, and where is the justice in that? I intend to have a word with the Captain when up-there. We are all the product of our actions, I say, and to even the ballast I think I should live at least a few decades more than the common mortal and stay of young appearance 'til the end. I shouldn't need to die at all, much less bone-crooked and skin-wrinkled—but if I must, I could as well check out with a tight complexion and a young maid in my arms. This is my kind of justice.

But, back to the business we have together you and I. You shall find that this story has no other purpose than to preserve my life for posterity and, of course, to show you how much better I was then than you are now. And you shall like it and be intrigued by it and remember my name. That's all I ask! Merely to live a bit longer, if only as a word on paper or an adventure in some fool's mind.

And if I forget some things, or if I make up some others, let it be - you'll never know it. There is only so much a head can bear for a mouth to say. But I will persevere! I know myself. There is nothing I've started and not finished. Beside one or two things I have yet to remember I've started. Even secured one of them dictator-phone to help me keep my word and make it easier on these hands. And, why not? Scribbling is for wonks and bookworms and hard is it for the hand that sparred for years with a dagger to toy around with such small trinketry as pens.

I have bestowed upon Rose, my nurse, the noble task of setting my words to paper, and for this she will be royally compensated. If you think I am a poor old man, then you are a bigger fool than Mrs. Schultz on the third floor, who tries to cheat me at my game and seduce me into telling her where my loot is. Ha! Smoke me dry and cuss my name! I shall never surrender to that old hag! Not even an un-fledged naiad, with tender lips and scintillating eyes, of no more than forty springs could tempt me to lose the fruit I have so sinned to acquire! I will defend my fortress with the price of my innocence. And I should lay a few on your back, you ingrate, for doubting my integrity, or my charac-ter—or the former of the later. But I shall do that later. Now I'm tired and can't find my medicine. Where did I put those scurvy pills?

Eh, well... What was I talking about? Let me rewind here... Can't find it. Cursed be the Machine and those who made it!... Ahh, here we go. About laying a few on your back? Oh, I might've spoken rashly; in fact I like readers and wish I had a few right here, right now. I would call them listeners not readers, but I would treat them as fair.

Well, now. You think you know pirates? You've read of them in your novels or seen them in your picture books? Fabrications! There are no stories told by the real men of the sea and should I stay silent, never will be. So bless your fortune and open a wide ear for, as incredible as it may seem, what I will tell you from now on is entirely true. You have my word.

CHAPTER 1

WHERE YOU SEE HOW A HERO IS FORGED

That being said, I'm famished. And thirsty. More thirsty than famished. I can't yarn on an empty stomach with a clear head. I haven't had my liquor for ages now. It is to wonder how long a man can last without it... By heavens, I'm turning into you, you half-breed son of a cur! And you, you can't spin my yarn. It's mine, not yours. Rose! Rose, can you hear me? Give me my liquor and you shall have your story. Rooose! Where the hell is she? May all the dogs in hell have a bite of you!

Now, where was I? Let me rewind here... Bless me, this pipe! It's what keeps my head afloat these days.

Hum... Hum... Ah! At the beginning? Blasphemy! I thought I was nearly done... Let's start before I finish....

And I was born. Pulled into this life, like most of you, naked and clueless. Abandoned and deceived, and in no position to argue the meaning of all that, I set about crying and kicking and leaking for I was sure the end had come. And like most of you, I persist in remaining as clueless as in the beginning, although, I hope to end it somewhat covered.

But, as I am trying to make it rather short than long, I shall simply say: "And I was born." There. The story has begun.

I happened in a little town atop of a rocky mountain a thousand miles away from the sea. It was one of them faraway countries you'd never hear of unless a calamity wiped out half the population or some lunatic grew a radish so large, a man and his mule can cool in its shade.

Unaware of your ignorance, or that of your forefathers—for at the time of my birth you were but an idea—worriless of tomorrow, worrisome of today, I grew up amongst promising radishes and impending calamities, and was oblivious to the rest. I was raised by my parents with help from the Almighty, and both parties worked hard to keep me of this world—one, likely, judging me too young to meet, the other having no choice—for more brainless and reckless a youth rarely survived to see hair on more spots than his head.

Things I have done in my tender years, should I be more liquored and of better humor, I would spin a tale or two about. Alas, my head is now clearer than a young maid's honor and my desire to entertain you, at this moment, matches the opposite of my wish to amuse her. Blame Rose for it all! That's what I do.

So we'll go straight from those years to the ones I spent in school, where I succeeded in getting myself expelled from every institution in the city, and from there to the time I left home to seek my fortune with nothing but ten crumpled bills guilted from my distraught mother, and landed myself in a small German town on the wet banks of the Rhine.

That is where all it began. Had it been anywhere else, this story could be now that of a—a worthy miner, or a chicken farmer, or a famous criminal, or—God forbid!—even a teacher. This last choice would be most hurtful, for you must know that I was as fond of school as a sailor is of a gap in his hull…though, had I set foot in a country in-habited solely by young student maids with no mentor and without prospects—forgive me!—a teacher I would be and never complain. Alas, Germany it was and not the young maidens! My sorrow matches yours.

So says an old proverb, "He who steals an egg today, tomorrow steals an ox." Well, a penniless man must stay either honest or fed, I say, and I—owning more pockets than coins—chose food, since it is known that honesty can eventually be bought back. Now of course I could've chosen to work for my food, but the problem with work is that first you must work, then you get paid, and just after that you can eat—and if you're too hungry to follow through, I ask, what do you do? When you loot for a meal, you eat it right there; what you owe gets put on your tab and later you pay—much later. My hunger was such that I opened my tab that very day and over the years I fear it has grown to the size of a healthy book much like the Bible (though some-what less holy).

Once I had filled my stomach, I longed for a coat, and once I was clothed, I desired to fill its pockets, and once I did that, well, I thought of it as a sport. Owing to my light feet and my slender body, I was soon quite a successful thief. The most successful one in those parts I'd like to think, though I'm not sure anyone else saw it that way.

As fate would have it—for otherwise I would probably be in such a sad state as you, reading a story instead of telling one—one day I was caught. Not by the law, but by something much, much worse. Something that resembled a man, but didn't deserve the name. I have seen many of them wretches in my time; hell, I've slain more than I can count. Sent them back where they came from. But Ruzban was my first, and it just so happens, one of the nastiest. The scare I lived through that night owes a great deal to his appearance. But I suppose I must tell you how it happened first:

It was one of those days towards the end of the summer when the fruit weighs ripe on branches and the leaves begin to wonder. The mid-afternoon hunger had caught up with me as I was returning from an adventure, let's call it that since it concerns not our present story, in the old part of town and which had ended with a long chase involving a pack of mouth-foaming dogs and my behind. Fortunately, a tall fence had saved them a bigger disappointment as there wasn't enough of it—my behind that is, for all of them to go around. So, buttocks unscathed, I drifted into a local store, owned by a Turk named Hassan, one of few places where I could procure packed meats, and cheeses, and the occasional sweets. When I say procure I mean steal, and when I say occasional I mean daily. Old Hassan was one of those trusting storeowners who didn't think to question your integrity as long as you bought something; and, as always, I was planning to buy a bottle of fizz, for it was cheap and too large to fit inside my clothes.

So there I am in the back of the store, filling my pockets with salamis and cheeses when along comes Hassan, all red and holding a long wooden cane in his hand. He says something about mirrors and when I raise my eyes I see that the treacherous Turk has installed them all over the store! As I stood there staring at myself from twelve different directions, he laid one on my back with the conviction of a man that had been cheated too many times and with the might of one decided to right the wrong sooner than later. I judged it unnecessary to try to deny the crime, or to complain, or even to wait for the second blow that was coming even more vengeful than the first, for old Hassan was now oiled up and ready to sell some justice, and made for the door rather hastily, my meal pouring from my many pockets. On the way my arm caught on the edge of a case of ale, pulling it down. This accident, which at the time I considered fortunate, as it stopped the madman from following me, today upsets me the most, for though I prefer hard liquor, at this moment I would sell my nurse and her clique for one of them bottles of sweet golden liquid.

But follow the man and not his goose. I saw the exit and knew my salvation lay just one step away. Hassan knew too and cursed at me in his maternal tongue—which seemed a very fast one—but abandoned the chase on grounds of his lying flat on his stomach in the debris of what was once fine August beer in its bottles. I turned around and made faces at him and mocked him a bit. My way of bidding farewell, for I knew I would never step foot in his store again. I had no idea, though, how right I was! As I leapt outside I found myself wedged between the sidewalk and a gigantic palm. Its long, warm fingers draped over my ears. I tried to move, to turn around, to turn my head, to open my mouth. In vain. The palm pulled back and two hands wrapped themselves around my waist, lifting me straight into the air. I raised inquiring eyes to see who could own such fine fleshy instruments, only to find my view obscured by a large set of gold teeth as brilliant as the almighty sun. Their owner carried me, as you would carry a child that had spoiled itself, into the street where he unceremoniously threw me into the trunk of a fashionable automobile, parked on the curb. As I squeezed between two spare tires, I thought to myself that there was nothing at all fashionable about that trunk. I squirmed like a worm in a can and kicked and punched the hood until I realized that I was the only one there who could feel the pain, and decided to restrain myself.

What seemed like centuries later, the car stopped, door opened; feet stepped, clench unclenched, and the hood rose. The fresh air slapped my face like cold water. It was dark outside and all I could see against the starry black canvas was the set of bright golden teeth, now married to a pair of ivory eyes squinting at me with suspicious friendliness. A superhuman force lifted me out of the trunk and held me up as I, in my own rights as a kidnapped man, treaded the air with feet going miles a minute. I soon gave up and lifeless lay in his hands not unlike a puppet in his master's. As I was catching my breath, a voice which seemed to drift on a whiff of air from another realm, whispered softly, "Do you know what a eunuch is, child?"

Thorns grew up and down my spine. Had the wind spoken? Had I dreamed it?

But then it chortled. Lightly. Gently. Like a sated hyena. "Do you wish to become one?" it asked.

I raised terrified eyes to the behemoth. I hadn't seen

his lips moving, but the fact that he was half-naked and contemplated me joyously offered no comfort. His head was hairless and his gigantic bust bulged at my eye level, its smooth, oily skin casting back the light of the stars like clear calm water. Half his chest was wider than my body and was covered in scribbles like ancient runes, as was his arm, which was certainly thicker than my head. He was wearing light pants of coarse fabric that swished against the straps of two boat-like sandals. Catching the gleam of the dagger jutting from a monstrous sheath attached to his leg, I grew softer than a wet cloth. Was I going to become a lady?

This might not be that bad, you say; gals are in many ways better off than us men. I say, I wish you were here so I could slap you one! I loved the dames, and still do; I loved them with all my means and hoped they'd love me back—becoming one of them, well... I'd never thought of that. On the other hand, you say, many a man with larger heads than mine or yours swear that all of mankind's troubles come from that which hangs not far from his derrière, and that the loss of it would make the man a peaceful animal. Which I wouldn't dispute, had it ever been proved. But, since none of them thinkerlings ever dared to experiment with the theory, we'll never know—the use a philosopher makes of his stones in the real world is more theoretical than practical. And, why are we having this discussion? Maybe you should stop interrupting and listen to the story! I wasn't scheming to enslave the world; I was just a hungry young man whose plans involved, in one way or another, his manhood. You youngsters out there know what I am talking about!

So, I decided I must be dreaming! I was born such a lad who thinks that question should be the last a man should inquire of another man, therefore it just wasn't possible! But, implacable as fate, it spoke again, "You are not dreaming," it hissed. "I shall make you one tonight." Ahh! How I wiggled and squirmed when I realized that it was indeed a serious matter! If you have ever been kidnapped and roughed up, held close by a half-naked, full-sized giant in the dead of night and the middle of nowhere, contemplating ladyship, then you know how I felt. The speed my feet reached! Sparks would have flown had the giant dropped me to the gravel. But he held me there, effortless and patient, until I finally tired, then put me down and spun me around, his hand wrapped around my panting neck.

I could see we were on the still side of a forsaken road in a valley between two hills. The silence was such that it almost forbade disturbing. Not a frog's croak or the chirp of a cricket, not a leaf wrestling with the wind. It seemed as if everything, even the moon, now hidden behind the edge of a lurid, sharp cliff, was afraid of the behemoth at my back. Unaware of all this, smiling like a giant, golden-toothed cherub in the eerie half-light, he stood gazing down the expanse of the road, exuding an inner peace that was having just the opposite effect on me. I stared after him, while inside my brain fear ate away at my wits.

Finally, when I felt like I could take it no more, my nose picked up the scent of a lecherous perfume, sweet and heavy. The kind used on corpses that have spent too much time above ground. But, I hadn't time to think twice about it because, from nowhere and before I could even blink, a hand jutted out and clasped my nose in an iron grip. I froze. It came from the same side with the hand that was holding my neck. In a flash I thought the giant grew another arm!

"This nose… what a pleasant surprise!" the voice rasped.

It has been many years since, many more than you can count, but how could anyone forget something like this? My nose, my nose was inside someone's palm, and I gasping for air like a fish pulled out of the sea. Have I told you about my nose? Then you know it's quite the memorable thing! But it didn't deserve this treatment.

Without letting go of it, the arm stretched and a person came into view. That should've relieved me for it proved I wasn't in the hands of the unnatural. It didn't.

Now, I'm looking for my words here to describe you the man that showed up next, because if I can get you half as scared as I was, you'd surely wet yourself. Still holding onto my sniffer he came around and at first I couldn't see him, "Lucky, lucky, lucky!" I heard. "This nose…" He vigorously yanked up, down and sideways as if he wanted to rip the thing out its damned roots. "Mmh, just what I need!" He gave it a healthy squeeze and a few more yanks, then released me and tapped on the trunk of the car. "I'm already in love. Set him up here, Babar."

Babar, as that seemed to be the name of the smiling beast, hoisted me up by the scruff of the neck and dropped me on the trunk. The other man pushed him aside and came closer. The moon chose exactly this moment to peek from behind the hill. He was of medium height, thin as a skeleton, covered in silky robes, and at first my eyes dawdled on a thin strand of hair gathered in a tail that started from the top of his head. But it is what I saw below that scalp that froze the blood in my veins! Each side of his face was marked by two deep scars that cut down from his forehead, splitting his eyebrows in half. Below the eyes they continued, running along a nose like the beak of a vulture through the middle of his cheeks all the way to the jaw. And this was not even the most horrific thing I saw! His lips were! Even in the dim light I could see that they were missing, replaced by two horrible irregular furrows where the flesh had scarred in uneven crumples. I think he was smiling because those dry shriveled folds were drawing a sinuous line across his face. At the left corner, small, sharp teeth were showing through.

"I see you like it," he chuckled and those thick brows shifted independently of each other looking in fact as if he had four of them. Even his lips, or what was there in their absence, moved in a strange way and at first I didn't understand what he was saying. He laughed, "Are you listening, child? You look like you've seen the devil." He laughed again and clicked his tongue. The giant reached down to pull an immense dagger from a sheath on his leg. In my hand, it would've been a sword. Without losing one carat of his smile, he swung his arm and planted the knife in the trunk of the automobile between my very legs not one inch from the inseam of my knickers. And everything else those very knickers were holding.

"My name is Ruzban," the lipless mouth grinned. "This here is my servant, Babar." Another click. Babar gave the knife a lazy trust, splitting the metal like cardboard, and I could feel the fibers of my trousers twang against the blade. I was frozen in a state of terror, my brain still incredulous of the twisted creature its eyes were glued onto.

"Do we have your attention now?" Ruzban asked.

I said nothing. The strange movements of those mutilated lips; clear, unchopped words coming out from behind them; the sharp cold, steel pinned against my dear parts… This was surely a most fascinating dream! The sharp, cold steel pinned against my dear parts… I saw an inhuman glint in his eyes and the mouth opening for another click. …cold steel, really cold steel! I nodded frantically. Maybe I wasn't too sure this was a dream after all. "Good. I wish I could hurt you first, but I don't think you will be able to do what I want of you tonight. Did you think you could?"

None of what he was saying made sense to me, but when I saw he was expecting an answer I quickly acquiesced. "Are you sure?" I realized my mistake and shook my head violently.

"All right, my little friend," he said, "I'll let you be a boy for now and if you help me, I may, hmm, smile, hmm, kindly upon you, but if you betray me… I'll make you a girl. Do we have an understanding?"

"Yes," I let out.

"I want you to get me something from the house on that hill." He was pointing to the hill on my left. "Do you think you could?"

I nodded.

"Good, I knew I could trust you." He cocked his head, touched my face with his hand, ran a twiggy finger on the edge of my nose, got closer to my ear and huffed a putrid waft of air, "Now that we are friends, you wouldn't think to betray my trust, would you?"

I swallowed a knot and answered as confidently as possible, "No, no, sir. I can do it no problem."

The inside brows moved down while the outside ones went up, his stare was riveted to my face, "You said you wanted to keep all of your parts, my new friend?"

I felt a glow of sincerity wash over me as I replied with a breathless, "yes, yes" for I really, really did.

"Good. Because, you see, Babar is missing his, and should you think to betray me…hmm, he will catch you, cut them off, and feed them to you one by one."

At these words, the mountain of a man wrenched his blade out of the trunk with a screech and waved it before my eyes, grinning as if he truly believed that was the best thing that could happen to me.

And there, my beauties, would have ended your dreams of meeting the man of your yearnings, and lads, the hero of your study!

Chapter 2

Where I polish what I forged

Visiting was she? And there she goes calling me a mean old man! Old? Me? Ha! A wee one, not taller than my knees! Just like them lasses, ever wrong. To prove it, her mother comes quickly, wipes her tears and says, "He's just sad honey, that's all." Sad? Me? Ha! If she wasn't so comely she'd've tasted my wrath! Or my stick. I think both. But, I'm always nice to them wenches. No matter how young or old… And to you Rose, my warden from hell…. I'll get my hands on a bottle one of these days, then we'll see… I can almost taste it!

But as I was saying, I'm always nice. Not sad, not old. Just better. Don't like children more than any of you out there. As for the wee one, I only pulled my cheeks apart with my fingers, stuck my tongue out and crossed my eyes over my nose. You know, a funny face. She didn't giggle as any normal child would, instead, she made an even funnier one and started bawling, spewing tears and spit like there was a fire to put out. Of course, I laughed. Wasn't I supposed to? And she goes and calls me sad. That will teach me to be nice!

A pirate is a fragile thing, I tell you. People judge you, people fight back. It's a lot of work.

So, where was I last night? In my bed, you say? Ha…

The story goes, in order to keep my stones, I was to steal something. Steal what, you might ask?… A photograph! There I go, out and telling it before I even found it out myself. A mixed up thing, this narrating business, I tell you.

"…a photograph," Ruzban said, "from a… hmm… woman. But the house is empty now," he added.

I stared. I was expecting some exotic and unobtainable treasure that required the skill of a master—which naturally, I thought I was. A photograph? And nobody home? If this were your story, I wouldn't believe it. All the misery I'd been put through, for a photo? I couldn't make sense of it. I would've done it for a warm meal, which, by the way, I hadn't had since home.

After providing the whereabouts of the picture and a reminder of what would happen to me should I come out without it, Ruzban handed me a lantern and ordered us to leave. Babar pointed to the path and we took to it.

I couldn't help but admire the mountain of a man. His skin was chestnut, tight and smooth like that of a baby. He had one big fleshy nose and a pair of stretched, plump lips that seemed to have been molded into an eternally, sincere—yet to me very confusing—grin. His eyebrows rose and ducked with each stride he took, like thick black caterpillars, while, in the moonlight, the surreal glow of his mouth reminded me of those genies awakened from a lamp, ready to grant you three wishes. He moved with the easiness of a cat sliding soundlessly through the trees. He was indeed a giant, easily over six and a half feet tall, blanketed in layer upon layer of thick muscle that surged and eased, undulating with every step in a mesmerizing dance. The sight of his dagger curbed somewhat the joy I had felt at leaving his master, for I knew I couldn't outrun him and was pretty sure that with one stroke he could slice me in half.

We soon found ourselves in an apple orchard. The trees were heavy with the fruit, and from time to time, here and there, one would fall to the ground with a thud that shattered the deep silence, making my heart quiver and giving my legs a jolt in the opposite direction. Slowly, we made our way to the top of the hill.

The trees ended a hundred feet from the back of an imposing building. Its sharp edges, its dark silhouette looming over the treetops populated my mind with barbaric temples and images of ancient sacrificial rites. There were two levels, with thick columns at each corner. The tall windows were covered with shutters, and no light whatsoever filtered from inside. There was no fence or garden of any kind around it, just short grass; its dew scintillated in the light of a moon that was laughing at us from just above the chimney.

Babar turned to the left, keeping to the shade of the trees, which was hard because he was taller than many of them. He bent his back and beckoned to me and I saw that he was taking us to the front. Arriving at the corner, he slipped out of the shade and, with small, fast steps, slid to the foot of the stairs where he squatted down. I followed in the same way. He turned to me and put his index finger over his lips, then smiled. I wondered why the need to keep quiet, since no one was supposed to be home, but I nodded and smiled back. What else could have I done?

Was he supposed to wait for me outside the house or was he to go back down to the road? Ruzban had said that he would wait at the car, but didn't give Babar any orders. And afterward, what? Would they really let me go?

It crossed my mind that perhaps the object was a bit of evidence, proof of some long-lost royalty or other such conspiracy. I had read once in a book that it was possible. Royalties get lost all the time. Especially when helped by a shifty-eyed, back-scheming relative. And if this was the case, I figured I'd be the feller who is discarded, probably on the same line that he was introduced, before you even find out his name. The helping character, I think they call it. It saddened me because up till then I seemed to have been the main character of my life and had some control over it. Now I was just a pawn.

Agile as a monkey, Babar climbed the stairs and, arriving in front of the door, pulled something out of one of his pockets and went to work on the locks. There were three, but one by one they clicked affirmatively to the twitching of his tool. My last chance would be a bar or chain on the inside, I thought, but the gods were favoring the genie, for the massive door finally creaked open. He caught it and pulled it slightly up to stop the noise, then waved me inside.

With my heart at the bottom of the sea, I gripped my lantern to stifle its rattling and stepped into the darkness. The door pulled behind me. I could see nothing and was tempted to light the wick. Instead, I waited for my eyes to settle in, all the while listening at the door to hear Babar's leaving. For what seemed an eternity I neither moved, nor even breathed. Then, as I heard no sound from outside, I carefully turned around, pulled the door open again, and peeked out into the night. If he hadn't been there, I would've escaped, and you would have no story. But, alas, there he was, a few steps down, eyes and teeth glowing in the moonlight. I closed the door again and breathed deeply. No choice but to go forward. Comforting thoughts came into my mind, as often happens to the condemned man not yet facing his end. Maybe I would be fine. Maybe the cat is not as black as it looks. I was a thief, no? And what do thieves do? They steal. I was so close… Just a few steps more. Take the cursed picture. Give it to him. Perhaps outrun him on the way back. If he had it maybe he wouldn't follow me… Then again, maybe he would, and if I am caught… I reached out a hand to the wall to steady myself. You see the predicament I was in, then, my beauties?

I turned around to face the darkness, concentrating hard to keep from shivering with every bone in my body. The wooden floor creaked warningly under my first step and my heart stopped right there. I listened. No sounds whatsoever came from inside the house. On tiptoe, I put myself another step closer to the wall. The floor there moaned slightly but seemed to forgive my weight. I crept in this fashion, feeling my way down the hall. I passed the study on the left and the room on the right, just as Ruzban had foretold, and safely arrived before the two large doors at the end of the hall. *Halfway there,* I thought. Of course I was wrong, but there was no one to correct me. By now, my eyes had gotten used to the darkness and I could see a set of handles.

I stopped, breathed deeply, genuflected hurriedly and caught one of them. I pulled up to stifle the noise as I had seen Babar do, then pushed it down, praying that the door wouldn't be locked. Ruzban had said it wouldn't. But he also said I'd be missing bits if I returned empty handed, so I didn't think that such a small thing as a lock would qualify as a deal-breaker.

The door gave way to my gentle pressure and my heart fluttered in my chest. I leaned against and it opened just enough for a head to fit. I bit my lip and put mine inside.

It was a large room. The light of the moon filtered shyly through crannies in the window blinds and relieved some of my tension: I shouldn't need the lantern after all. I stepped inside ever so sheepishly. There were windows on two walls, telling me this was a corner room. To my left, stood some tall furniture and a desk beneath one of the windows. The fireplace loomed in the shadows of the far right. I was to cross the room if I wanted to get to it.

As I glanced toward the place I was to direct myself, I observed in the center of the room a large dark structure with poles on each of its four corners. I froze in horror, realizing it was one of those canopy beds. This was a bedroom!

I hesitated, not knowing what to do. It was one thing to steal from a house, another to steal from a bedroom. If the woman was there? I didn't put lying past Ruzban. Poor old thing, if she was of weak heart she might have a shock waking to a stranger hovering in the shadows. Was she there? If she was, she was certainly not snoring or breathing heavily, because I could not hear the faintest noise in the dead silence. Perhaps she had heard me and now was holding her breath. Or maybe she wasn't home, after all. Tormented at first, then relieved by these later thoughts, instead of keeping to the wall, I stepped toward the center. I had to know if she was there. Don't ask me why. I wasn't the wisest of lads.

The floor was healthier in this room and I was able to move soundlessly. I reached the head of the bed and saw that it was empty. Untouched. Relieved, I let out a large quantity of air I hadn't known I was holding. Around the bed I went quicker and more carelessly, until I stood before the fireplace. *Just get it and get out*, I thought. Optimism had caught up with me and I was planning afterward to try sliding out one of the windows. Maybe, I could outsmart the grinning demon.

I peered at the fireplace in the murky light, and indeed, as foretold, there was a mantel. I rose to my toes for it was higher than my head, and looked for a frame, or something that could hold a photograph. Fate was smiling on me again. Perhaps even laughing. For there were two such things there.

But, I've always been a resourceful lad, known to have carried in many instances more than one thing in my hands at a time. I also felt that I wasn't paid—if I can say that—to solve mysteries; so I resolved to take 'em both and be done with it. Then I'd take the window out, and if the giant gave chase, just pitch them left and right to distract him. That was the plan and I was proud of it. It seemed top-notch. And probably would've worked too. But Fate is one of them females, and they mostly never agree with the plans I make.

As I reached out to take hold of the loot, I heard a loud noise behind me. I spun and fumbled with the lighter until the lantern was lit. The rays bounced out and, for the second time that night, my eyes fell on something horrible, not two feet from my face; something like a devil, yet more frightening. It had only one eye and an abominable expression. Its lips were curled back and the lonely eyeball blazed a hole right through my very soul. I screamed but my scream died away under the frightful howl released by the demon, and I felt a heavy, sharp pain rain down from the top of my skull and into the roots of my teeth. Relieved, and, with your permission, seeing more stars than are there in the sky, I promptly dived into a deep sleep. Undoubtedly, it was the best thing that had happened so far.

But no good thing lasts forever. When finally I recovered my senses, I wished I hadn't. My head throbbed, but as I found myself tied, I couldn't check for damage. I was sitting on the floor with my arms spread, strapped to the poles of the bed. The light of my former lantern was projecting into my eyes, manned by some unseen hand. As my head cleared I became aware of an extremely unpleasant voice saying, "…I've been waiting a long time for you. *Für alle Hunde in der Hölle,*[1] now talk!" The voice rasped like two millstones scraping along one another. A strong current of alcohol and tobacco wafted into my nostrils. I moaned and tried to move my head away from the beam, but the slap of a heavy hand brought it back into the light.

"You move when I tell you, you *hurensohn.*[2] Who sent you? Talk, or by God I'll drag it out of you one fingernail at a time!"

1 • *for all the dogs in hell*
2 • *son of a whore*

"Nuahhh!" I cried, for I remembered the horror I'd seen before blacking out, then managed, "Anything! I'll tell you anything!"

"You will?" the voice seemed disconcerted. "What's this all about, you deceitful bastard? No one's ever talked." The blade of a knife slowly split the beam of light before descending under my chin and onto my throat.

I felt its chill on my skin and I, I'm not proud to say, released the prettiest whimper than the world has yet to hear.

"Now they're sending children, phew! Where's your weapon, boy?" the voice asked.

The merciless light was hot and blinding. "What weapon?"

"Are you trying to make a fool of me?" the knife pushed deeper into my skin. "I know you have a weapon. God himself wouldn't dare face me without some sort of protection."

"Please," I wept. "I don't know what you mean. I don't have anything."

"Well, I didn't find one on you, but you could've hid it somewhere."

"I had only the lantern."

"I'm holding the lantern," barked the voice. "What are you doing here?"

"They sent me to steal a photograph. Please…"

"Stop your bawling!" it ordered. "What photograph? Who sent you?"

"They, Ruzban and Babar. A photograph from the mantel."

"And you expect me to believe that?" it said.

"It's not a lie! Please, Ruzban, he's in the car! In the valley! Babar is outside the door," I was spitting the words out faster than a gun does bullets. "I didn't want to! I swear to you! But he gave me no choice. He… he threatened…he asked me if I…he would have…"

I began to babble as panic swirled through my head.

"What?" it barked.

"My…my…chop off my…!" I blurted, attempting to nod in the general direction of my pants.

"Consider it done," the voice said. The head rose up just behind the curtain of the light. "Somebody's outside my door, heh? Wait here!"

It wasn't as if I could've done anything else. The light turned off and I heard the heavy cock of a shotgun as a massive shadow left the room, leaving me to contemplate my miserable fate. A moment later it returned and with it the blinding light.

"There is nobody outside."

"He was there," I said. "Ruzban said to meet at the car. But I checked—after he let me in, I opened the door and he was still there…"

"Shut your trap boy and answer my questions! Where is the car in the valley?"

"I don't know; it was between the hills."

The creature seemed to muse a while over my answer, then it lowered itself towards where I was sitting and a gruesome head interposed itself between me and the light.

As I said before, it had only one eye, the other covered by a black patch. The valid eye was unexpectedly blue, and large, and blood-shot, and around it skin shirred in hundreds of little wrinkles that made it look like a trap for unsuspecting little boys such as myself. Long oily hair from which time has nibbled away the color partially covered its forehead, yet in the half-light, the face itself appeared rotten, as if a one-eyed mummy had been mystically revived and was now glaring at me. The nose was thick and squat and it breathed with a powerful blow that raised in my mind the image of a cornered boar. The mouth, with lips the color of eggplant, curved down in a wicked arc and was chewing the butt of a cigar. Through all these horrors, and in a state of shock, I suddenly realized that, despite the presence of an honest moustache, it was the face of a woman.

"If you lied to me boy…" she growled and blew a cloud of smoke and liquor in my face, "if you lied to me, I will kill you and bury you beneath my trees just as I did with all the others."

With these words she rose and, carrying the shotgun and my lantern, left the room in quick steps, surrendering me to the dark and my ropes.

Kill? Bury? Others? Words I don't like unless I'm the one saying them. Or I'm fighting, or have a treasure in sight. That's about it! At the time none of these good things were happening to me so I just hung there, like a thief on a cross. Where was the glory and riches I had dreamed of? For you should know that I had great dreams when I left home. And, as I never—to this day, I say—learned better, they all involved thievery. But now, caught in my own deception, I was to die a terrible death at the young age other wiser lads begin to enjoy life. Madly, I began to struggle with my ties. But my hands were too far apart, and as I was sitting rather than standing, pulling on the ropes didn't do any good. The massive bed wouldn't budge an inch. Was it nailed into place? I tried to twist, twirl, put one leg around my neck... at some point I was sitting on my head. Nothing worked. On the cusp of a quarter hour my only accomplishment was that I had drained myself of strength and moisture—the latter soaking my clothes; the former, floating somewhere in the air—yet my ties were now tighter than before and were cutting deep into my arms. I lay defeated when I heard heavy steps approaching. She stood in front of me looming darker than the night.

"There is no car in the valley, boy. You've lied to me and sealed your fate!" I saw that she was wearing heavy military grade boots before the light hit my eyes and blinded me once again. "What do you have to say for yourself?"

"I don't know," I muttered defeated.

There was a pause. Then she grunted heavily, displeased. "How did you come to be in my house, boy?"

I gave her a summary of the affair—how I was just a petty thief and not even a very good one, how I had been kidnapped and forced to enter her house by a madman and his giant.

"Phew!" she spat, interrupting me as I got to the bit about Babar dangling me above the ground. "That's a fine tale you're telling, my boy. But I'm tired of tales. There's nothing in them for me anymore."

She circled me with deliberate steps as a cat does the mouse. I realized with horror that she had made up her mind. She went to the windows and pulled up the blinds. I could see the moon, full as a pearl and probably my last. She, my captor, turned herself to the glass. "I can't let you leave, my boy. God forgive me. If it's not you, it will be me and I'm not ready, not yet. For now, I'd rather be a monster than a corpse," she said. Her voice had grown softer.

Then she straightened her back and spun around hitching the shotgun to her hip and cocking it in one fluid motion. "Say your prayers, boy…"

"Y-y-you h-have to f-f-find him!" I cried, staring death in its two-barreled face. "Can't miss him! Ruzban, his face! It's all but gone. And its lips…"

"What did you say?! What about…" she bellowed down at me, and the gust of her rancid air closed my mouth on my behalf. With dangerous quiet she hissed, "His lips??"

Incapable of speech, as the shotgun had snuck un-steadily to rest against my nose, I simply stared up at her with what I hoped was a very truthful expression.

"What about his lips?" she whispered as my heart thud-ded in my ears.

"They're badly cut," I moaned from underneath the barrel.

"Like someone took a pair of scissors to them?" she prodded.

"I… I guess? He said his name was Ruzban."

She slowly retracted the gun and let it fall limply to her side. "He never told me his name. But I know him well…" she trailed off, losing herself in thought.

I kept silent, contemplating a different bearing. My

future. I couldn't find a thing that I liked. Between the loss of my manhood or my life, it was hard to choose.

She suddenly set the light on the floor, moved back a step, and stood up. "You…you, my boy," she said, "How did you know about that man? Ha! If it's really him that sent you, we both know what he sent you for. Out with it. This time, the truth. Why are you here?"

My mouth had gone as dry as pumice. "…a photograph," I rasped.

"Again with the photograph!" she boomed. "What a child! Don't you want to die like a man?"

"The photograph… on the mantel, he said…"

Her fist hit the board next to my head. Hard. I heard it split.

"Which photograph?" She picked them up and shoved them in my face, "This one? Or this one? There are two here. At least get your story straight! Why would you want a worthless picture? Which one should I bury with you? Both? They mean *nothing* to me."

My vision was blurred, but the light was now on the floor and, as she moved them toward me at a slight angle, I caught sight of a figure behind the glass of one of the frames. I felt like knew that face.

"Uhh…" I said, my eyes snapping to her face. But she was frozen. She turned the pictures around and watched them for long seconds, gun resting in her elbow, legs apart, like a frozen grim reaper awakening to deliver damnation. I closed my eyes, for the wait was more unbearable than what was to follow and I promised God right there that I would build a church and become a monk should I escape with my life from the place. Over the years, I think I owe Him more churches than hairs I have in my beard, and if He keeps an honest tab, I'll tell you now—I fear meeting Him.

And I waited. And prayed. And waited.

I finally opened an eye and found that she was still there. Unmoved. The silence was such that I didn't even hear her breathing.

"Für alle Hunde in der Hölle," she said at last in a thick whisper. "Who are you?"

She slowly lowered herself to my level and caught my hair, turning my face toward the light of the moon. It was still as beautiful as any I will ever see. Then she caught me by the nose and pulled hard. It was painful, but I was getting used to it. Anyway, I welcomed the pain. Meant I was still of this world.

"Who are you?" she asked again, but her voice was more of a murmur now.

She didn't wait for my answer; she stood up, and rushing, almost running, went and turned on the light. Four lamps in the room lit at once, blinding me for a moment. I closed my eyes as she came thudding back.

"Mein Gott!" she rasped, "I had forgotten that face…"

I opened my eyes, both fearful and hopeful at once. She drew out the knife, sending a fresh wave of panic through my body, but used it cut my ropes. Relieved and bewildered, I rubbed my arms. I stood up shaking, and took a better look at her while she, herself, was studying me. She was as tall as I and stout-built. Every feature I have described to you yet was still true—for a more daunting powerful being I have never laid eyes on. Ruzban had been nasty and chilling and frightening, yes, but he compared to this woman as a thunderstorm compares to a hurricane, as a swampy marsh to the craggy mountain looming above it. She had only one eye, the other covered by a black velvet patch. But what an eye! Oh, but what eye! More penetrating than a red-hot spear, more adamant than a hunting lion's, more unforgiving than the Devil's! Over the years, I have looked upon a million pairs, I have made most of them drop beneath my gaze, but I could never argue that eye. Now, it was dissecting me like an insect.

"You…" she said.

Silent I remained, and submissive.

"Here!" she finally said, handing me one of the pictures.

I took it. It was the portrait of a man and I was right to think that I'd seen it before. For there, my worthless friend, there in that photo, dusty and gray and aged by time, looking back at me, stood the face of a man with eyes that could've been mine, wearing a nose and a mouth that, should you replace them with the ones from my face, would still be the ones I carry to this day.

I know that I mumbled something, but inside me time stood still. The frame felt weightless in my hands. Too many things in one short night. Should the same events catch me now, I doubt my heart would take it. There was no mistake; even disregarding the eyes and mouth, the nose was more evidence that anyone would need.

I don't know if I have told you about my nose… You

should see the thing! It's unmistakable, unbounded. It's fearsome. It's like a work of art. Or a jab in the eye. No matter where I go (unless I walk backwards, of course), it barges in a few seconds before me, proudly trumpeting my arrival.

And there was my very nose poking back at me from the behind the glass. The man in the photo was…*me?*

"It's been so long," she said.

"What…? What…?" I asked, for better words I couldn't find.

"My husband," she replied as she slowly went around and sat on the bed. "Dead now."

Had I been a man in his right mind, I would've taken this opportunity to run away, but I wasn't. I was a stupefied boy with a large nose starring dumbfounded at a photograph of himself.

"But…how…?" I heard myself stuttering.

She shook her head, "I don't know," she said. "But there is a connection somewhere."

"We're related?"

"I don't know; he was an army officer when I met him. It was during the war, so maybe he was stationed in your country. But somebody *does* think you're related. That's the reason you're here."

"What do you mean?"

She lifted her head and her eye flared again, "Of course that he sent you here to be caught, you *dummkopf.*[3] They're growing desperate. And so am I!"

3 • *idiot*

"What do they want?" I asked, a little afraid I might ignite her fury once more.

"I don't know if it's a *they*, or a *he*, a or a s*he*, but it's something related to him, Orlin," she said as she jabbed the photo. "For years they've tormented me." Her voice became a groan. "Sending man after man, thief after thief after it. They all died before I could find out where they were coming from. Then, all of a sudden, nothing. For almost five years! Not a peep! I thought, perhaps, at last, I might live in peace...Then *you* show up."

My mind barely registered the last of her words for it was caught on an earlier phrase. "The others...did you kill them?" I asked in spite of my better judgment.

She looked back at me and I could swear I saw death floating between us. "I did."

I gulped so dryly it caused pain in my ears.

She continued.

"Yes I did. All but the first one. The others... some died fighting, some crying, but none talked. I had no choice. The first... he came back... I wanted it to stop. *I want* to stop it!"

Then she sighed and looked away, "You can't understand. For twenty years this has haunted me. I've lost the thing that was dearest to me. The only thing I could ever have loved. Twenty years... Do you know what twenty years means?" Her harsh voice had lost its strength. Of course, I knew what twenty years meant: my entire life. She clenched her fists. It was all I could see, for her face was still hidden when she reprised.

"He is dead, but nevertheless, he found a way to torment me. Why? Why couldn't he just die? Just… just die and leave me alone… leave me to live my life…"

Her fists were now white. "And this *hurensohn*, the one who does this to me? When is he going to stop? Is he ever going to stop? Only death will stop this… It's me or him… or she…or they, I don't care if it's Satan himself! I will go after him and I will suck the life out of him like he has sucked the years out of me!" She stopped and turned to me, her jaw now granite-like. "This man you call Ruzban, he was the first one. He hurt me bad. Real bad! When he came back again, I caught him…and I made him pay. He holds all the answers. And this time, he'll talk!"

A filthy sneer worked its way from her eye down to her lips as she stood up. Crazy and demented she looked. "We will play his game, yes! It's what he wants! He is watching us and sooner or later will come out. And I will crush him …" she lifted her fists and squeezed them until I saw a drop of blood drip from her palm. I stepped back, for I imagined what it must be like inside of those hands.

"Ha! What a fool I was! Sitting here, waiting… as though he would dare show himself. It's time to go on the attack! Ha, ha! *Für alle Hunde in der Hölle* the time has come!" She lifted one of her huge fists towards me, "I needed a sign. And you are it!"

"I…"

Why hadn't I run? Why didn't I still?

I was terrified, that's why. Instead, I heard myself saying (politely, mind you) that I wanted no part in it the scheme.

I didn't finish. She leapt with a speed that would shame a well-trained athlete and before I could blink was in front of me. She raised her hand, caught my chin and lifted my face so she could fix me better with her demonic eye. Then she growled the words that seemed to have driven my destiny thus far: "You have no choice!" She continued as I swallowed my terror in great lumps, "Listen to me, boy. That nose saved you once from certain death, but only once. You owe me! Come. Or die!"

Our gazes locked for several seconds before she stepped back and shook her head. "You came here to seek your fortune, no?"

Sniffling, I shrugged, for I didn't care much for that any longer. I just wanted to escape the nightmare.

"Well, look no further!" she laughed. "Together with your nose, I can make you rich beyond your dreams, or any man's dream for that matter! Come with me and you can have it all. I don't need it; I'm an old woman. I could die any day. But, you can be sure of this: I won't die before I catch the monster and make him pay."

There was something in her voice that caught my attention. I looked at her: she suddenly seemed more human. Things don't have needs, I realized. Nor does the devil. But she was yearning for something. So much... I could see it in her eye. Oh, I tell you—for a fleeting moment I could look in that eye! The first of very few times. And I saw hope.

And I took pity. Pity for the devil. No, not the devil. In that moment just an old, tormented woman with a teary eye and a broken heart.

"What can I do?" I asked.

"You can come with me," she answered.

"Where?" asked I.

"To find a treasure," said she.

Chapter 3

I tell a story

Today a most unwelcome melancholy has taken ahold of me, and it squeezes my heart with soft fingers, searching for a weak spot to pry apart. I need my ship, my crew, my island. Where are the long nights under the stars with only the songs of the sea to cradle my dreams? Where is the whisper of the wind? And the rolling of the waves? If you haven't lived it, you can't understand. You, as I did when young, think the sea an empty and desolate place; but you couldn't be more wrong. In the morning up on the deck the rigging sweetly moans like a contented lover; the happy sails chatter amongst themselves, telling stories the winds have brought from distant lands; the sea rocks you like a loving mother whilst the sun smiles as gentle as a father... You can't but smile back. So much contentment! Being content it is what being happy means, I tell you. No sadness or desolation for hundreds of miles. Nature can never be as empty as a heart can be—I say, for I've seen it in your cemented cities, morning frowns passing each other in their solitary courses, each jealous of the birds of the sky and of the fish of the sea for the freedom they have. That is desolation, my friend, that is loneliness.

Ah, melancholy! It's not yet the time or the place. Just wait until I tell of the days I spent in the easy-house, or when I speak of the fair Anna. Oh, Anna! Where are you now? Did cruel time nibble your skin as it has mine? It matters not, I say! Inside, I'm as fresh as the day I met you.

Yet, I have to abide by the rules of narration, so I shall keep with the present story, which demands at this point that I tell another story.

When last we spoke, I told you about Sigrid. I have also told you that I found myself bound to follow her quest. She didn't allow me a choice, but still, I could've run away that night, for she gave me a room to sleep, all for myself. I could've slipped through the window and over the balcony and seen my way out of there. But strangely enough, I was feeling safe with the woman. Drawn to her as a moth to a burning candle, you might say. She had spoken of a treasure, but I imagined it to be somewhere close at hand. Not for a moment did I think we would have to cross the world for it. Had I known, I might've chosen the window.

The following day she was again the woman I had first encountered. What a character! As one of those wit-rattling, paper-wasting scribblers would say: her character exceeded in strength what her body lacked in grace.

She said she had a few jobs of little significance to be done as she prepared our departure. She would pay me she said, and I could send the money home, to my family. I gladly accepted for, as I was set in my mind to follow her, I would've done it anyway. Not that you or anyone else would have done otherwise: when that fierce eye and that starless patch set upon you and asked for something, you felt there was nothing else to be done…as if a demon, whose will was your wish, had spoken the words directly into your mind.

"So you can work at anything?" she asked, watching me intently.

"Yes," said I, wary of her question.

And wary for nothing I wasn't. The cursed wench was testing me! For the next two weeks I worked like a ship-boy on dry land at the feats she fabricated for me to accomplish. She supervised my every move. When I cleaned the stables, standing to my knees in muck, she cheered me on with words like: "Watch out boy! Here comes another batch," (which is to rephrase it nicely) or "Hurry up boy, the cows are waiting to show you what *they* can do!" Later, I had to distribute the manure in the field with a wheelbarrow as she ran like a sheep-dog, sometimes ahead, sometimes behind, prodding and rushing me with a stick. She didn't seem to suffer of any of the inconveniences associated with old age. She moved faster than a woman half her years and, from the stories I heard, was stronger than a bull. Quite literally. Some of the lads swore they saw her knocking out with her bare fist a bull that had escaped from the barn into the orchard and was indulging in apple frivolities. As fantastic as it first seemed, watching day after day that wrinkled face, where strength and determination mightily inter-wove themselves with a strong dose of insanity, the legend began to feel true, and she began to grow in my head as steadily and surely as the catch does in a fisherman's tale. As a result, I hardly blinked when the pitchfork broke and she asked me to use my hands—I simply agreed that it was the best way. For quite some time after, whenever my hands approached my face, the stench reminded me of this truth.

When I emptied the beehives, she assured me that I needed no protection, for these were domesticated bees, warm-hearted and good-tempered and ready to surrender their hives as a cow is her milk. "Just speak with them and let them know you're there. They will yield to you," she smiled, putting on a suit, gloves, and veil. I was either at a loss for bee-appeal or the mad woman was lying, for, as they swarmed all over me, I tried speaking to them, even sprouted a song, but in the end settled with screaming and crying. I flapped like a lunatic and slapped myself, half demented, until I couldn't tell which pained me more—the butt of a bee or the side of my hand. Next morning, looking like a champion boxer after a fight, I applied for a day off. I couldn't even open my eyes, for my cheeks and my forehead had swollen almost together; and my nose had reached astronomic proportions. After examining it, and saying that it could be seen from the moon, Sigrid brought a bag of ice, poured it over my head, then took out a knife and aimed it straight at my neck. I jumped up asking what she was doing.

"So, you can see, huh?" she said putting the knife away.

"Not at all," I mumbled, but she perhaps understood "like than an eagle," for she decided, "Then you can work. Today's job is easy, it may even help your condition."

Cleaning calcium deposits from the walls of one of them swimming holes in the ground, it was. Now, I reflect that it had indeed helped me. You won't understand, I suppose, unless I tell you that the basin was filled. *The water,* it turns out, was to be my salve. She explained that she was planning to empty it after I had cleaned it, for reason of economizing water. I think she was also economizing cleaners for the water was green and filled with a colony of gossiping frogs. For hours, ignoring their mockery, I arduously scrubbed the walls. The nose proved a blessing in this instance for I had only to point it up to take in air from the surface.

During these trials, as I shall call them, I was living in the house and took my meals with Sigrid and the cook. A strange relationship they had, those two. Unlike with her other servants, I never knew her to yell or even grunt his way. Hell! I never heard her curse at him…

Cursing—ah! She could curse, believe me! And yes, she did! The veteran grandfather or invalid uncle that mother doesn't let you visit on account of the vocabulary they've picked up in the company of men or pain, Satan himself after a meal of perverted priests—even myself, liquored up and ready to fight—would have to bow before her as the foulest mouth there ever was. To repeat here even the shyest of her ejaculations would make your head explode, princess! So I will content you with her favorite, *Für alle Hunde in der Hölle,* or "For all the dogs in Hell!" if your German is rusty. From there on you must use your imagination.

No. There was definitely something different about Sigrid and her cook, Albert. He was a humble man. He wasn't and old man, but to put an age on him would be a mistake, for so physically imperfect he was and so shy of character, that lest be his mother, I'd most certainly tell you wrong. He was of medium build, skittish, as I mentioned, and bore a small hump on his back. A better teller would say "he quietly carried a small hump on his back," but as I am nothing of sort, I will only say that the man had a small hump and was quiet. He carried his burden limping, as one of his legs, for some reason, stood crooked; but, above all, he was the proud owner of a glorious moustache that would've stricken jealous a champion artist or a philosopher—you know, one of those types who express themselves better through facial hair than through their work. In fact, the moustache was the only thing proud about this lowly and submissive man. Imagine an old, rotten mule with a healthy, shiny tail and you've seen Albert. It was black and thick, without a single white tainting strand, and stood straight and rigid and in your face. The mustache, not the tail.

He seemed to love that moustache, Albert the cook. Every few minutes, after pressing it to his lip, he licked his fingers and in a quick, graceful motion curled its tips upward. Their connection was unmistakable. From under it, as I have told you, the mouth spoke not often; only when asked, and then with a strong accent. He watched me with a devious eye from the day I arrived like I was there to steal his cookware or his secret recipes. But, I didn't mind and set for myself to cheer him up with every occasion I might get; which was well intended, but never done, for he kept his distance and avoided me as much as he could.

As for my situation, surely God was making me pay for all my past sins, and probably for some of the future. And as if under a spell, I paid and paid, and never got paid myself. Sigrid seemed to have forgotten about our deal and I was feeling that everything in my future involved a stable and manure of some variety. However, at the end of a day filled with particularly ripe and steaming mountains of the foulest summer's leftovers, almost at the end of my wits, the spell finally snapped and, ready to abandon ship, I began planning my great escape. Little did I know that I was to learn that my plans don't really matter, as long as there is someone out there bigger and stronger than I.

With my birthday around the corner, I decided to celebrate it as a free man, even if need would be to steal me some food and some bubbly drink from a market store. I did my duties on my final days with doubled eagerness and a secret smile that made Sigrid chomp her cigar harder and frown her eye. The night before the blessed day, I said a prayer, made my demands, promised in exchange a life of fasting and abstinence, then slipped out the open window and into the night air quieter than a fox into a chicken house. The sky was moonless and so dark I couldn't see the tip of my nose. The air was cool and a vague, smoky odor floated to my nostrils, but by the time my brain had worked through a thought's worth, it was too late. As my second foot set on the balcony, I heard the cock of a gun and a piercing beam of light (which I easily recognized as that of my former lantern) locked with my eyes and froze me up.

"You've made me wait two nights, boy," said a calm voice, which I need now describe to you just as much as I *don't* ache for a bottle of gin. "I should give you a beating for the first one and shoot you for the second," she added. Fortunately, no curses were uttered, and my intellect, already warmed up with fear and surprise, detected no anger in her tone.

To say I wanted to take a stroll or fancied an apple

would've been unnecessary, seeing I was carrying a bag containing my poor effects. So I kept my mouth shut.

"You know how you told me that your family is poor?" she continued.

Indeed, at some point during my trials she had asked questions about my family and I had described the place of my origin. And of course, I had painted myself as some kind of hero who left his home to spare his family another mouth to feed. Now, though she could only see my eyes, I shaped a sad and wistful face as if to say that it was the longing for home that had pushed me over the sill.

"I have sent them enough in deutschmarks to feed a hundred idiots like you for a hundred years," she said.

Had she said she grew another eye, I would've been less surprised. My mind calculated that the sum necessary to feed a hundred idiots like me for a hundred years would be enough where I came from to buy a good chunk of the country, and I began to feel lightheaded. As a wave of guilt washed over me, I lowered my head and attempted an apologetic thank you, which came out more as a grunt.

She turned off the light, stood up from her chair and stepped closer. In the dark of the night I could only guess her presence, for it was, as I told you, pitch black. She leaned forward until her mouth was near my ear. "Don't do it again," she whispered softly. I could feel her foul breath when she spoke and a cold shiver ran down my spine. "Follow me to the kitchen!" she ordered. "It's time I tell you a story."

I followed her as a lamb would a wolf wearing his mother's skin. There, she set the lights, gave me a chair, fetched a couple of bottles, sat down and so began the telling of a tale that was to forever solidify my allegiance to her and her quest, and—as by now it must've been well after midnight—the only gift I received that day of my birth.

I will now pass it on to you as I remember it, and I shall tell it as once, in my youth, tales were told to me by a man not much older then than I am now…though in front of a fire, surrounded by his herd of goats, and not in such a cold and pitiful place as this one is. You see, he had caught us, my friends and I, in the act of stealing one of his kids (with the serious intention of roasting it over a fire, for we had heard somewhere that until you have tasted thus cooked young goat, you haven't tasted heaven). He kept us prisoner for the entire night, and while his dogs watched over us with wary eyes, told us tale after tale of magical lands and wondrous feats; tales he had heard from his own father, and his father from his father, and now he had no one to pass them on to because his only son had abandoned the family to become a medical practitioner somewhere in the city. He put forth goat cheese and goat milk and we ate and drank, and felt guilty, and asked for more. And we listened to him, the dogs growling at our every move, and dreamed of them. And so shall you, unless you chose to skip forward; for dogs to watch over you, I have not.

So, here it is…

Once in a faraway land… Ha! She would've sooner set fire to a village than start out this way, but now *I* am the shepherd, and I shall begin as it pleases me!

There was once in a faraway land, I was saying, a maid who—if we are to believe the story, and not what I thought when I first met her—was of the softer sex. She had a sister that, as I suspected and later found out, was the fairest of them all.

Now, it so happened that the king of that country was a short, nervous man with a tiny mustache. It made him look quite the buffoon during those grand speeches he so liked giving, and rather than being in awe, the world laughed. This would enrage him and he would have great fits where he would stomp his foot and shake his little arms and demand respect, but that only made him look funnier. Seeing no end to this comedy, he decided to do what every short fellow commanding a great army had done before him. He decided to conquer the disrespectful, ignorant world.

I wouldn't be telling you this if our maid had not fallen under the spell (or myopia) of one of his young captains, an Orlin von Lindgren. As one misunderstanding never happens alone, they married. She, as the code of good wife demanded, manned the home, while Orlin went off to fight the little angry man's battles, and there distinguished himself as brave—even wounded. Not badly, that is, but enough to be rewarded an extended leave, which of course pleased the wife.

Too soon, however, her joy was cut short, for he began spending his time at her sister's residence. Some say it was because of the parties she threw, some say he liked the society—the sister, you see, had a reputation amongst the upper echelons that preceded her at length; her receptions were renowned and it is said that even the man and his mustache attended once or twice—I say he must've acquired eyeglasses.

An ordinary captain would only read of these gatherings in the morning paper or dream of them from a dug-out, but Orlin enjoyed as special a status as any of the high-ranking guests. And revel in it he did, and the alcohol more than the rest (or so I was told), reserving for his wife only those hours in which his myopia had been restored by its ingestion.

Alas, in the end, the war did not go as planned. Which is perhaps the only thing to be planned when plotting a war. Coming upon an inevitable defeat, those of the sister's social circle who had neither fallen for the cause nor because of it, decided to stow away some little odds and ends they had picked-up here and there by their travels in the business of war: gold, diamonds, precious jewels, and the like. For this they needed a ship. The admiral, being one of them, provided. One vessel would not make a difference in a lost war, he said—unless it carries pirates, I say!—and a Captain Gunther von Eichmann was given command of it. Much to our lady's dismay, for first mate he chose the young Orlin.

She cursed and cried, damning heaven and hell alike, for she knew the many perils that awaited those who would undertake such a mission. But men like von Eichmann have a nasty talent for making requests sound very much like orders. And so they departed.

With the end of the war came the scattering of the conspirators—those few who had not meet with a swift end, that is—to the four corners of the globe, never to be heard from again. Of the siblings, one was left to wait for her husband; the other, more practical, set to make guests out of the new establishment, which proved to appreciate her offerings as much as the old one.

For years, our misfortunate lady awaited Orlin's return;

long years, filled with the biting of nails and collecting of wrinkles. That is, until she was contacted by a solicitor somewhere in the eastern hemisphere with news about a man who had just passed away. In his will Orlin had left her an envelope containing a strange piece of paper of what looked like a detailed location of a place where something was hidden. But it didn't say what place or where it was. So she understood that this was only half of the map to the location of her husband's ship's cargo. Thinking the other half would follow soon she set to wait once more. And waited. Finally, puzzled, saddened, angry, and already half-mad, she gave up and settled down with someone else.

If you think her ordeal ended there—leaving her to enjoy a life of peace—then you are as right as you are virtuous, and worthy of my hand, I'd say, perhaps once or twice. For more mistaken you could not be. Her ordeal, the *real* one, was only itching to begin.

"The first one came in my second year of marriage," she said, as I recall, discarding a bottle. "I would have given him the map, but he had to hurt me first, the sick bastard. And he did. I wanted to die. Part of me did die that night. Since… God have pity on their souls, because I don't. That *hurensohn*, the one who hurt me, Ruzban, you named him, came back. I wanted only to make him suffer… I took my time as he had done with me, but he escaped before I could finish him. I don't know how, but he did. Then more of them followed…" And so she kept on, and on, and on aiming a new bottle higher and higher.

You must understand that the game she described played on for quite a long time, no side scoring but in blood and madness; for as determined as was the mysterious personage to get at her map, the more determined was she to make him pay for his persistence. Though it seems, the only ones being fed were the trees, whose apples were big and red and sweet and quite famous in the region.

Remember that half of that map was missing? Well, years later, the second part made its own strange way to the fair sister's hand, this time accompanied by a letter, said from Gunther, demanding the sisters meet him at its end. Such a thing is easy said, but nearly impossible to accomplish for two very striking reasons: first Sigrid loathed her sister, who she blamed for her misfortune, and little can even a great treasure woo a wounded woman's heart. All the more profound, however, was the next one: Gunther was dead. Apparently, he had been captured in some country and hanged as a war criminal.

So, home they stayed, and as no attempt was made to steal this second piece, the sisters concluded that its sender was the one who had tried to acquire the first.

She stopped here, put her elbows on the table and laid her head on her arms. Her breathing was heavy and wheezy. As I was waiting not knowing if I should leave, I heard her mumble, "But then, that idiot had to go and steal it..." So, I waited for I had no idea what she was talking about. A few moments later, some healthy snores convinced me that the show was over.

That's all I found out that night and so have you now, but in the end you are in a much better position than I was because you already know something I didn't at the time. A marvel, that is! A marvel that neither the sisters, nor their mysterious aggressor, nor even *I* could have foreseen. Something inexplicable and wondrous. Something that would change the course of everyone's lives as effectively and admirably as I will now end this little tale. Something, had you seen it, you know you'd beg for more. Something I call: magnificent.

And that something, as you most certainly have already guessed, was someone.

And that someone my beauties, was me.

Chapter 4

Where the adventure begins

There was meat in my soup today.

Did I tell you about the wretched cook? Can't remember... Anyway, I do love my meat. Where I come from, meat was a privilege rarely enjoyed. Once, for my birthday, I remember, I discovered some in my potatoes. Never did find out if it appeared there by accident or if my poor mother had sold some of her inheritance to put it there. Otherwise, such a special opportunity required a death in the family (and preferably one who had a leg of lamb or pork butt stored away for their kin to split—lest in vain they should have died) or a miracle, such as the day a flock of wild geese landed in my grandparents' yard. Ah, and what a feast ensued! The king of kings wasn't thus honored upon his death, for liquor we had—as we could make it from anything the earth produced—but meat, as you now know, was rare. Kin from seven villages arrived. And the villages with them. Ay, no occasion to celebrate was ever lost by my people! Eating itself was one of those. The engorgement even brought forth love and two spontaneous weddings occurred. After all, the meat was there…Alas, a young chick myself, I had dreamt of drumsticks and juicy breasts, but got served necks and heads instead. Gnawed those bones all night, I did; gnawed them into dust.

Ah…meat. Though I always preferred it to fish and relished the first bites to be had when my ship came at last into port—none has ever tasted as sweet as the morsels I savored in my malnourished youth.

Today I found meat in the soup. Hm… Did I tell you that? …There hasn't been much of it in our food lately and I have my suspicions that the cook is keeping it all for himself—or selling it on the black market. On any ship, that would get you skinned alive! Eh…

So, I caught up with him in a corner, somewhere in the basement where the kitchen lies and I gently let him know that his back would meet my stick if he didn't give up smuggling and leave the meat in our food where it belongs! He protested at first, saying that he was not the cook, only the night manager; but I wouldn't be fooled. I lifted my stick up in the air and told him that I won't have it. I know when a man is lying. And what do you know! He confessed to it all. Stealing meat for years, he was. Figured we couldn't chew it anyway. Ha! You see what a little old-fashion interrogation can do?

But to keep with the story, there is another kind of flesh that holds my attention. A kind I like more than that in my soup, but which I didn't discover until after we landed in Venezuela. Why Venezuela you might ask? Because that's where Sigrid's sister was to be found, the sister in possession of the other half of the map we needed for our quest. This put Sigrid in a foul mood, for I hope you have gathered by now that they weren't the best of friends. As for myself, I could not have been happier. No young lad dislikes traveling or the prospect of wealth.

So, I spent the next few days around the house dreaming of great adventures and making serious plans to settle down afterwards in a country that smiles kindly on harems. It is every man's dream.

Two days before our departure, without words, Sigrid handed me a set of papers of the finest German quality. The photographs attached to some of them could hardly contain my gracious nose. At no time, before or after, did my close-up images make any sense—they usually look like a nose with a patch of hair behind it. You need space to examine my magnificence. Yards of space. I also found out that Albert the cook was to accompany us, which surprised me to a certain measure. What benefit was a hunchbacked cook on a long and perilous voyage? But she cared little about my opinion and was herself a danger greater than any I could imagine—so I resolved that she knew what she was doing.

The night before our departure, I couldn't close an eye for excitement. The unknown, the unexpected, I could smell it. It had promise and hope, lots of it: me getting rich, me getting popular with the ladies, and if possible, me getting a tad taller and handsomer. There was a dab of angst somewhere in there, squished between my future fame and my conquering personality, but I never let it bother my joy, for the young mind rarely sees the clouds before it rains. And thus it should be, never the other way around. Ah, curse me, do you think I have changed? In a heartbeat I would give all the gold I have to be back in that time. Half a heartbeat! I would dream the same things and make the same mistakes all over again, with double the eagerness. If only to be young, with eternity before me and a tight skin over my skull!

We left in one of Sigrid's carriages. Mighty she looked up there in the driver's seat, sucking on her cigar, odd eye evening you out. I can see her: long, heavy skin coat, dark brown and blackened by age, solid high boots below her knees, wide-brimmed hat… Half way to the aerodrome she passed the reins to the boy at her side and turned to glare at us with menace.

"This voyage is *my* business," she said, "so you'll do what I say. I'm the one they want. When they strike, and that they will, leave them to me! Understood?" She stared us down for a couple of seconds, me in particular. Then she turned back.

Little did she know…

A couple of aeroplanes later we landed in Caracas. The city was on fire. Or that's how it felt to me for I had never breathed such suffocating air. Unaffected, Sigrid strode down the busy sidewalk like a mighty general in the midst of plebeian troops, cursing and shoving everyone out of her way, in search of one of those taxicabs that carry people from one destination to another—while we battled with the luggage. When a large automobile old enough to be in a museum, smoke coming out from more places than its back, pulled along, she stopped it victoriously and ges-tured for us to throw the bags in the trunk and ourselves in the rear. "Hotel Royal, Mercedes!" she ordered. No *por favor* or anything. The driver didn't seem to mind and we were off, dodging pedestrians, bicycles, children, cats and carts. However, half hour into the trip, he abruptly brought the car to a stop, got out, and darted off down the street, disappearing into the bush several hundred feet ahead. His speed coupled with his distressed gestures made me think of someone that had eaten something that didn't fall right with his stomach and was now rushing to mend the situation. We glanced at each other, but before anyone could say a word, a subtle smell wafted toward our nostrils, seeming to confirm my unspoken suspicion. I tried to open a window. It was stuck. I asked Albert to open the one on his side. He couldn't. I tried the door. It didn't budge. It was then that I noticed the gas pouring through the vents and the last thing I saw before my eyelids fell was Sigrid smiling triumphantly, like she had planned the whole thing. "*Gut!*" she mumbled and made herself more comfortable, as if settling in for a beauty nap.

I was sweating, a greedy priest at the final judgment. My pockets were full of gold and God was watching me with a raised eyebrow. The loot felt heavy and tight and was hindering my respiration. I wished I could drop it somewhere but he wouldn't take his wary eye off of me. Then he began to snore right in my year, which confused me to a certain degree, but not enough to wake me up. His foul breath, however, succeeded where the noise could not. I opened my eyes and saw no God. Saw nothing in fact. Sigrid's patch, one inch from my face, acted like one of them black holes, eating away the light. She was snorting and puffing like a steam locomotive.

I cried out and rolled away. I say rolled not jumped because I found myself confined to myself by a segment of cotton rope, as a sausage to its casing. Sigrid looked like salami.

Curse this! Now I'm hungry.

Before we had time to share a thought, a door creaked open and the light sprang in. The same instant I curled into a ball to protect my softer parts. There in the entrance stood Ruzban and Babar.

The fear of meeting them again had given me nightmares. In a way, you might say, I should've gotten used to the idea, but I have found over the years that nightmares prepare you for the real thing about as much as getting wet prepares you for drowning.

Ruzban glared at Sigrid, "Finally!" he rasped through maimed lips, "You are finally mine!" He advanced and used his foot to kick a bewildered Albert out of the way. "Nothing will save you now!"

Grunting, Sigrid rolled onto her side to better gaze at him. They measured each other for long seconds. "That was my plan," she sneered. "You just played into it."

He planted a foot in her stomach and she folded around it like a jackknife, but somehow managed to spit in his face in the process. Ruzban growled holding his hand out to Babar. This one watched it with a bemused expression; then as understanding dawned, the giant patted his pockets and from one of them pulled a handkerchief the size of a towel. He handed it to his master who wiped the mottled skin with slow, ginger movements. "Enjoy it while you can. When I'm finished with you, I'll be the one winning beauty contests."

He turned, eyeing the rest of us appraisingly. I instinctively curled tighter, which seemed to amuse him. He nodded in my direction with what might have been a grin, before turning back to Sigrid.

"Now...give me the map." he barked. "I have searched all of your things. Should I have Babar also search your rotten cavities?"

Sigrid snorted while the slave's bright expression darkened as if a cloud had settled in above his head. His eyes flitted between her and his master, evidencing more than a little distress, and then flicked around the room, as if in search of an ally. They met mine for a moment, and I attempted to give him a nod of encouragement. How could you not sympathize?

"Or..." Ruzban continued," should I just kill your consorts one by one? What do you say? Are their lives worth a map?"

"Only to them," she replied. "But you'll pay for what you take. You still owe me from before. I'll add them to the sum."

He exploded all of a sudden with a fury that seemed to surprise even Babar, "Haven't I paid enough you vile hag?" he cried, madly kicking her kidneys, over and over. When he had enough, he bent down bringing his face inches from hers, "Or did you not get a close enough look?

"What life is it that you think you have condemned me to? Do you think I am here for my own amusement? I am here to make *you* pay! And pay you will!" he raged, lashing out with his foot again and again, every strike slowly pushing her across the room. When she could go no further, he staggered back and wiped his brows, breath uneven. "Each one of you!" he crooned, turning in my direction with a flash in his eyes. "Slowly, slowly. And over time, perhaps the scale will even. Then perhaps we will both be free."

Sigrid rolled around, eye thrown wide and nostrils flaring. "I've been free for years now, you *Hurensohn*," she groaned. "Free of my child, free of a normal life. Vengeance is all I have left. For you! You and the one who sent you! Just tell me who he is and I swear to God I won't cut your ears off. They were next, you know." She let out a loud, maniacal laugh, spattering blood on the floor in a wide arc around her mouth.

He had stopped now. His back hunched, his head between his shoulders. The silence was such that I could hear the drips of blood from Sigrid's mouth. Seconds ticked by. I watched the curve of his back, his arms dangling inert alongside his body, and I could see the shaking. He was not moving, but the flesh on him was. Twitching in short spasms beneath his light robes like from electric shocks. And the silence kept feeding on us. I was afraid to breathe.

"Nothing you say can touch me now," he muttered. "I will make you suffer like no one has ever suffered. Them, I could let go but not you." He went and kneeled in front of her and pointed toward Babar, "I bought you a gift. I found him in the filthiest, nastiest slum at the bottom of Mumbai. I fed him, I trained him. I made him what you see. When he cried, I whipped him; when he laughed, I whipped him harder. When he became a man, I stopped it. Yes, I did! I needed somebody faithful to me not to his urges. He can handle you."

He ran his tongue over the frayed edges of his mouth.

"Let me educate you. I will start easy: After I pull out your fingernails, I will cut off every little bit that sticks out of your body—pretty you up for the rest of the evening. Next, your limbs. Can't just cut them off. Need that stinking blood inside you, not on the floor. So, Babar will pull them far enough out of their sockets until they hang at your side for you to watch them and say to yourself, 'I can feel the pain, but why can't I move them?' Then I will rip your teeth out and skin you, but I won't touch your tongue, no. Because I will want to know how you feel. I want to hear it. Your eye, I will spare, too. I want you to watch me as I do it, see the pleasure I take in my work. And a pleasure it will be, repaying you for the kindness you have bestowed upon me," he paused, running a hand down his ghoulish face.

"But…if you give me the map, I will give you the promise of a knife in your heart. The boy and the old man will go free. So what do you say? Make your choice now."

Sigrid seemed to ponder. But it only lasted a second. "I should have killed you when I had a chance and spared this man the life you've given him," she said. "Now, it's too late. I offer you the same deal. Tell me who sent you and I'll let him go and I'll free your soul."

"Enough! Babar, bring the chair!" He turned and faced Albert and me, "You, brothers, will now see a spectacle you'll never forget. I almost envy you. But then, you may be next, so perhaps *envy* isn't the right word…"

Now, you must understand that I was then just a young lad with a tender spirit. In not even a month's time, I had experienced things that would turn most of you milksops into loons. Hah! Despite all these trials, I still had my sanity—though not for long, I thought, for I felt that an important threshold was certainly to be crossed that day as a most potent dread began to bore through my stomach. Whatever was about to happen in that room, I knew for a fact that did I not want to see it. Too many things at once can destroy even the most stoic mind. Now, bring man gradually through adversity, and in time you will see how he hardens; the muscles of his brain growing as strong as the muscles on one of those lads who spend their time lifting things up in the air only to put them back down. For everything in life—for life itself—time is the key. And curse me, time is now my enemy!

Albert, the cook, was lying on his side not far from me and looked no better. His moustache seemed to have lost half of its pride, and the part that was supposed to point to the ceiling hung loosely in the air like a broken limb while large drops of sweat dripped from it and from its sibling like silty water from two broken pipes.

The chair Babar brought was a heavy, metal type with armrests. He made sure it was well anchored to some beams jutting out of the cement floor before standing up and going over to where Sigrid lay. He picked her up and threw her as you or I would throw a rag, onto his shoulder. She didn't protest or curse or spit, which, even in my state, I found most unusual.

He brought her to the chair, dropped her next to it, and cut her ropes with his knife, for tied as she was she couldn't have sat. With one of his huge hands he held her wrists, and with the other lifted her up and sat her on the chair. Just as he prepared to tie her hands to its arms, a thing most… should I say *extraordinary* happened.

There was a short burst of air, which I would've ignored

but for the fact that Babar looked up somewhat surprised, and hesitated. He shook his head twice and reprised what he was doing but his movements were now slow, his strength leaving him. He then faltered and stopped to steady himself, but his legs seemed to have grown weak. Without a sound, his chin fell onto his chest and he, himself, slumped forward on top of Sigrid.

She swore and hustled to push him off, but the colossal mass weighed a ton and it took her a number of seconds to free herself.

Ruzban watched these events motionlessly, seeming powerless to move. By the time he had made up his mind and taken a step toward his servant, Sigrid was halfway out from underneath the giant, a victorious grin on her face. He let out a howl of frustration as he spun and disappeared through the door.

Cursing like the demented, Sigrid grasped Babar's dagger and flew after him. She came back a while later, mad as hell and still cursing. *"Für alle Hunde in der Hölle*, I had him! I had him!" She wildly kicked at the body on the floor before striding to where we were and freeing us. While she was cutting my ropes, I noticed something different about her patch, but her head was against the light and my mind hadn't yet recovered from the day's events. I couldn't tell what it was.

"Let's get out of here," she said once we were on our feet. "Our luggage is upstairs."

"What about him?" I asked, gesturing toward Babar.

She gave me a harsh look and replied, "He's just a big child. Besides, he's going to sleep at least half a day. If you want to carry him, be my guest."

I looked at the sleeping giant snoring peacefully with his humongous cheeks squished against the concrete, his big lips flapping together like a pair of loose sails in a gale, and decided that I did not.

CHAPTER 5

WHERE THE ADVENTURE CONTINUES

He was a god, and I, his meal.

Dirava or Tanodirava-something, somewhere in the Guineas... Said to live amongst his tribe in the body of a wild beast. Wild pigs or kangaroos, you say? Perhaps a parrot or a scary, hairy bat? No sir, no. It had to be a tiger. And while we're at it... big as a whaler. I don't know why, perhaps because his kind don't live there, perhaps because he was the first one they'd ever seen—I didn't think to ask.

The wretched critter... I am known to lack fear of man, but fear of beasts is a whole other thing. I can still see the golden glint in his eyes, I can feel his powerful nostrils feeling me, the blast of their hot breath on my face... The tribe captured me and my second mate with the idea that a pinch of a stranger, or two, tender and rare in those parts ha! might improve the god's mood; seemingly, he was a moody one. Is it because of the lack of diversity?—they must've asked themselves before they realized that the answer lay inside the question. Mankind has known since its beginnings that it's all about diet with these gods. They like meats. All sorts of them. A few live on nuts and carrots, it's true, but the grand majority likes to chew on bone. Or smell some good burning flesh. And an imprisoned god should like diversity more than the free-roaming ones. It's only natural. See, I've just given you the entire human mythology. Wasn't hard at all. "When the gods are happy, the hunter is lucky," went this tribe's religion. The whole of it.

So, you understand there was much at stake. Luckily they'd relieved us of our ropes before throwing us, uncooked, into the pit where his mightiness dwelled. He snatched my man right from the air. Dead before touching the ground. I watched him devoured in front of my eyes.

He was a behemoth, that tiger. You should have seen how our captors screamed and chanted and beat their sticks and blew their horns there on the edge of the pit, the scoundrels…

The beast, or the god—I wouldn't want to be sinning now—decided to keep me for breakfast, as he seemed to like his meat…uhm, twitching. For now, like a good kitty with a full stomach, he had curled up in the corner for a nap. And they danced and celebrated above us all night long those devils, undoubtedly in anticipation of the next morning's performance. Fires were lit and fiery liquids were brought forth. And they danced some more and played on their drums and one of them, apparently a better hopper, or dancer—if you wish to call it that—or simply more drunk than the rest, flask in one hand, spear in the other, fell neatly into the pit. The beast lifted his head, opened one eye, licked his lips, and went back to sleep. And so, I clubbed the drunk and drank the liquor, and with his spear I killed the monster. 'twas a pity, for he was a beauty. Took my time and struck him right in the heart. Not a sound came out; he jolted in surprise, and heaved a long sigh, settling quietly back into place. Ah! My god turned out to be a bit more resourceful than theirs! I broke the spear in half, and, under cover of the singing voices and the beating drums, used it to climb out and disappear into the dark jungle. I had to survive a week there, gin-less, chased by a maddened, godless tribe, feeding on roots and larvae and other vile crawling critters, sleeping in marsh-mud to my neck, waking up every morning with a pint of blood lost to those blood-sucking marsh-leeches… Not a pleasant memory, that one… What was I doing with it?… Oh hell, I can't remember. Rose you take it out when you get to it, you hear? I've been trying all morning to work this machine but can't for the life in me. Every now and then the buttons get stuck and the cursed thing gets moodier than a tribal god on a diet of domestic meat. … I was once part of such a diet… Ah-ha! Now we have it.

So where did I leave you yesterday? …Oh, I remember! How could I forget? I love this part! This is the part I would live again. Every day.

Here I go…

Twice, I had escaped that Ruzban and believe me I was counting my blessings. My legs were shaking as we exited that wretched place. We had found our luggage on the first floor, emptied and thoroughly searched and the house seemed deserted. Not a scrap of furniture about the place.

Outside, Sigrid stopped to light the butt of a cigar. I slowed down and tried to steal a better look at her patch. Something suspicious had happened inside and, in spite of the joy I felt for escaping one more time with all my bits attached, I was still curious. How had she put the giant to sleep? Her hands had been bound all along.

Seeing me rounding her like a dog a bone too big to carry, she took out the butt, spit next to my feet and grunted from the corner-mouth, "What you gawking at?" I hastened to not say a thing, busy as I was moving legs to a distance I considered safe. She grunted again then started walking.

From the street it appeared that the house was situated on the shady side of town. Its dusty brown streets were littered with debris like some storm had just flown by. Tiny, neglected shacks lined the curb, with unpainted fences of which the sole purpose seemed not to enhance appearances, but to cut the view of the daring passer-by to the dubious happenings on the other side.

Albert was visibly upset and I offered to carry most of the luggage.

"Dank you," he said.

"This must've been very hard on you," I said, marching along him.

To my surprise he answered, "*Nein*, Albert iz old und my life vas, vat do you say, boring," he said hesitantly, fetching words from that place between languages.

"But we could've been killed."

"If Madame Sigrid ok, I am ok. I go vere she goes."

"What do you think happened to that big man back there?"

He shrugged his hump, "I don't know. Fery..." and he couldn't find the word.

"Strange?" I helped.

"*Ja, ja,* fery strange!"

Happy that he was finally talking to me, I asked him more questions about his relationship to Sigrid, as she marched ten yards in front of us trying to find a way out of the slum. He had been working for her for a long time, since she had married with Uber, in fact. Upon decoding, I realized that Uber was a name and not another butchered word.

"Uber," I said, "who is Uber?"

"Madame husband," came the answer.

"I thought his name was Orlin."

"Zhat vas zee first one, Uber vas zee second."

"Oh, the second!" I said, for I remembered she had told me she had remarried, but as she had mentioned it only once and spoken fast, between tight lips like it was something she regretted, I had forgotten.

"*Ja, ja,* und one day Uber tisappeared und Madame levt avter him next day. She come back sree mons later veez patch…"

"Oh!" I said, for I was under the impression that Sigrid had been born with the patch there on her face. "And Uber?"

"I never see him…"

We had to stop there. Sigrid had finally spotted a taxi. She had jumped into the middle of the road, forcing the driver to stop and, ignoring his objections, as well as his client's, sat herself next to him. Next to the driver. The poor passenger, she had removed by pulling him out by the ear all the way to the sidewalk. The woman took safety to heart. The driver who had missed his chance to speed away was now banging his head on the wheel. She sat herself next to him, I said, unaffected, and forty minutes later we puttered up in front of the hotel.

It was an old edifice of some fancy style—which I ignored as much then as I would now—but which showed some need for renovation. There were blackened stone lions roaring down at us from four tall columns and in the center, above the entrance door, a Madonna with undulating hips, hands opened to the sky, was crying decades of clammy, pasty bird droppings while praying for our souls. On the door there was a sign saying: "*Solamente con la reservación*" and I wondered if Sigrid had made one.

I was looking forward to a good night's sleep: after what I had been through and, if there is a balance of things in this world, it was the least I deserved. However, life doesn't care about balances—I found this out as soon as we entered Hotel Royal.

I didn't know much about hotels; I hadn't had the pleasure at that time in my life of visiting too many of them. But this one was most unusual.

Upon passing the first door, there was a small empty space where we hardly fit with our luggage, and of which the purpose escaped me. Behind it, there was another door, which after a short wait, rang, and opened when Sigrid pushed down the handle. Impressed, I expected to see a reception of some sort. Well, you are right to guess that there wasn't one. Instead, after a number of steps through a dark hallway, before us opened a large room, in the style of

a saloon, dimly lit and decorated with paintings depicting
… well, I should describe them to you: there were bodies
of ancient men and women (I say "ancient" on account of
the robes they seemed to have worn before it all started,
and not because of their age) entangling themselves in a
confusion of limbs, heads and other parts in such a scan-
dalous admixture, that were I more ignorant, I should have
believed that they had been set to stew in some huge barrel.
Only there was no barrel. Here and there, an arm with a
hand holding a cluster of grapes or a goblet rose in the air
as if some had been wishing to have a bite or make a toast
right before other bodies fell from above weighing them
down. A most interesting sight, I tell you… I observed it
for a good while, for I love history and I passionately suffer
the presence of art. But before I could completely satisfy
my thirst, my eyes were drawn to the room where an even
more glorious sight awaited my young eyes. And I thought
it was every little bit as glorious as the most glorious thing I
had ever imagined.

There were large divans and armchairs, many of them,
indiscriminately thrown about the place and which were
covered in red velvet with black decorations. That's not
all, in fact, that's not even important. In these chairs a few
noble gentlemen sat. Which is also not important, I'm just
mentioning it for the sake of the picture in your mind.
Some of these honorable men were talking, some were
smoking cigars—each rejoicing in his favorite activity. One
thing all of them seemed to favor equally was the company
of a group of scantily clad girls, all happily giggling, and to
whom I attribute my subsequent loss of interest in the mu-
ral of art—for, I say it again: where art makes me sigh, life
makes me cry. And cry at this sight, a man with a heart that

beats and blood that runs, would, and should, and must! Tears of joy, let him weep! Hallelujah!

Oh...

Another group of damsels, as mirthful and entertaining as the first, though dressed as house-maids, French I suppose—or some other nation famous for wearing less while doing chores—carried drinks and refreshments throughout this merry assembly.

Thinking back, it was one of them poetic views. I have no knowledge of any scribbler ever recounting something like this, but I'm sure there must be some out there, as it was too much for one's eyes to take in without making the soul sing. Blessed, at birth, had I been with skill at crafting words with meanings and rhyme and all that, or in this moment with a bottle of something, I'd try my hand at it, for no other reason than to impress the damsels and enflame the young lads. For, it is known that inside every pirate hides a poet and a minstrel. And some other characters, not convenient to our present parable. And I say, what better occasion for these artists to poke their heads out than the presence of glorious beauty or of a liquid with some proof to it? The presence of both, you say? Well, you're right, bless you. But you shall sleep unschooled tonight, my friend, for I have none of these things here. Blame Rose!

To come back to this lyric sight, besides confirming my suspicion that there was something wrong with the hotel, it had as a secondary effect the sudden loss of my ability to speak, accompanied by a most curious dislodging of my eyeballs, which were now protruding out a few good centimeters. They would've most likely popped out of their sockets just like wet soap from a child's hand had I not caught a glimpse of Sigrid. Deeply disturbed, I turned back to the maids.

They were all lithe and handsome as I would bless you all to be, my beauties. Most of them were wearing to the sight, if memory serves me, not much of anything at all, or more of their skin, if it lessens your guilt; and what a delectable rainbow of skins it was, thin and curvy, light and dark… A few, dressed in outfits that didn't seem to fit with the general, angelical décor, confused me, for they were carrying objects more appropriate to the situation we'd just gotten ourselves out of. Others seemed quite religious in their adornment and I wondered what they were thinking to associate themselves with the first ones. But mysteries I was starting to get used to.

I may repeat myself, but so far, in my wildest dreams and my richest fantasies I had never believed a place like this one could exist. Later, I found out that even *El Presidente* occasionally stopped by in periods of great electoral stress, or mid one of the many *las revoluciónes* that the country seemed so fond of.

Under the guilty impression that I may have sneaked passed the gates of heaven, I fell prey to a reverie of a most philosophical nature, and, naturally, ignored the question that a graceful soubrette, of French accoutrement, was posing me.

Her name was Anna. Ah Anna, Anna… The most beautiful memory I will take from this world! Blame me, for in this story she plays a small part even though she has the foremost role in my heart. You see, we started out well, then it went downhill—the necessary path when you are as crude as I was. But, I am getting ahead of myself…

As I said, she was speaking to me and at first I ignored her. When I finally turned my head my eyes wrapped themselves around a waist of skin like silk with a ring hanging outside its bellybutton. Which bellybutton I thought was smiling at me. So, I smiled back.

She was of exquisite proportions and, as I found out later, not even French. Everything was present in amounts fit to please the gods; my eyes kept going up and down her physique and couldn't settle anywhere in particular for every morsel seemed as intriguing to my young eyes as probably the new continent was to the eyes of Columbus.

Her attire? I would remember it like it was yesterday and would take my time painting it too, but as my wide eyes were searching her body for more of it, trying to record it in my mind for you, a slap on the head stopped me cold.

"...go bring Marlene darling." I heard Sigrid saying to the girl.

Anna made a little curtsy and turned around. Now I attempted to record her from the opposite angle, but it wasn't meant to be, for a voice from behind made us all jump:

"And what do you seenk you are doing eer?"

I spun around.

There, in all of her splendor, like a goddess descending upon her subjects to deliver final damnation, stood a majestic female, towering over us all! Red as a burst of fire, her silk dress cast the generous curves of quite an imposing woman in a breathtaking glow, strikingly beautiful with smooth, even features, and of an uncertain age. A black shawl, also silk, covering her naked shoulders and part of her extremely generous bosom, strongly contrasted with the platinum hair that flowed uninterrupted down to her waist. Her full lips, pinched and disgruntled, were covered in heavy lipstick, as red as her dress. She was magnificent standing there on the second step of the stairwell! She had a crutch, which she held under her left arm with the majesty of a queen wielding her scepter. Curious, I dropped my eyes and saw that she must be missing a leg, for only one pointy black shoe peeked out from under her voluptuous dress.

"You know why I'm here; you know the reason I'd ever come back to this place," answered Sigrid, in the same tone, stepping up the stair to even eye contact.

The queen measured her with contempt and declared with an even voice, "I told you zhat if you ever came back eer I would *kill* you. You are finished for me since zhat night."

As if by magic the saloon emptied, girls removing customers by a different set of stairs, leaving the two forces to defy each other on the battlefield.-

"And *I* told you that if *I* ever saw you again, *I* would kill *you*…" replied Sigrid undisturbed. "But then, he came along," she extended an arm toward me.

Slowly, the queen redirected her eyes. Several knots squeezed in my throat and I swallowed them one by one. I felt like a virus under a microscope, as she studied me silently with no expression on her face. Then she turned around and, without a word, but with supreme dignity, hopped up the stairs. We followed her, Sigrid leading the way.

In her office I expected more biting contempt, but

a mind is always as strong as its curiosity. Just past the entrance she dropped the crutch and jumped upon me with both arms open exclaiming "Oh, *mon Dieu! Mais ce n'est pas possible*, oh *mon Dieu!*" She hugged me, and kissed me, then caught me by the chin and turned my head in all directions, sizing me up with two eyes as blue as her sister's. "*Formidable! Ce nez, formidable!* It looks *juste* like him! What iz your name, little boy?"

Glancing toward Sigrid, I gave her my new name, though it came out with more of a quiver than I would have preferred. "Varik," I said.

"Varik? *Mais*, what name iz zhis?"

"It's his name and that's all," retorted Sigrid, serving herself a cigar from the box on the desk. She smelled it, broke it in half, and lit it with a match that she pulled out from hell knows where. "You drive me crazy, you know. With your stupid French accent. You are German for God's sake."

Marlene ignored her and said to me, "I am Marlene, *mon beau*. A noze like you... *ce n'est pas possible*, I would recognized it in a sousand. Are you my little nephew Varik?"

"I don't know..." I said.

She caught my nose and shook it, "*Mais oui, mais oui*, you are ! Your noze betrays you. Iz real!"

"He can't be your nephew, I was the one married to that bastard," her sister added from the top of the desk where she was sitting.

"Orlin was *juste* like my brother, I seenk I can call him

nephew."

"Ha. More than your brother, I'm sure, you back-stabbing…"

"What do you mean by zhat?" Marlene stood straight, and the question was almost a yell. "I told you many times zhere was noseeng weez me and Orlin." Then, she lowered her voice as she said to me, "Don't listen to er, she iz crazy. Orlin was good man."

I could do nothing but nod.

"He may have been," Sigrid reprised, "until he met you, you corrupting debauchee; then he left me to go off to his death with one of your clients… and I paid for it! All because of you; I have lost an eye and… and much more. And you? How did you pay? Enjoying yourself in a whorehouse as the chief *Hure*,"[4] she said and in a gesture of disgust turned to the side and spat on the floor.

Marlene released a cry, let go of her prop and suddenly pulled me to her billowing chest scaring the hell out of me, "Zhis iz not a *bordel*! Iz a ouse of *petites plaisirs*!" I could feel the words vibrating through her bosom. "*Certains hommes* need to relax after zheir wives. Like Orlin from you. Zhe man was tired after eez work, Zigrid, and eee was tired after you: 'Orlin do zhis, Orlin do zhat, Orlin be like zhis, and Orlin be like zhat…' you drove eem crazy. Eee came to my party by eemself, I didn't call eem. And I told Gunther not to take eem along, but zhat *salopard*[5] never listen to me. I aave already told you zhis. And Uber iz not my fault, you know zhat."

"Another bastard; good thing he's also dead."

4 • *whore*
5 • *bastard*

I thought I was about to join them for where I was there was not enough air for the three of us. Was doing my best trying to breathe through my eyes, but it didn't seem to work. "You killed eem…" she lamented, as I was fighting for my life.

Sigrid made a noise like she had something stuck in her throat. But, that was just scoffing. She went and opened one of the many mahogany cabinet doors, pulled out a bottle of bourbon and brought it directly to her mouth, "Let's put everything on the table," she said after half of it was gone. "I didn't kill him. He betrayed my trust and tried to kill me. The bastard got what he deserved, but it is not me who killed him." Then she installed herself comfortably on Marlene's chair, boots on the desk, lit a new half-cigar and aimed the bottle to the ceiling. They both seemed to ignore that I was growing limper by the second.

"But who?" asked Marlene, and in her surprise she finally let go of me.

I felt like I was being reborn. Soft legs, blurred sight, the need to pee without the need to care where, all the signs were there. When I regained some of my strength, hesitantly and staggering, the first thing I did was bend down, pick up her crutch and hold it out to her. She smiled and caressed my cheek. "Senk you, *mon amour*. You are *un trésor*. I recognize *un vrai gentilhomme* when I see one!" And her arms flew wide open in a grand gesture. Horrified, I took my last breath, closed my eyes and mumbled a prayer, but to my surprise she grabbed her support and went around to the cabinet. She pulled out another bottle and a glass from behind the door to the left, filled it halfway, wet her lips, and said to her sister, "You left wizhout a word zhat night…"

"And without an eye. Ha! Eh, the past is past. I don't want to talk about," said Sigrid fiercely working her bottle.

(Damn it, Rose! Everybody's drinking but me!)

In sudden anger, Marlene lifted her prop and banged it on the floor, "*Merde!*" she yelled. "You don't want to talk, you never want to talk! You seenk if you talk you are not az big… I must find out the truth! I lost someseeng, you lost someseeng, and I must find out why! Zhees iz not finish!" Then she began to cry, her bosom dancing up and down to the rhythm of her sobs.

Still fearing for my life, I hastened to console her. I must say, I liked the woman at first sight even if she did try to suffocate me. Tears were washing down the powder that covered her plump cheeks. This time, she leaned her head against my chest and wept abundantly. "You are a good boy, Varik! *Juste* like Orlin," she said caressing my hair.

"Another back-stabbing leech…" mumbled Sigrid with contempt.

On the opposite side of the room, sitting on a chair, Albert had pulled his head between his shoulders and was watching the scene from under the cover of his hump. Marlene lifted her head, gazed at me and said between sobs, "I like you *mon fils*, but stay away from my girlz. Zhey are good girls, but your eart will be broken and you will become juste like Zigrid."

"My heart is *dead*," corrected the other shaking the almost empty bottle to see how much she had left.

"Varik iz a good boy, ee iz not mean like you. Your eart is dead because you are mean."

"I'm surviving," retorted Sigrid. "And should I remind you that you took my husband away from me? I didn't take yours, you took *mine*."

"Ee came to me because you were mean…"

Sigrid emptied the bottle, cursed at it, and threw it in a corner. I watched it roll back and forth between the legs of a chair. "He was my husband," she growled. "You should've sent him back! Uber, too… You are like garbage for flies! They can smell you wherever you go. Look! Now, this one's sniffing the pile!"

"Uber waz not my fault!" cried Marlene who by this time had made visible progress with her own decanter. (Damn you, Rose! There is a storm in my mouth and I see I take more pleasure in describing the liquor than what happened.)

"You know zhat! Ee came eer because ee stole your map," said Marlene.

"That greedy *Hurensohn*! He fooled me and knew you were the weakest."

"But I didn't give it to eem! Are you crazy? Aaaaah, you are zhe worst!"

"*Ja*, because I followed him. Who knows, maybe you wanted to split it with him."

"*Incroyable!* I tried to keep eem eer, until you came, but ee called someone and zhen ee ran away… I came weez you, no? To catch eem! But zhen what happened? You killed eem, you did!"

"Boy! Bring me another bottle!" Sigrid barked.

I darted as if propelled by a spring. Though Marlene

was the one I liked, Sigrid was the one I feared. I can feel the bottle in my hands to this day! Ah… what a fine whiskey. Showing initiative I picked up a glass and put it in front of her.

She watched me sideways from under her thick eyebrow, but motioned me to pour into the glass. "Fill it up," she said. She picked it up, she smelled it, tasted, and said, "*Die Hure* here is living the life…" and downed it with a gulp.

"I don't know what happened that night," she continued after a moment, "but in that explosion I lost my eye and Uber—kaput."

"Don't forget about my leg, you always forget zhat I lost someseeg, too. But, I'm appy I'm alive and my ed is not crazy."

"Your what?" Sigrid asked.

"My ed, my ed," Marlene repeated pointing to her head. "I can lose everyseeng but my girlz or my ed."

"You've already lost or gave away everything below it a long time ago," mumbled Sigrid sarcastically through the mouth of the bottle.

"I eard zhat!" Marlene cried, but you could see her heart wasn't in it. "At least I ave ope and I want to be appy. You are like…" here she searched for a word, smacked her lips with a grimace, "not tasty, *aigre* old woman. And you killed Uber, because I saw eem dead."

"No, I had just beaten him senseless, he wasn't dead. Someone was there; someone was waiting for him, a man. I think it was a man, I saw his back. I was too mad to think straight, to prioritize. I should've caught him first. Ah," she slapped her fist inside her palm, "If I'd only gotten my hands on the other son of a bitch… I know he's the one I want."

"Maybe we should give eem your map," proposed Marlene. "Because iz your map ee wants. And we finish forever weez eem. You stay eer weez me, business iz good."

Sigrid lifted her feet from the desk and stood up; she slammed the bottle on top of it, then came around smoking with fury. I backed up toward the other corner, almost bumping into Albert who seemed to have fallen asleep. She pounded over to where her sister was now lying on one of the large armchairs, and stopped before her, legs wide, fists on her hips. "You see this?" she bellowed and pointed to her patch. "You see that?" she showed Marlene's leg. "You want to have lost half our lives for nothing?"

"I don't know!" Marlene sobbed. "Maybe iz better to forget."

"NEVER!" Sigrid cried. "I will never forget! It must end NOW! And this time *I* am going to attack! Either I die or I win! No other way. I can feel him watching me. He knows I've left. We were attacked just before we got here."

"Ee iz here?" asked Marlene, pulling herself up.

"Yes. His henchmen attacked us. They slipped through my fingers. They will come back, though. I know that they will. And I will be ready to send them back to *hell*," her voice ground down to a dangerous growl.

Marlene said nothing and slowly sipped at her drink.

"Are you coming with me?" Sigrid demanded after a moment.

"I must," sighed Marlene. "You are my sister... But it will finish *mal*, I feel it right eer," and tapped her chest.

"I don't care," said Sigrid.

"Of course you don't care. You never do. And you bring zhis young Orlin weez you and you don't care for eem."

"He knows the risks."

"Yes, I'm sure ee knows. Ee's going to war weez crazy Genghis Khan. I must come weez you to take care of eem." She then turned to me, "Don't worry, I will come weez you. But leave my girlz alone," she added in a menacing tone.

I shrugged then nodded, for I hadn't done anything.

Yet.

Chapter 6

Where I hear my calling, but I'm not allowed to answer

And there I was. Like a fox dropped in the middle of a hen house. A fox that had never tasted poultry before. That was me, my beauties, that was me! Times have changed, huh? Still a fox, but where are the tender hens? Where is their happy clucking? Why am I surrounded by a chorus of geriatric gobblers? Cruel irony! Merciless faith! Just when I need a good hen more than ever. But then, I've always needed that more than ever. Can't remember when I didn't.

At the time though, it was a bit of a shock. Like winning a harem with a lottery ticket. Marlene's advice? Forgot it the second her mouth stopped moving. Forgot everything that entered my ears that day for I needed the space to store what my eyes were seeing. In fact, it's a miracle that I can recall enough to tell you, for my mind, the whole time they bickered, was sailing through another world altogether—the one from the paintings in the front hall. And guess who was holding the grapes this time? Guess who had a dozen or so of beautiful bodies piled atop of him? There was enough steam rushing through my veins to power a steamer and crush an iceberg, I tell you. I think I grew a full beard that night.

Next morning, tired as a soldier after a long and weary battle, I exited the room Marlene had given me and went to find some nourishment, for the body grows hungrier when the spirit does all the work. I asked my nose to make use of his gift and sniffed out the kitchen down the stairs below ground level. Albert was already there and for some reason (of a culinary nature, I'm sure, since neither could understand what the other was saying), had offended the cook of the establishment, a gigantic-bottomed lady, apparently of a delicate and sensitive nature when it came to food and ways to prepare it. Tears flooded her doughy cheeks and a stream of unfamiliar words poured out from behind her sausage-like lips. Shortly, she began, with surprising dexterity, to throw pots and pans at the poor old hunchback, clearly aiming for his moustache. Fast as a cat, smart as mouse, he hid behind a glass cabinet door, which of course shattered and caused a commotion.

Hunger pains assailing me, I had no choice. Hunger grows a boy bold, amongst other things, so I entered the war zone as a peacemaker. A few words and many gestures later, I succeeded in calming her enough to get hold of the coffeepot, which was undoubtedly next. Disaster avoided, I poured myself a cup, just in case, and began the negotiations, which went something like this: to the lady, "You, big food (open arms wide), mmm very good (eat air), bueno (rub stomach); steak, meat, grill (pinch her arm trying to show meat, get slapped; pinch my own, cause confusion).

"He (pointing to Albert) tiny food (hold fingers millimeters apart), cake, cakeos, very good, bueno (rub stomach), but not like you; you more important (feign worship). You make meat." I don't know if she understood, but she suspiciously glanced at me one more time, then she sighed and said "Ay!" and turned around talking to herself at a very fast pace.

Thus began my adventure in the house I-wish-I-had-never-left. There was good will in the air, a good egg in the pan, good coffee in the pot, a good life to come… I couldn't have asked for anything else.

My happy cruise was short lived though, for, as I was sipping coffee, luck suddenly changed her bearings and headed for the reef. Light and graceful as a silk curtain fluttering about dawn's first breeze, enchanting as a heavenly dream, and scented like a garden of thousand roses, an angel appeared. I watched her with coffee dripping from my mouth. I let it drip, convinced that I was dreaming and a little drooling should never interrupt such a dream. In the end, the delicate being hosting the kitchen took pity and gently slapped the back of my head. Alas, she might've intended it gently, but her hand weighed a ton or more, so my head received it as a ball would a bat and sped nose down into the cup of scalding liquid. The pain was terrible, the shame indescribable. I rushed to the sink and put my forerunner under a jet of water.

You might notice that I didn't say cold water. That's because not knowing the works of the cursed spigot, I chose the extreme of the two settings available. Naturally, the wrong one. The water that came through that pipe and onto my suffering organ was literally boiling. I covered my mouth with my hand to stifle a cry that would've flattened the building. I switched the settings and waited for the water to cool. I kept my suffering trumpet beneath the jet, breathing through my mouth, hoping the young lady would disappear, or leave and forget what she had just witnessed. After a while I lifted my head and dared a peek. She was sitting in the opposite corner facing away from me despite the fact that she was basically staring at an empty wall not even a yard away. I hid my pain in the soft of the elbow and shot out of the door. I took the long way around the table, though, just to steal a glance at her. No beauty ignores me and gets away with it.

Yes, it was the same girl from yesterday.

I must forever avoid her, I told myself.

The mirror in my room revealed a nose reminiscent of the size and color of a monkey's derriere, peeling in some spots. By my present standards it didn't look that bad, but at the time I was mortified. Ah, the drama! I cursed the gods and my luck and the moment I had left home. If only I could disappear here and appear somewhere else, I didn't care. Ruzban, I'd have welcomed back before appearing in front of any girl in such a fashion. I promptly resolved to never leave that room.

But I was hungry. My meal had escaped me and the last had been… wasn't sure but at least ages ago. Anything more than four hours seemed a long while at that age, and I was sure it had been longer. Besides, it's against a young lad's nature to stay put more than a moment. Or, to keep his word. So, twenty minutes later I was ready with a plan.

I had spied, the previous evening, not far down the corridor a room where the girls went to change for the night. In fact I was spying the girls and the door happened to be in my way. Fortunately, it had a keyhole. By now you should know me. Anyway, I hoped that I might find there a large hat to hide my monstrosity while I went back down to the kitchen. I wasn't planning on wearing the hat on the nose, mind you, just to hide under it while I filled up my belly. Faster than you'd count to ten, I was in front of the door. I knocked, I waited, I peeked, I entered. No one was there but a couple of mannequins and rows and rows of costumes, enough to fit an entire carnival. I looked for hats. Well, there were hats all right, but not the kind I imagined. For instance I hadn't imagined feathers. Half the lot had them. The rest were in colors no respectable pirate would dare show on a deck. I wasn't a pirate yet, you say? You're right! So, I tried on a couple.

Haha, how strange it feels to reminisce all this. I thought I had forgotten most, but as I think of it chronologically, it all comes back to me like it was yesterday. I told you most anything has happened to me. This is just some of it.

So, you would think I should've just given up. But let me tell you, I was myself then as much I am myself now and this pirate never gives up. Especially when hungry. A lion would be more likely to give up on a wounded zebra than this lad on a meal. As I was telling myself all this, not because I like talking to myself in ladies' boudoirs, but to reassure my masculine integrity of its… well, integrity, my eyes fell on a dark veil wrapped around a mannequin's head. The head and the lower face were hidden, just the eyes were visible. Now you see where I'm going. I didn't, but I still put it on. It looked like someone had pitched a tent over my mouth, but I didn't care. Except now my shirt and pants made me look ridiculous. Let's try on the top, I said. And done. I ceremoniously disrobed the mannequin and put the top on. I remember it had a V shaped base pointing at my navel, leaving my hips uncovered. I had a thin and tight body that luckily never displayed much hair, legs included. I say this because the skirt, though long to my ankles, was split on both sides all the way up to my, uh… unmentionables. So in order to hide those I had to roll them up to a size that, by my today standards, would make them, uh… unnecessary. The belt had little bells and jingly bits about it so I chose another one, wide and leathery from a costume down the line.

Since none of the shoes fit, I had to go with a pair of open toe sandals. This lad wouldn't do things halfway, no sir. You may laugh now, but know that later on I often used disguise when the need arose. Mostly with success.

After a couple of twirls in front of the mirror, to check for possible giveaways, I put a shawl around my shoulders and was prepared the room when a feeling that something was not right nudged at me. Something was amiss. Parts were missing. You know what parts I mean! I was flatter than the back of a Christmas cookie up there. So, I divested and chose one of them bosom-cupper thingies that lay about the place. Never knew you needed a team to put it on, so after some trials I just stepped inside it and pulled it up like it were pants. I used my old socks for filing to make things look livelier.

And so began the long trek for breakfast.

I arrived in time for supper.

Here's why:

At first, everything looked like a success. I passed a couple of giggling girls on the corridor who stopped and greeted me. I turned my head to the side and, holding on to the shawl, tweetled-tweetled-doo at them from the tip of my fingers, trying to hide as much as possible of my hands. They tweetled back and reprised their way unwary. This wasn't so bad. I was proud of me. Master of disguise today, tomorrow an international spy, I told myself. My career options had doubled on the spot.

So proud, my feet got lighter, my shoulders straighter, I was flying down that hallway. I could almost taste eggs and ham. As I put my foot on the first stair a hand caught my upper arm from behind and I heard, "Aisha?" I tried to keep going, but the grip was firm. "Goodness, you must be very strong!" the voice said as I was struggling with its owner.

Finding, I didn't have a choice, I spun 'round and came face to face with the girl from the kitchen, which was the same girl from the previous evening, which was the same girl I'd had a couple of unchristian dreams about during the night. All three of them stood there smiling at me with a pair eyes like blue stars on a sunny day. "Your kind of dancing must be quite an exercise, you are so toned," she said poking my stomach with a finger as I concealed my surprise with a gasp and the gasp with a burp. "Good, you ate. Marlene wants to see you. Come!" she said and she caught my hand pulling me down the stairs. Her voice was like honey on butter.

My feelings, you ask? In waves. At first it was the despair for the eggs and ham that seemed to fly away. Then excitement, for I was holding a soft and warm hand and, to tell you the truth, I hadn't done much of that before. In fact I couldn't remember a time when I done it at all. In fact I didn't even try to remember for I knew I never had done it, damn you, vow of sincerity!

Next, came fear. Did she say Marlene? And how had she not realized the fraud? The answer came almost immediately as she pranced down the steps light as a butterfly. "I'm Anna," she said. "You are the first real belly dancer we've ever had. Maria and Corine were the ones that had to fake it, but they weren't very good, so Marlene decided to get a true expert. Nice to meet you," she turned her head and smiled. I was holding the scarf around my face to double cover so I tweetled my fingers and squeezed out what I thought sounded like a giggle.

It must be destiny, I told myself. The place is full of lasses and she's the only one I keep bumping into. Not that I was complaining. I was still hungry, but at least my eyes were feasting. She seemed very young, the youngest of all the girls I had seen so far. She wore a light shirt and low candy-pink pajama pants that revealed the immaculate skin around her hips; her hair the color of ripe wheat flew freely over her shoulders and her eyes were a blue only the sea can match in depth. What was she doing in this place? I asked myself. She seemed content. The smell coming from her made me forget the danger I was in. Until she stopped and knocked on a door I recognized.

"Entre!" Marlene's voice came.

I followed Anna through. The game is over, I thought. What will Marlene do to me? Nothing she could do, I judged, would be as embarrassing as letting this girl see my nose in the state it was.

Both sisters were there at the desk bent over what looked like a world map. Marlene had her back to us. "What iz it? I'm busy now," she said.

Sigrid released a cloud of smoke, lifted her head and glanced at me. She seemed lost in thought, but I knew she had more senses than a heard of cats so I shifted and tried to make myself as tiny as possible behind Anna's body. Eye still on me, she puffed her cigar, sucked on one of her molars, grunted at something only she knew and looked back at the map.

"This is Aisha, Madame. You said to bring her."

"Le Colonel learned of er arrival and wants zhe first dance. You know how much ee insisted, ees campaign in Africa, zhe camels, zhe dancers, blah, blah, blah… *Mais il paye bien, alors…* Ee iz waiting in the Pasha Room. Teach er zhe rules. No touching, eh! *Juste dancer.* You stay and watch." She said all this turned halfway.

"Yes, Madame."

Anna curtsied and she turned around and exited. I tried to imitate her gesture, but I almost tripped myself. To this day I'm not sure, but before I got out I thought I saw a small grin on Sigrid's face.

Now I was in real trouble.

"Oh, I forgot to ask, do you speak English?" Anna asked when outside.

I groaned something and with my thumb and index showed "Very little," all the while looking around for an escape. "But, you do understand me, no?" "So, so," I did with my head, and was about to start sprinting when she said, "Did you see her sister? Real scary, no? And there is a boy with her," she giggled.

Yes, she did. She giggled. I know it's not much, but any hormone-crammed zitter out there will tell you that that's plenty. At that age I was practically teaming with the stuff to the point that some mornings I could taste it in my mouth. So I didn't run. Of course, I wanted to hear more! I bet you do too, but that's all I have. Next, she caught me by the hand and it was all over.

She dragged me in front of two double doors. On our way we met and greeted some other girls but I was in another world. The sneaky foxy minx! She *had* noticed me! While she had made it clear that the contrary was happening. How do they do it? You think they don't even know you exist while they have you priced to the last tooth. I'm not like that. When I notice a beauty, she'll hear about as soon as I lay my eyes on her. Or see the drool marks if she's exceptionally fair.

"Ok," she said, once we stopped, "It's your first time so don't worry." She got closer and stared intently at my eyes, "Are you crying?" I shook my head and stood back. The cursed veil was rubbing on my nose and the pain was making my eyes water. "I love your eyes, they're gorgeous! Can't even see your make up, you *are* good! Oh, don't let all this upset you," here she gave me a hug and her nose came near my chest. I saw it twitching a little. "This is a great place, Marlene is the best madam. She'll never force you to do anything you don't want to. Just do what you're so famous for—dance—and you'll forget the nerves in no time. This client, he's a little strange, but a big girl like you should be able to handle him. He knows he shouldn't touch you, but I'll be in the next room watching through the camel's eyes, just in case. If you need me just bang the wall and I'll be right over. Don't worry," she added, "you'll do great." I was still hugging her when she opened the doors and pushed me inside.

And there I was, my sorrowful friend. Like a virgin on the sacrificial altar. Even dressed as one mind you. Resigned to his fate, stood I, the future greatest pirate of all times, about to shake my belly before a—

Was that a snout I was seeing? Incredulous, I advanced two steps. A mystifying sound of zither and cymbal was flowing through the air; the room itself was dim-lighted painted dark red with golden trims and was furnished mostly by pillows of all sizes scattered across the carpet. A screen of transparent curtains, pulled half way, divided it in half. Behind it, in the center, a cluster of pillows was grouped around a table set on small legs on the floor. Large plates with foods, the type you don't use silver to eat, lay there and, at the far end, from behind some pillows, a snout, a real animal's snout was making its way through one of these plates emptying it of its contents with the ease you would your pockets should I ask you to.

Two steps later I discovered that it belonged to a hog. It was wearing a military jacket and an officer's cap.

It looked up at me with the nonchalance and smuttiness of a pig that was used to ordering people around. It grunted.

"Colonel?" I mumbled.

"Oink," it said back.

From the description I had thought the colonel may be fat *as* a pig, not a fat pig. A real fat pig with a curly tail and everything.

Then it hit me: it was a trap. Those crafty wenches!

It's hard to describe the humiliation I felt. To play such a prank on a sensitive lad as myself I felt was pure cruelty. If only I could dig a hole and hide in it. I imagined them in the next room watching through the camel's eyes laughing their hearts out. The camel's eyes. On the right wall there was a painting of a caravan moving through the desert fighting a sandstorm. The leading camel and its handler were realistically depicted in the foreground, the rest of the convoy being half hidden by waves of blown sand.

Upset as I could be, I approached the painting. The handler's face was covered but the camel's glassy eyes seemed to judge and pity you the same. I felt like poking them with my fingers, but in the end just took a blanket and threw it around the frame. Any minute they'll burst in laughing, I thought. They'll laugh even harder when they see my nose, I thought. I hope they choke and die, I thought.

As I was preparing mentally for what was to come, I heard a wild scream and from nowhere something heavy landed on my back. It was so surprising that a-tumbling I went squarely on top of the pig. The pig went flat on the carpet legs splayed at its sides. It began squealing like one about to become pork, madly struggling to get free, large ears slapping at my face. Two arms tightened around my neck and a sharp voice yelled in my ear, "Die now, you double crossing wench!" Choking, I jumped up and started running around the room slamming my back on each of the walls. Unsuccessfully. In desperation I ran towards the table in the middle, leaped in the air and landed the thing on my back on it and me on top of the cursed thing.

The arms around my neck went limp and I was able to take a breath of fresh air. But only one before the pig, now mad with the awareness of the brevity of life, ran head first between my legs.

I saw most of the stars in the universe and heard a fat lady singing an aria in my head. Phew, it's so vivid I'm hearing it right now. Lots of a's and o's! In the end, I rolled to the side holding what's left of my groin.

Many breaths later I inched up and glanced at the table. It was broken to the floor, food scattered around it, but on top of it lay a half-naked half-man. He had long disheveled hair and a beard. His miniature torso was as hairy as the beard; fortunately he was wearing pants and boots. The traumatized pig was now grunting in a corner, head under a pillow.

I picked up the jacket and the hat and held them up. They were small, child size. Was this the colonel? I wasn't sure what to believe. The door remained closed, and I might've killed a very small person, perhaps even a bearded child! Was he dead? Upon inspection he wasn't, he was just playing so on account of being knocked out. The smell of him suggested that he'd been dipped in a barrel of Filipino rum.

I was fixing to tuck him under a dresser, when I heard a knock and Anna entered. "I'm sorry, I tried to… I have to check…," she got to say before her eyes widened considerably. Since what she first saw was one of the boots coming off of the near-naked little bugger I was holding upside down in the air, by the legs, I could almost feel what she believed.

"What are you doing with the colonel?" she asked.

I quickly threw him on some pillows, and shrugged my hands backing up quite embarrassed. So, it hadn't been a prank? How was I to explain?

"What happened here?" she looked around. The room looked like a crew of pirates just had a social gathering in there. Or, a social gathering where at least one pirate was present.

I've been invited once to one of those by a baroness that had taken a liking to me. I did my best to lift my eyebrow when I asked a question or keep my pinky up while emptying them bottles. I think it was a success. Two day later I declared the castle independent territories, I raised a flag made up of a pair of the baroness' knickers on its main tower, pillaged every room of anything that had any value and when the army arrived, fortified myself inside the wine cellars. I surrendered two weeks later, second day after the wine ran out. There will be times when there won't be enough liquor. Remember that.

But this situation was a great deal worse! I couldn't declare my innocence without revealing my true identity and worst of all, I was sober.

"Who *are* you?" Anna's voice followed me down the corridor where I was sprinting as fast as I could. I should've just stayed and explained, but I'd never done that before…

nor ever since, so I don't know why am I even saying it!

What to do now? Where to go? I was thinking I would just return to my room, change back and nobody'd be the wiser. Ever!

But you see, I was still hungry. And you know that spells trouble. As I was cascading down the stairway, I was certain that no matter what I should lock myself in and never come out until my nose healed. I didn't care if I starved to death. But when you're young, there is nothing more uncertain than the thing you're most sure. By the time I got to the next floor I felt so famished that now I was certain that I couldn't make it to my room unless I put some food inside my belly first. So I kept going all the way down. The kitchens, I thought, should be the safest place now; no one would think to look for me there.

Pleased with myself, I passed through the eating hall and snuck my head inside the main kitchen. There were two persons going about their business around the stove, while another was slicing down some big chunks of boiled beef. I watched him mesmerized trying to contain the monsoon inside my mouth. He finished, scraped everything inside a big bowl, and from inside the oven pulled out a ham big as my head that he started to treat also to the knife.

I was going through the torments of Hell when someone called from the other room and he put down the knife and left. With the voracity of a dinosaur, I leapt to the ham and grabbed it with trembling, greedy hands. I dropped it right back for it burned. I took down my shawl and wrapped it around the loot. So packing ham, I initiated the pullback to friendlier territories where I was to devour it in peace.

I was a yard from the door when who do you think steps through it? That's right, the gracious hippo I had met that morning. My plight was to go on. In her hand was a thick piece of pork skin on which she was chewing; her eyes flicked from my eyes to the oozing package I held dearly against my chest and then back to my eyes. In a flash she understood. A deluge of foreign curses and slaps washed over me as I tried to sneak past her. Alas, a fly couldn't fit; she was wider than the doorframe. I backed up but see my way blocked by the other two employees. In desperation, I uncovered the ham and attempted to make a meal of it right then and there. But woe is me, I was still veiled. The cook reached out and grabbed the pork butt from my hands with inhuman strength. Let your tears flow!

She didn't expose me; she didn't even care to know who or what I was. Maybe she'd already guessed, I don't know; all she wanted was for me to peel a cauldron of potatoes and scrub the deepest, most inaccessible corners of the kitchen to a shine that would make any rat turn back and go wash its paws. All this on an empty stomach, imagine! I was so hungry not even the dirty rat would have been safe in my presence… You think I didn't try to escape? Phew, she kept herself between me and everywhere else with such success that I was still there by the evening meal.

Dinner was the only meal the residents of the Hotel Royal made an effort to take together. A large table filled the center of the mess hall. Each evening everyone sat down and waited for Marlene to come bless the meal. It sounds strange, but there was a unity of all the employees and a respect surrounding their mistress that I only later understood.

So I wasn't expecting much when the kitchen Cerberus put a large bowl on my hands and pushed me through a door. She wanted me help set up the table, I thought. So I barged right in the middle of Marlene's benediction. I froze. The serving spoon didn't care and slipped to the ground. Marlene raised her head, looked at me then finished with an "Amen."

Everyone sat while I scrambled to set my bowl anywhere on the table. Behind the veil that was covering my face, I was sweating bullets. But, if you didn't understand yet that it wasn't my day, you should go back to counting your fingers. A hand caught my arm as I was about to spin around and sprint out of there. I tried to keep going but the grip was strong, and strangely familiar.

"Say *Aisha*," said Anna looking into my eyes. "How was your day?"

She had a smile on her face that froze the tip of my toes.

"Wonderful!" answered a girl from my other side. "Nikki took me shopping. The city is marvelous!" She had dark hair, a slightly hawkish nose and full lips. She looked up at me with large black, eyes and said, "*Salam!*"

"But nothing out of the ordinary happened to you?" insisted Anna squeezing whey out of my arm. "Did you get in a fight, by any chance?"

"A fight? Why would I get into a fight? The people here are so nice!"

"So you didn't deceive anyone, today? Make a fool of them in front of Madame? No one confessed things to you things only *you* should hear?" Anna growled through her teeth. Her eyes were spewing lava.

Aisha looked confused while I, with superhuman effort, struggled my arm free and ran.

As I was about to exit to the kitchens—a wild scream. I heard that before, I thought in the second before a small hairy chest slammed into my face. Two puny legs wrapped around my waist, two smaller hands clench my throat and a sharp voice cried, "Sabotage! Sabotage!"

The impact sent me flying backwards. With the Lilliputian on top of me, I slid a good distance and came to rest with my head beside Marlene's metal foot. She calmly looked down at us, pulled a big ladle from a pot on the table, shook it well and brought it down upon my assailant's head. He softened and spilled himself over my face and I got to take another in-depth look at the dense jungle decking his tiny bust.

"How many times must I say small drinks for zhe Colonel," said Marlene looking with severity around the table. "Ee waz once betrayed by *une danceuse* and zhe *alcool* come up to eez ed and make eem crazy!

"Donna Belan," she turned to the matron cook, "see zhat ee wakes up in eez room. *Et* bring pleez *une* plate for my *neveu.*"

And that's how I got to eat. Phew, it doesn't seem so eventful now! But for the whispering, or the laughs, or the fact that I had to turn my face if I wanted to see my spoon, or the pair of eyes stabbing me from across the table, it was the best meal of my life.

Following that, I decided to never leave my room. Then I saw the stupidity of it. If I do that who's going to enjoy the company of two dozen or so of young beautiful lasses? Not me, that's who! So, I spent the rest of the time willing my nose to get better so I can get out of there. And it did, and I did.

And you'd think that I'd have learned my lesson…Ha, I never learn, I refuse to learn. I'd have to sit down to learn.

A couple of weeks later I was great friends with all of the hotel's residents. All except one, as you may have guessed. She avoided me like I had the pox. This didn't slow me much as I thought there were plenty of fish in the pond. The fisherman shouldn't starve just because the enchanted little fish doesn't bite, no? But still, there was a spot in my heart that was soft for Anna, so I done my best to wear her away with silly jokes at the table, or funny faces as she sped past me in the hallways. It didn't work. To top the cherry with the cake, just before we left Hotel Royal she caught me with my pants down. In fact they weren't down, they were hanging from one of the two beautiful chandeliers that ornate the saloon, but the point is that I wasn't in them.

You see…

Marlene and Sigrid were out that day making secret preparations for our trip. Being early in the afternoon, the hotel was almost empty of clients, so, a group of girls and I decided to play some games.

It started out innocently and we were having a merry old time until the rascal inside of me proposed that we play for dares. I figured them being so many and I only one the odds were clearly in my favor. I had a few dares in my mind

I was going to ask that were to make me a very happy man. So, it came as a terrible surprise when I lost the first round. I figured they cheated, but since I couldn't prove it I had to obey. I had been dared to sing a song, since everyone knew from a previous experience that I couldn't sing to save my life.

I started in a low key and with little enthusiasm, but twenty something beauties had their eyes on me, so timidly I started sketching a few of them cancan steps, you know, just to get a few laughs. The cheers inspired improvisation, and the steps got bigger and more confident. I was a riot, I thought. This turned out better than I'd expected. The music came on and I did a twirl or two and shook my booty to the left and to the right, which seemed to drive them lasses crazy. To keep the momentum, I reached for my belt and pulled it out and spanked my bottom a few times. They were rolling on the ground. My body was now doing rounds I hadn't thought were possible and my hips were rocking like Jonah's boat in the storm. Swinging low and swinging high I let my knickers slide to the floor, I put one foot out and with a masterful move I jolted the pair above my head. You know where they landed.

On the floor the delirium had reached new proportions. They were throwing money at me. Some of them had joined me and we were shaking it together. Dancing in your unmentionables is so easy, I was thinking, I should make it my profession. Not for a moment did I guess they were thus cheering because I was bad at it. I was so into it that I was inventing new moves with ...well, every move.

I was in my own world, perfecting a move which I thought deadly for the faint of heart, and which I now shall keep secret, and didn't realize the cheers had ceased. Impeccably executed, I opened my arms and eyes to receive my tribute and there before me stood Marlene, Sigrid, Anna and Nikki, a splendid Nigerian beauty with legs longer than a day of lent. The rest of my audience had disappeared.

Nose held high, with an expression of absolute and supreme indifference, eyes looking straight ahead, after dropping whatever she was carrying, Anna disappeared up the stairs. Sigrid removed her cigar and allowed an eloquent "Phew!" Marlene, on the other hand, hopped closer, lifted her prop and dropped it on my head, then exited in the same manner. Sigrid measured me with a squinty eye, as I rubbed my head, and said, "Be in Marlene's office in five minutes. Wear pants."

They were smoking at the desk waiting for me with no bottle of liquor in sight. I stared at the floor shuffling my foot like a guilty child waiting to see what's coming to him.

"We can't trust eem," said Marlene pointing at me. "Ee iz big problem. I told you to leave my girlz alone! Why iz Anna upset? You bring eem you decide. Maybe *juste* send eem ome."

"He is not a bigger problem than you've ever been," said Sigrid calmly. "He didn't do anything you haven't already done ten times worse. And why do you care about the little whore? We'll leave in two days, it's not like she'll see him again."

"She iz not a ooore!" cried Marlene banging her fist on the desk. "She iz like my daughter! And *justement,* she comes weez us."

"Don't even think about! You've lost your mind. This is not a school trip."

"*Exactement*, she grew up on a ship and knows ships. Unless you know to navigate she comes weez us. And Nikki too, she iz good mechanic. I seenk of everyseeng."

"I don't like it," grumbled Sigrid. "Young women around this idiot in heat. You saw what happen, and where we're going... I can't take care of everybody."

"You take care of your orny idiot, I take care of my girlz. I don't want to see eem around zhem!"

"All right, it's your ship after all... Now, tell him!"

"You'll know zhe location of zhe treasure in case someseeng appen to us."

"Me?" I said.

"No. Mon frère. Of course you! What language I am speaking? Even if you don't deserve it."

"But why not Albert, or one of the girls?"

"We need a young man in case someseeng appen to us."

"I don't plan to go anywhere until I get my hands on the *hurensohn*," said Sigrid. But, you should know anyway."

Just thinking of Ruzban and Babar I was very certain that I didn't want to know. "But, if they catch me..." I said.

"Don't worry I will make sure they don't," replied Sigrid enigmatically.

I had no choice. I memorized the directions to an island in the Pacific Ocean close to the Philippines. There were descriptions of things and places on the island where something called *die Beute*, was hidden. Later I found out that it meant, exactly, *the booty*.

"Now," Marlene said once I had recited the list twice, "I will destroy zhe maps and we are zhe last people on zhis planet to know of it. *Que Dieu nous aide!*"

"Pointless to say what would happen to you if you disappear or tell anyone about this," added Sigrid from behind me.

"Pointless," I repeated, convinced, and with no intention of ever betraying the woman.

I went to sleep with a heavy heart, repeating the directions in my head, and yet, I couldn't stop wondering at the perils Orlin and Gunther must've gone through to bring a boat all the way to that forgotten place. It must've been all an adventure. Not my kind of adventure though. I was fairly convinced that the life I wanted involved more of *die Beute* I had just discovered in Hotel Royal and less of *die Beute* on a godforsaken island in the middle of nowhere.

CHAPTER 7

ADVENTURES AT SEA

Hah, Rose you wretched warden from hell! I'm just letting you know that wheels are in motion. Did you think you would stop me forever? Ha! I've sailed against the wind most of my life, you vile woman! Hehehe! By the time you hear this I'll be drunk as a sailor, that's what I'll be! The honest way. And you can't stop me! No one can.

I'll keep along with the story for this is why I'm here, but know that I'm scheming, that's what I am, I'm scheming like a pebble inside an honest' man boot. I'll get my liquor if I have to bribe a thousand angels or need kiss the devil on the mouth!

I can still remember her name. It sounded strange to me because at the time I couldn't speak French. A very proud Marlene was giving us a tour and as I was looking for opportunities to get back in her graces, I asked what it meant. I remember she couldn't translate it. She stuck out her tongue and started panting and drooling. "Are you sick?" I asked.

"Idiot!"

"What kind of name is that 'Idiot'?"

"You are zhe idiot, idiot, zhe boat iz not idiot. Iz like when zhe dog aaz eet in eez body."

"In heat?" I tried to understand.

"Yes."

"Oh," and I winked at her.

She slapped me over the head, "Idiot. When is too much eet in zhe body and ee drinks water."

"Ah, when the dog is hot. Drooling, you mean?"

"Yes, yes, but not ezactly like zhat. More like…like… nicer."

Well… Her name was *La Baveuse*.

We pulled anchor and hoisted sails the next Monday at first light. Since lately the country was hosting more revolutions than an old woman fake teeth, Marlene had her anchored in a small bay an hour outside the capital, ready for a quick getaway should the time come. She was under a hundred footer, two masted schooner, ivory sails, wooden hull and six cabins (one which I shared with Albert). A smart diesel engine made port maneuvering a breeze.

I can see her now. She was a beauty to sink your teeth in! A bit old, not too old to drag her feet though, enough to be graceful, wide sterned—a bit much for how I like them now—but enough to keep up appearances. As a woman past her prime, she yet competed with the younger ones for the eyes of the public, and made up in experience and refinement what she lacked in freshness or speed. She heeled seductively when riding and gently bounced when under way, and as much as I ignored her on that passage, so do I remember her now with fondness.

Needless to say we were expecting a lengthy passage, and I will not bother you with the details of it. Save a few instances which I will describe to you next, my callow state of mind, untuned to the call of the waves, perceived it as dull and long and dreadful. Thus is the sea for the ignorant. You need burnt skin and salty eyes to grasp its beauty, and peace in your soul to appreciate its tranquility, neither of which I had. Long days, identical days, chased each other across the expanse and all my eyes could see was water below and the sky above, broken only by the occasional crack of the sails catching wind. That is something to drive a restless youngster mad, I tell you, especially one shunned by the rest of his crew.

A fortnight after leaving our last stop in Costa Rica, the wind died and with it everything else. All but the glaring eye of the sun, that is. We started the engine and under its tug *La Baveuse* resembled a tear dragging a trail across unblemished crystal. If before the trip was boring, now I wasn't sure I was still alive. I had to pinch myself to see, and doing it was all the excitement the days afforded me. I later took up fishing, something until then I would've not cared to know even had it been promised to get me to heaven. When the line yanked for the first time the adrenaline almost killed me. You might say I was hooked. Next, I took up swimming. The hot, dead air was suffocating my skin like an impenetrable blanket, so I spent many days bathing in the cooler waters with disregard for any danger that might come from the abyss below.

Until, danger came…

The day was like any other, and nothing let on that I

would have then my first adventure at sea. I woke up as usual at noon, went to the kitchen, had my coffee, endured Anna's indifferent look, ignored *Les Terribles'* (that's how we were calling them now, the crazy sisters) ritual fighting, snorted at Nikki's daily joke about my nose, and mounted the deck. The air was stale, not a bug in sight, "nothing was stirring not even a mouse"—as a better teller once said. I jumped in the water to cool myself and make some noise. The silence was deafening. Practicing my back stroke, I heard another splash. For some time now, I had dreams of Anna coming to join me and hopefully watched for her golden hair to spring from the depths; instead, the shirt-covered bump of a human stern surfaced, followed by Albert. My surprise overcame my disappointment for I hadn't known he could swim. Instead, he proved to be a better swimmer than I, and I was compelled to stop racing him when he had beaten me twice. I pulled out a rubber ball and we began playing catch.

So we had been playing for a few minutes; myself, I was about forty yards away from Albert and thirty from the boat, when I heard screams. I turned around and saw Nikki and Anna yelling and waving their hands. Their voices were scrambled together and muffled by the splashes of the water so that I couldn't make out anything at first. Pleased and surprised by Anna's sudden change of heart, I was thanking the gods when fragments of their screams began to make sense: "… ark…ark…shark!" Shark? The second most frightening call one can hear at sea. I spun around and signaled Albert: "Shark! Shark!" He acknowledged it and started swimming toward me. I didn't lose any time and did the same toward the boat. When I got there safe, and they had pulled me in, Albert had still twenty yards to go. Alas, form abaft a large shark fin was closing in fast.

"Gun…gun!" I yelled "We need a gun!"

"Maybe Sigrid… but there's no time!" Nikki said.

I turned around with the intention of running under the deck for a gun and collided head-on with *Les Terribles*, each armed and taking long strides to the rail. "We're eer!" roared Marlene.

They took shooting position along the rail and waited. Marlene let go her crutch and leaned on the railing.

By now Albert was only a few feet away, and you could see the desperation in his eyes. Closing in, a gigantic dark form stalked him from beneath.

"Shoot, shoot! What are you waiting for?" Anna screamed.

In a moment of rare bravery, I caught the rail with one hand, swung down the ladder a few steps and reached out to the struggling man. Two more strokes and he was against the hull. I caught his arm and with an effort that pulled a loud cry out of me, yanked our Quasimodo from the water.

I looked back frantically. The fin had disappeared. I stepped on the deck and barely had Albert climbed a few of the rungs when a huge hole with a thousand teeth opened beneath his legs. Two shots went off almost simultaneously and the shark fell back. A small bloody cloud appeared in the water. Sigrid judged it not large enough to have come from a mortally wounded beast of that size.

I bent over Albert who was catching his breath, spread like a lobster on the deck, and, you know I always joke to diffuse a tense situation or to brighten a scared soul, it's in my nature, so, I said laughingly, "This shark has no manners, he wanted to eat you uncooked."

A strong slap to my head sent me sprawling on the deck. I saw red and leaped around ready to hit somebody. Nikki and Anna were standing there, eyes bolted to me, no love coming through. Snorting like a wild mad hog, I tried to see who the culpable party was, but to this day don't know. I do have a suspicion it didn't come from Nikki. I tightened my fists and stared back at them for several long seconds. There was nothing I could do, you agree. I turned around and went to the storage chest where I remembered seeing a spear gun.

That shark is going to pay, I said to myself. Determined, I pulled a piece of meat from the ice box, coincidentally that day's dinner, and armed with the gun, headed for the deck.

"What are you doing?" Nikki asked, while Albert lifted a frail hand towards the hunk of meat and moaned: "Zhat iz dinner, beev Stroganov."

"Not anymore," I said still angry, charging the gun with an aluminum spear. "Make it shark Stroganoff. Where is it?"

"It has disappeared, you idiot," answered Nikki who evidently didn't have any confidence in my abilities as a harpooner.

"That was a great white, boy; you can't kill a great white with a spear that size," said Sigrid, throwing her wet cigar in the sea.

"No? I'll show you, you old hag; consider yourself lucky I don't aim at your fat behind," I yelled, again, from the safety

of the inside of my head—my courage, though aroused, only went so far. Hell, I was mad! *Chased by a shark and saved an old man's life, only to have my nose slapped into the deck. And now they make fun of me? I am the man around here! I'll show them.* Had there been someone weaker than me on that boat, besides the girls of course, I would've punched him a few times right then and there, with no reason. So he could tell you too, how it feels. Instead, I just said in a defiant tone, "This shark is mine! And I'll do whatever I please!"

I held my breath as I saw her throwing me a slanted look, her eye squinting inquisitively, but she shrugged with indifference and left. Relieved, I breathed deep and imagined myself showing my friends a photo of me and a thousand pound shark. *You are better than all of this*, I worked myself up as great warriors do before a fight, *in your veins runs the blood of legendary hunters such as... or as...* The legendary ones seemed to escape my mind for the moment; nevertheless, when I opened my eyes, I was another man. *I'll show them, yes! I'll show them!*

"Albert, go heat the stove," I said with the majesty of a great hunter just before he gets ready to complete the act which characterizes the very essence of his existence.

I didn't wait for his answer, nor did I listen to the women's complaints, for I was scanning the waters in search of the beast. I caught a glimpse of a dark shadow ten feet off starboard, the opposite side from the ladder Albert and I had scrambled up. I directed myself there, followed closely by the two girls. As a great hero on his way to become a legend, I ignored the presence of the one for whose presence I yearned for most. A huntsman, a true one, in the moment before the kill becomes one with his prey, and in that moment I was a shark, the king-hunter of them all. Thinking of women makes you vulnerable and weakens your hand, if you know what I mean. *Just show them who the man is here! Do that while ignoring them! That's the secret!* I said to myself as I pushed my chest forward and flexed my biceps.

I attached the piece of meat to some fishing line and threw it overboard. Then I lifted it back up until it barely touched the water. *Watch this, weak creatures! Watch the hunter at work! Don't I deserve to be loved and cherished by you all?* Thus my demeanor spoke at that hour.

The shadow didn't move. Just floated there, tantalizing, beneath the surface.

"Come on boy, here is your food!" I yelled. "Come on, I know you're hungry. It tastes better than Albert." (A little humor goes a long way with women.)

Five minutes later, I was still flexed in the majestic position, but alone. The girls had left searching for better entertainment. I dropped my gun and I was about to give up when from the corner of my eye I realized that the dark spot was growing bigger. I reclaimed the weapon and aimed at the meat, heart pounding. "I will try shark fillet, grilled shark, shark soup, shark stew, shark..." I didn't finish: a conical snout pierced the surface, followed by a cold, dead eye looking straight at me. The gigantic mouth opened showing rows upon rows of arrow-shaped, serrated teeth. The chunk of meat, of a serious size, looked as big as a baby's thumb in a lion's mouth. The glance of the lifeless eye froze the blood in me, but only for a wink of time. Then, I aimed and fired.

Since, I have often replayed the event in my head. I can see myself pressing the trigger whilst the wave created by the shark lifts the boat. I see the spear being thrust out; I see myself wobbling, trying to regain my balance, and I see the spear missing. Though not completely. It enters the flesh of the beast's snout not far from his left nostril, and stops after exiting on the right side about a foot's length, nearly even with the length projecting from the left. The last sight I see before he drops back into the water is that of a shark wearing a silver-white moustache, swallowing down a large chunk of meat.

The next moment, as I had forgotten to attach a line to the spear, he was out of sight. I reloaded the gun, properly this time, and waited, but in vain. The ungrateful Albert refused categorically to donate more bait and I had to give up on the fantasy that had been destined to make me famous amongst the greatest fishermen.

Next day, life was ready to follow its normal course. I woke up as usual; had coffee as usual; I ignored everyone as usual, and jumped in the water. As usual.

The routine ended right there, for I jumped right back out. During my short flight overboard, I had perceived a dark spot tarnishing the crystal clear surface, about thirty paces away. By the time I made it back on board and found the binoculars, the spot had crept closer. Through the glasses, I could see the shark, the same from the previous day. I recognized him from the new feeler on his snout, which he (can't say if proudly or not) wore without any sign of discomfort.

Unsure if he would know to properly show his gratitude, I, from then on, had to give up the water. The shark was there continually and, unusually, near the surface for I could see him most of the time. Sometimes he would go missing for a few days and, just when I thought we had finally got rid of him, he would appear the next morning smiling under his iron whisker as though he had played some joke on us. In memory of his famous cousin Moby, I baptized him Moustache Dick.

Moustache Dick was a smart shark. I can't say on a shark scale, but on a dog scale, he was probably in the upper percentile. He acted like one, too. I tried to hunt him again in the followings days, which soon turned into weeks, but he always kept his distance, just like a dog that had learned its lesson. I used as bait just about everything we had on the boat that I thought a shark might enjoy. I got myself slapped, cursed at, and even chased with a loaded shotgun for borrowing different things that belonged to my mates. The shotgun was Albert who, one day had a breakdown over me stealing the meat from the freezer, entered Sigrid's cabin without knocking and, under her confused watch, picked up the gun and began chasing me around the deck promising that *I* would be the main course of the next meal. I'm telling you, the old man could move fast when provoked. I escaped with my life and didn't ever touch his meat again, but I did persist in my effort to convince Moustache Dick to approach the boat. I even cut myself and let the blood drip into the water—in vain. As I said before, had something weaker than I been around, I would've probably used it as bait, I was so desperate. Enduring such a trip, it doesn't take long to get obsessed with the smallest distraction, and I would've given anything to get another shot at him. But no matter what I tried, I tried in vain, for he never did approach the boat.

In the end however, my obsession gave place to admiration and respect. I even fished for him; each fish I would stun with a blow and throw back in the water to my shark-dog. I can't say if he ate it though, for I forgot to tell you that in the days following Albert's adventure, the wind had finally picked-up and the boat was now moving fast.

Before long, we berthed in Majuro Atoll of the Marshall Islands. I went ashore with the hope of finding some books to keep me company for the second leg. On account of space, there wasn't a book store on the tiny island, only a liquor hut, a market place featuring fruits and vegetables, island medicines, and, since one is rarely enough for even the smallest community, another stand selling the local moonshine, which made *Les Terribles* twice as happy. We replenished our provisions at the marketplace and at a small table in the corner I discovered an impressive collection of magazines featuring lovely maidens on the cover. Intrigued and much more, I bought one of each. If need be I could read pictures as good as words. Indeed, walking to the boat I found myself so drawn into the lecture that I almost fell over the pier.

Moustache Dick was still there when we returned to sea and the first thing I did—actually, the second, the first being to read one of my new books from cover to cover—was catch him some fish.

This part of the trip was far more exciting than the previous. You'll see: First, thanks to my reading material, I had something to pass the time. Second, God was breathing over the water and our ship maintained good speed. And third, we had entertainment. The kind I would've rather enjoyed as a spectator. Nonetheless, as there was no place for an audience, I found myself obliged to participate in a few of the nightly displays put on by *Les Terribles*.

Wonderful recitals! I will speak of them in musical terms for, to a foreigner who didn't speak our languages, the yelling and the cursing could surely have sounded like some kind of opera. Having more alcohol than food in our reserves, the sisters opted for self-sacrifice and halved their meals while tripling their liquid rations. As a result, the show often began soon after lunch and lasted until one of its protagonists passed flat out. And if you say that too much music is exhausting, know that there was some variety in the content of the libretto, which helped us cope. And of course, we had no choice. They had the instruments. Classics such as "It is your fault," or "I'm going to kill, you *hure*," or "I have lost a limb because of you," with shotgun accompaniment, improved our musical knowledge.

Two times I happened to find myself on center stage, in a heated dialogue with one soloist, her tunes bringing warm feeling to my heart. And my pants. With the risk of falling out of your graces, my beauties, for by now I surely must be the hero of your fantasy, I must tell of it for I feel the truth should prevail no matter what.

First time, Sigrid disgorging of artistic passion and probably blinded by it, mistook me for her sister and sang to me in solo "I got you *Schlampe*,[6] you are dead." In vain I tried to get within sight of her bona-fide eye. She was holding her instrument firmly in front of it and together they followed me like a duck at the fair. When I mentioned that

I wasn't the *Schlampe*, she answered that she grew up with me and knows what a *Schlampe* looks like. I insisted that I was a man, thus my thick voice, but as her voice was two octaves lower than mine, the argument sounded more like its own rebuttal. When the climax was about to be reached and the final note to be released, I closed my eyes and let go. Totally. Fortunately, another note, discharged by the real *Schlampe*, hit the mast above her head and caused enough of a distraction for me to have time to faint and disappear from the diva's visual field. I woke up ready for a change. Which I did in my cabin.

The second time she confused me again, this time with her deceased husband, though she didn't say which one, and resolved that I deserved a dedication. I protested, for I felt unworthy, but I couldn't deny her a few dance steps when she got more insistent with the trigger. Then, she gave me chase about the entire vessel and cornered me on the deck. Resigned and freshly relieved, I stepped inside the life ring and jumped overboard. I hadn't seen Moustache Dick for the past days and hoped he wasn't a music lover. Fortunately, he hadn't attended the concert that night. Needless to say when Nikki pulled me back on deck sopping wet, I was in need of another change.

I booked tickets at topmast after that and from there enjoyed full performances in the luxury of my box. Such artists! What talent! I often wonder how they survived those recitals. God bless them! And God bless liquor for it brings out the artist in us every one!

Eventually, we arrived in Palau—the last stop before Calbosa Island—physically and mentally exhausted and, at least in my case, with no change of clothes.

CHAPTER 8

A MOST INTERESTING CHARACTER

Rooose!

You foiled my plan, Rose! Damn you! You'd better take care, for one of these days I will... I will... do something! I schemed and paid good money and now you drink it, eh? I'm sure you do. It's good liquor, Rose. Don't spoil it. Drink it. Drink it for me, you wretched wench!

I know forces are gathering against me. I feel them... Things are not right! They've found me. And I need my liquor to fight them. You'll see Rose, you'll be sorry! They know I'm spent and weak. Have you sold me out? Have you betrayed me like so many before? I'm still here, am I not? And my Judases? They rot in hell, where I sent them. Keep that in mind, Rose! Ah...

This woeful story will be the end of me, I tell you! You and that scurvy nurse are to blame. You started me on this and now I can't leave before I've finished it. It's not like me to leave a chore undone. Yes, I call it chore! Where on this blessed planet have you seen a ripe man, such as myself, spin a yarn on a clear head. It's madness, I tell you! My grandfather, heaven has him, used to spin yarns *only* on payday, and *only* after the necessary stop at the tavern. It warmed his soul and reminded him how much he loved the little ones waiting home. He didn't care that Nana (upset for she had expected—she had known!—that the old dog would come home smelling like a barrel of liquor stored in a smoke-house, but, and she had said it every time, she hoped for once he would miss the tavern on his way home), yelled and beat him about the shoulders with the big sweeper made of straws that she had whipped out from behind the old stove. Under a shower of blows and damnations (starting with the threat of divorce and ending with her own self condemnation, for she had wasted her life, as she could've been a famous comedienne—or even a singer, a singer's life would've been better than this life!—with this man who comes home muddled as an ox), he, happy as a newly wedded middle-aged village wench (for that's what the tavern is doing to the spirit of many a man), would pick us little ones up on his freshly swept shoulders, carry us into the barn, throw us down on a pile of hay, give us each a fistful of candy from his pockets, sit himself down in front, pull out his spare bottle (for no man in his right mind left the tavern empty-handed), taste it, sweep his mouth with a back hand and shout, "Heh, heh, my rowdy little imps, have I told you the story of the charmed wolf and the lucky prince?"

"No!" we would say as one.

Of course we'd heard it many times, but he would never tell it the same, nor did it matter, for that was a magical time. And, under the inquisitive eyes of Buttercup, our old cow, he would start… The night long he would spin tale after tale until the last of us succumbed to the sweet smell of hay and the enchanting sound of his voice and fell face down, thoroughly asleep. Then, he would lie next to us and together, we would dream of the prince that ate the golden apples, talking wolves, horses that could fly higher than dragons, or other such marvels that had been planted in our minds, while Buttercup watched over us like a ruminating fairy godmother.

Aaah, those were the times, my pitiful friend...

Now, I should get back to our adventure for little we've sailed, and much is left...

For you to understand the state of despair I was in before we anchored in Palau, I must tell you, my beauties, that of the rare instances in my life when I craved something more than your company, this was the first. After the immeasurable stretch of days I had spent on the water, I would've sold all of your souls for a piece of dry land to set my foot upon, just as now I would do for a bottle of something. Strike me for I'm a sinner!

By now my hair was long and the sun had taken away the need to discolor it; my skin was dark and leathery, about the color of a nicely roasted piglet, and walking through the docks I proudly observed that I didn't look much different from the occasional sailor. The sea had done in a few months what would've taken life a few more years—made me a man. Or at least made me look like one, for I dare acknowledge, in my head I was almost as undeveloped and crude as most of you living there, outside my window, unfortunate souls.

This said I feel better. And, God bless my pipe, for it's the only thing that keeps me alive at present.

So I made my way through the docks happy to have something still beneath my feet and confident that no one would guess from the look of me. I had just crossed half the planet on a ship—that made me a real sailor, right? And a real sailor has many needs and even more appetites following a long stay at sea, no? As I knew my literature, when he docks, a sailor requires three things above all: a piece of meat—big and juicy as a maid's lips should be; liquor—lots of it, a river of it; and the society of merry damsels who are thirsting for company. Having not yet befriended the bottle, the second didn't seem that important, for at that time and that age I was everything else more than thirsty. But, as a practical young lad, I thought that a place where I could satisfy all of my appetites at once would be most appropriate and took on the island in search of it. Of course, I was searching for a place more like Marlene's hotel since the solitude and the literature I had recently mastered had helped keep the memory fresh in my head. Anna's refusal to acknowledge even my presence had hardened my heart and I was sworn to ignore her as much as she ignored me. Just to show her. The sea is full of fish, I told myself, and magical or not, they all taste the same.

So, well-motivated, I walked the cursed island in length and roamed it in width, then I canvassed it again, ignoring its natural beauty, and found myself bound to conclude that the gods of depravity and immorality had missed this forgotten place when they spread their seed in that part of the world. Betrayed as I felt, by the afternoon, hungry and thirsty and blasting those gods for their incompetence, I set to stop in the first place I saw, to work on my stomach's hunger and throat's thirst which by now had eaten away all at my other senses to the point that I would've sold your soul anew, my beauties, this time for a can of stew.

My eyes lighted on a tavern of sorts, set on top of the cliffs, its bamboo awnings nosily rapping the wind. I stepped inside. It appeared to be one of those places where the drinks are cheap but the food is good, and I fit right in with my new looks.

I sat down like a man in his own right, commanded a jug of ale and asked the host to prepare me the largest chunk of meat he could find. He asked what kind of meat, I said I don't care as long as it came from something with hooves. I thought that was a pretty smart answer for a real sailor like me, then I emptied my glass at once for a sailor is always thirsty. Not a minute later, the strangest creature pulled a chair from under my table and casually sat himself in front of me with the assurance of a man that had indeed been invited not once but twice.

I found myself looking at a wild man, old as I could only guess, for the lower part of his face was bedecked by a huge beard, and the upper covered in thick hair probably not brushed or washed since the day it grew in. The skin below his eyes and on his neck was burnt by a thousand suns, but his eyes were fresh and gleamed at me with smug brazenness. He smelled of tobacco and salt water and dead fish and up to that point I never had seen a sea-dog more true to the name. If not for my growling stomach I probably would've welcomed him as a specimen worth studying. Instead I saw him as threat to the integrity of the piece of meat I was about to receive.

I looked around, half the place was empty. "Excuse me sir, this is my table…" I said to him.

"Aye junior," said he to me in a hoarse voice, "this table belongs to the establishment, but in me goodness I'll share it with ya," and he installed himself comfortably. Then, with stone hands he rubbed his legs and groaned deeply like a man who had just climbed a mountain, "Ah, me limbs are best on the nodding deck, I tell ya. It's the hard land that kills 'em." And he gazed at me from under his heavy brow somewhat curious, somewhat amused.

His accent was strange, but I was too deficient to guess its origins. His demeanor was strong and confident, yet not forceful or unpleasant, so I just looked back at him unable to say anything for a while. But, as I was still determined to eat my meal alone, I picked up my ale and the jug and stood up, "I got here first sir, but I don't want to argue with you…I will move myself," I said turning.

"No, but sit me yung friend," he insisted, catching my arm and forcing me back down. "I like ya. One should have company in drinking. Drinking alone is fer losers and misfits and lonely old maids and ya're not one of those are ya?"

Well, I was feeling like one, but not ready to admit it, so I said, "No, I'm only by myself and I should point to you sir that most of the people in here drink by themselves."

"Eeh, safe to presume all losers and misfits…"

Still, I hesitated. I was indeed craving some company, obviously less hairy and with rounder forms, but I felt the old dog wasn't giving me an option. And I don't like not having an option. Well, I don't like it now. Then, I was getting quite used to it. So, I set back the mug and waited.

"Say, yung fella," he said in a merry voice, "if ya fancy the first round, I'll take care of the rest then."

"Don't worry about it, mister," I said doubting he had anything to take care with.

I ordered another jug, the biggest they had and filled his and mine.

"Thank ya, me friend, God bless ya. God bless this yung lad!" he cried loudly standing up and holding his glass in the air; then he emptied it in a single gulp. A few customers caught by surprise lifted their drinks half-way. Then he raised his chin up, heaved a deep and contented sigh and moaned with pleasure, "Ahh, I tell ya what junior. I'll give up saying me prayer tonight if ya fill her up again."

"Sit down, what are you doing?" I yanked him down and quickly refilled his mug.

"A generous lad deserves recognition and ya're a generous one."

I told him to stop calling me that and I'll buy all the drinks.

"Done deal mate, I told ya, ya're generous," he responded with a wink.

My meat arrived. It was one of those slabs as large as your head and thicker than two of my fingers laid side-by-side and judging from the price, it must've come from some divine beast's rump. But I didn't care; I was planning to spend all the money *Les Terribles* had given me, for next I was to be rich anyway. I saw a twitching under my guest's thick beard and seeing his eyes riveted to the sizzling meat, I realized he was licking his lips. I groaned as my own mouth was flooding under a hailstorm. "Ah mister, I can't eat when someone is watching, here…" I asked for another plate and shared the meat and everything else with him.

He blessed me again, grasped it with his hands and began chewing it like he was on a holly mission and that was going to save the world. Grease ran down his beard and onto his clothes where I suppose it fed some even more exotic creatures living in the fabric.

For a while we didn't talk, the sound of chewing and the smacking of the lips paying tribute to his healthy appetite. He finished his plate, licked his fingers loudly enough for everyone to hear, tinkered with his index and thumb inside his mouth, pulled out a piece a meat from between his teeth, looked at it, put it right back and swallowed it, filled up his glass, drank first what was left in the jug, then emptied his mug, set it on the table and exclaimed, "Ahh! Let me order, will ya," and turned to the bar and ordered not one but three more jugs. "It'll save some leg; they might run out, ya know…"

I didn't say anything, being preoccupied to cut my meat into small cubes and eat it delicately as taught I had been, but had never done before. His presence made me exacerbate my movements, as I should prove to anyone watching that we weren't together and only an unfortunate circumstance had brought us to share the same table. He watched me with interest for some time then began talking.

He was a fisherman, the best in those parts—I had his word for it—he knew the Pacific like the back of his hand; his fame was so widespread that the creatures of the sea quivered at the sight of his "barque", as he called it. Unfortunately, at the present time he found himself barqueless, for some terrible incident had relieved the seas of his terrorizing presence and, obliged to sojourn on dry land, he was honoring the island establishments and their patrons, such as myself, with his companionship.

"Oh junior, I tell ya… the sea is a beautiful dame, all dear and cuddly before ya marry 'er, then…" here he paused reverently and watched for a while as the waves beat against the rocks below. Then he pushed his cup away, grabbed one of the jugs, swung it to his lips and half-emptied it with one gulp and brought it whomping down on the planks of the tabletop. "Ya marry 'er, fer she is sweet and peaceful, and ya think that's how she's going to stay… Oooh, but a fool ya are!"

I finished my food and bravely emptied my mug, "What? Why?"

He turned to me with hollow eyes, "Don't ya marry her, ya hear me? Don't ya marry her!"

"Who?"

"Her…"

"How…"

"Don't."

"Why?"

"Because ya'll never be yer old self again, junior. She will glom onto ya like barnacles onto the hull of the ships; ya'll think she fancy ya till one day when she'll make ya sorry ya ever drank a glass of water. And that's as true as me name is Ros Nir. Captain Ros Nir!"

As the message was somewhat cryptic, I asked again, "Why?"

He watched me as a teacher would his worst student and began, "She has in her belly critters the man never laid eye upon, beasts of all shapes and figures the sun itself denies its shine and warmth. They're scary and dreadful, but the danger lay not there, fer ya must be dead before ya'll get to know them; the creatures that roam her lands should trouble ya, fer they better in every way the monsters from below. And those ya meet when ya're alive me friend and ya wish ya was dead and buried and never born to a mother before they finish with ya…"

Another gulp, another jug.

"I used to think meself the king of her; she proved to be the queen of me. She must've been angry and weary of me pretense, fer she took me barque and meself and beat us fer days and days or nights and days, I couldn't tell light from the dark, north from the south, the up from down—that mad she was. Me whole crew perished then, but that was a blessing, fer she reserved fer meself the worst and a thousand times I wished I was dead before…

Then I tell ya, stay away from her if ya fancy yer life. Best, go home and marry a lass and make a good brood of little ones and tell them stories ya figure yerself in yer head, before ya get to live them and be sorry…"

The ale was good, his voice bewitching and his tales more than enthralling. I was making a serious effort to follow his words, but gravity soon overcame my will to look anywhere else than at the table and my head was wobbling in all directions trying to acquiesce to his words. The captain seemed not bothered by my gradual descent towards the table and proposed a new toast and another turn, which I obliged, for a new revelation had come over me: I liked this yellow liquid.

Two jugs later, I felt the need to relieve some of the pressure created in me by the serious quantity consumed and confidently stood up with the sober intention of attending the privy situated somewhere in the back. I promptly fell nose forward on the table to my left, fortunately not occupied at the moment. My companion, who had gotten over the sorrowful stage and was seeing now more joyful times, more or less carried me to the latrine and held me by the back of the shirt while I attempted to pretend to aim.

"Say junior," he asked, "would ya have a place for a worthy sailor on yer boat, wouldn't ya? She's calling me and I'm getting rusty. I've been out of a job fer some time."

"But you said… she is a… a…" I could hardly scramble.

"I said she is me queen junior, and I am no king of her. Once ya've known her like I do, there is no turning back. Ya long fer her like a baby fer the bosom of his mother."

"Soly mate. *hic.*" I answered with a hiccup. My tongue was having now a mind of its own and was trying to tie itself in a knot inside my mouth, "It's my not chip… my ship…my passenger."

"Aaaah, pleasure cruising we are taking then…"

"No, no, it's… sshhh," I motioned him to get closer, "*hic*…it's a seclet."

"Aye, a secret ey? Ya needn't tell me mate; a secret's meant to be kept."

"I tell you maybe not… maybe yes…"

He carried me back to the table and sat me down. There

my cursed mouth wouldn't see itself shut. "You see," it said without me allowing it, "because of the seclet…sshhh…I cannot take me with you. No seclet… I come with you."

"No worries mate, too bad it's a secret, I could've helped ya. I know these waters like me back hands."

"Me too… maybe after I come back from Calbosa I'll buy you a chip like this big… like twenty long feet…" I said, feeling all of a sudden very generous.

He lifted his head and squinted his already narrow eyes, "Calbosa Island, ay?" he asked, trying to get hold of my eyes. "Calbosa Island? Are ya sure, junior?"

I put a finger in front of my lips, "Sssshhhh, *hic*…mate, hold your norses…. I say nothing."

"Ya said Calbosa Island."

"No, I didn't, *hic*... It's a seclet."

"Ya said it!"

I beat my fist on the table and cried a loud "No!!" then hiccupped even louder.

He backed up, "All right, matey, then ya'ven't said it. But, there where ya going, be it or not other than Calbosa Island, because ya'ven't said it, what is yer purpose?"

I waved my head and my arm in the same time, "No pulpose…just vacation."

He reached over the table, caught my collar and pulled me closer, "Ya said ya're getting rich there. What do ya mean by that?"

"Just vacation," I repeated.

His breath smelled like staled beer. He looked at me

long and deep, while I, more or less, was watching his broad nose which was as purple as a plum can get. "Ya lie to me, junior. But, I'm glad. Me senses were right as ever," he said between his teeth.

I shook my head and squirmed like a distressed worm and pulled myself off of him, "I don't say nothing. Leave me alone!"

He slapped his palms on the table and was all of a sudden merry again. He apologized saying that the liquor had clouded his judgment for he simply wanted to give me a hug. Then he filled my mug and toasted, "Let's drink fer yer health, me friend!"

I lifted my cup and emptied it. The feeling of being drunk was new to me. I liked it. All my hopes and dreams seemed within reach. I felt in love with the world and with her creatures.

I stretched across the table and put my hand on Ros Nir's shoulder, "Don't woly vely old dog, *hic*… I will take care of you, *hic*… I will take care of you," I, unintelligibly but confidently, said. "You… you… my friend now. I… I take care of evlybody."

He patiently accepted my demonstration of love, then said, "Many things ya might find on that island of yers, me lad. Terrible things. Are ya sure ya're ready to know them?"

"What…?" I asked unable to hold my head high.

"It is said that she is cursed."

"Cursed?" I understood the word but couldn't grasp the meaning, "what do you cursed mean by … Not that I go, because I don't go there."

"It is said not a soul ever set foot on that island and was ever seen again."

"Ha?"

"There are strange creatures, dark creatures, on that land, me lad, creatures that shun the light of day, dwell on dark places and feed on the flesh of the man. Crews of men have been ripped to pieces before the very eyes of their captains…"

"…lipped to…?"

"…ripped to pieces, mate, ripped to pieces. Devoured while the blood was still warm and their hearts still beating. That's how they talk about it. In me long years I've never set foot on it."

I couldn't hold my head and it landed on the table with a bang. I was fortunately far enough from the edge for my nose to steer clear of it. He helped me raise it and set it on the back of my hands, then continued, "If ya're going to Calbosa Island, I know of only one man that can help ya."

"Who?" I asked trying to open one eye.

"Captain Ros Nir," he answered majestically.

"Los Nil? … I don't know," I said.

"*Me*, junior! The greatest skipper the sea has ever seen!"

"You? But you said *hic*…lipped to pieces…"

He leaned over me, "Oh, don't ya dare step on that land without captain Ros Nir by yer side." He stood up, slapped his hands on the table and declared aloud for everyone present to hear, "Captain Ros Nir knows no fear! Captain Ros Nir, yer honored to see before yer eyes, has no rival on the sea! Some might tell ya otherwise, but ya don't listen to them, no one equals him nine seas over!" He looked at me fiercely, "Time has come for this captain to visit that accursed island. See for himself if the legend is true."

I looked back at him with difficulty, "You said you no boat…"

He sat, "Aye! I don't need a boat, junior."

I was tottering like a flapping sail in the morning breeze, but I still managed to gulp down the last drops in my mug. "No?"

"No. I need *yer* boat."

"Aaa, me no boat." My head fell sideways on the table and pulled with it the jug which lay to rest on my cheek, the last of the ale slowly oozing inside my lips and down my neck and chest. I still muttered, "No, no, no boat…"

"Yes mate, yer boat it's going to be, that you wish it or not. If ya want Calbosa Island I'll give ya Calbosa Island."

"Shh! Seeeclet…"

"Eh, don't worry junior! Yer secret is safe with me. Ya sleep now. Captain Ros Nir is going to take care of ya."

That's all that I can remember now. Rest assured; it's a load more than I remembered the following day.

CHAPTER 9

HE THAT LOOKS FOR TREASURE
FINDS PIRATES

Next day I woke up blasting the gods of liquor and he that will ever drink again. I was out on deck like a pancake, the sun's snickering beams biting at my behind. Inside and out, parts of the body, unfamiliar to me, were screaming in pain. The sights I set my eyes on were waggling as if I was on a ship at sea, and until I held my head with both hands I observed not the rigging and the hoisted sails or everything else around me that would've taught a more aware mind that indeed it was on a ship, and at sea. I couldn't remember how I got on board, but I cared little, limping toward the kitchen to find some respite in coffee. The pot was empty. Disappointed, I rushed back and emptied my stomach over the side. This only furthered my sadness.

I recalled seeing no breakfast on the counter where it usually awaited me. More dead than alive, I knocked on Marlene's cabin door planning to complain about the situation, as I was sure my two foxy foes were conspiring to starve me. I had also recalled someone warning me the previous day about our island, and I was planning to say something on the subject. Sigrid's voice ordered me to enter. Inside, the sisters were sitting around a table, drinking coffee, smoking cigars and playing cards. Not a bottle whatsoever in sight. Surprised, as well as confused, I forgot why I had come.

Sigrid turned her head sideways so she could watch me and asked, "Well boy, how long you going to stand there admiring us?"

"Sorry," I managed, and after a moment or two got out some bit of sense, "I met a man yesterday…"

"What man?"

"A man with a beard… dirty beard…"

"The vagabond who brought you home last night?"

I scratched my head and said just, "A… well…"

"I told him to drop you on deck, then he asked me for a job. You were disgustingly drunk."

You worn-out gargoyle, I'll drink the ocean if I want! It's my right and you can't stop me! I yell now at you Rose, but at Sigrid, you can be sure, I whispered it inside my head.

"What about zhat man?" Marlene intervened.

"I hired him."

Marlene recoiled like she couldn't believe it, "You ired zhe man?" while I released a "Whaaat?" long as a thirsty day.

Sigrid pulled out her cigar, "He looked like an out-of-work sailor and he said he knows these waters. We need a guide, he needs a job…"

"You forget zhat we have a dangerous mission? We don't need ozher problems."

"Don't worry, I will get rid of him when the time comes," Sigrid said, calmly sticking the cigar back in her mouth. "Somehow."

"I don't like zhat you ire wizhout my consent."

"I don't care what you think. It's my expedition."

"Iz my boat…"

I left them arguing and returned cautiously to the deck.

There on the main, at the halfway, eyes closed, half-covered nostrils poking out from behind the beard, but wide open to receive the best of the salty breeze that was drawing the sails that morning, stomach filled with my morning meal, stood captain Ros Nir. He was holding the swab, as a pioneer would ready a flag to plant into some new land. He turned toward me with the majesty of a newly crowned king, "Fer all me ships me eyes laid upon, none worst this barque! It shows like it's been sailed by a flock o' rats, if even so… Ya have a lot of scrubbing to do, me boy. Go fetch soap and a can of sand and I'll show ya."

"What?" I asked

(It was true though, keeping a proper deck had been possibly the last of my priorities on that voyage.)

"Ya can't have a boat and sail it and not clean it, matey. Do ya wash yer face?"

"Yes, but…"

"Ya wash it because, ya have it and ya wear it. Same with a boat: ya use it, ya scrub it. Every day, like religion. Number one rule in the book."

"What book?"

"Book of the sea, me boy. Ya live on water, ya use water."

I was preparing to say something in regard to his own condition, when I saw his eyes light up about something behind me, "Mother of God! Say me boy, unless me sight is fooling me senses, a most graceful maid appears to come hither."

I turned around and saw Marlene hobbling towards us. She used to stop and arrange herself after the difficult climb on deck; she would take a minute or two to pull her dress onto her shoulders and force her bosom back inside the décolletage, although she would usually succeed only in small measure—reason being the lack of fabric and the abundance of breast. This time around, probably excited to see our new guest, she didn't make the necessary adjustments and her generous offerings were halfway out there like a gift to the gods.

She pushed me away and stopped two feet from the lucky captain. In silence they measured each other. For some reason however, I didn't think she was able to stare in his eyes.

Then, suddenly Ros Nir let out a hoot: "Ayyeyayee! The most beautiful creature me eye ever laid on ya're indeed, me buxom beauty. Captain Ros Nir here to please ya," and he feigned a bow by putting his right hand over his chest and lowering his head, not too much though, but enough to up-grade his ticket from balcony to orchestra level. He enjoyed the show for half-minute, but she quickly lost patience and demoted him to the deck with a well-placed fist to his left eye. This quick change of altitude took him by surprise, for he lay there for a while.

"What a boom!" she exclaimed. "I will srow you over-board, dirty boom. Quelle impertinence! Zhis is *my* boat, mesieur."

Ros Nir got up with difficulty, bracing himself on the swab. Then he shook his head and a few small organisms flew to unwanted freedom. "By me honor, that is the stron-gest fisted woman to ever lay hand on me!" he exclaimed as if to himself, before turning to her, "My lady, it will be my pleasure to have ya under me command," and made anoth-er bow, this time holding his head as high as possible.

"Captain Dirty Beard," replied Marlene with visible outrage, "zhis is *my* boat and *I* command eer. You are a boom and you zmell bad. After you use zhat mop to clean the ship, use it on yourself!"

The captain opened his mouth to answer, but with supreme dignity the lady turned around and hopped back to her cabin. He held the position until she disappeared down the stairs, then, with clear excitement, "Arr, wild and feisty are we? Soundly rigged, what a solid stern! What a healthy jib! That'll be the most dainty ship I ever mastered. Arr, that'll be a hearty fight! Listen to me junior, no beauty is worth her price if she is not putting up a proper fight. The fiercer is she, the more pleasure she'll give ya," he said, caressing the mast, his eyes roving the deck.

"Now, I name ya me first mate and more honor than this never a boy yer age been accustomed. Go fetch that soap and let's scrub this beauty."

As a result of this promotion I technically became the last mate on the ship, but the old fool seemed so animated I didn't have the heart to protest. I went to look for what he had asked, somewhere at the bow, and by the time I returned he had disappeared. Soon, I heard great noise from below deck and saw the captain backing up the steps one hand on the rail the other holding a large cast iron pan fending off some imaginary blows, one to the right, one to the left. Only they weren't imaginary. Albert followed, holding in one hand a knife, in the other a huge metal ladle. He was fencing forward here with the spoon, there with the cutter trying to get at the poor seaman. There was yelling and screaming, both in English and German, intermixed with the clanging of the kitchen tools hitting the pan.

The girls appeared and Nikki inquired about the commotion. Purposely ignoring Anna, I explained that we had a new guide.

Meanwhile, the hunchbacked cook and the filthy seaman were dueling in full force on the deck. Albert was determined to get him, only you could see the captain had some experience in handling a pan. Unexplainably, I found myself cheering for him, while the girls loudly rooted for the cook. Ros Nir was dancing, eschewing blows and cursing, and I saw he was holding a healthy piece of bacon with his free hand from which, in between blows, he bit large chunks as he blasphemed to Doomsday come.

"*Für alle Hunde in der Hölle* what is happening here?" roared a voice, and for a moment the two warriors froze. "You," Sigrid barked at the captain, "what are you doing fighting my cook?"

Ros Nir took a bite and answered with his mouth full, "I was minding all me business and there I see the wretched humpback striking at me head …" He didn't finish for the "wretched" one let out an enraged cry and lunged at his throat with the ladle.

Sigrid brought two fingers to her mouth, pulled out the cigar butt, and with a voice strong as the angry sea cried, "Stop!!! Or I will throw you both overboard!"

They stopped. And with them the wind ceased its blowing, the rigging its baying, the timber its creaking…

"Zhis man iz a … iz a…" stuttered Albert, "iz a *Dieb*, iz a stealer. I catch him stealing bacon und spilled zee coffee…"

"On me honor, I haven't got the habit. I figured it fer dirty water…"

"What about the bacon?" Sigrid asked.

"Me breakfast."

"Zhat vas *all* zee bacon!" cried the cook.

Sigrid said a disgusted "Phew!" then inserted the cigar back in the corner of her mouth and continued, "What are you? Children? You, old man, go clean up your mess! Albert, back to your quarters. No more of this or you will both do it swimming! And you," the general addressed her audience, "what are you looking at? Everybody back to your business."

"Ya won't be cook on me ship, for sure, ya wretched hump…" mumbled Ros Nir behind Albert's back.

"Shut up, old man!" Sigrid snapped. "What do you know about Calbosa Island?"

I expected the same reaction as the previous day, but he surprised me, "Good fishing," he said without emotion, scratching his head and watching the distant horizon, "deserted, as I remember it. I can take ya there."

Sigrid turned around to leave, but once I recovered from my surprise I shouted, "That is not what you said last night!"

She stopped in her steps, "What did he say about it?" she asked, looking slantly at Ros Nir.

The captain had hastened to put his arm around my shoulder and pull me aside, "'ere matey, the spirits raised about me head. 'ere's no danger where we' going."

But she had heard him, "Danger, what danger?"

I paused, beginning to regret my loud mouth, then answered, "Monsters and…" I scratched my head unable to remember the details "… and other things."

"Nay, old wives tales and sailors jests. Seen the boy uneasy about the place and sought to scare him a bit. Just for the game. No worries about the island. Just as innocent as meself it stays."

She caught me by the neck and pulled me close, but scared of her eye I stared at the black velvet patch. "You told someone else about the island?" she growled.

I only could mutter, "No… I just… I don't remember…I was thirsty, and…"

She tightened her grip and raised her arm so I found myself on the tip of my toes. I could feel the burn of the cigar and the smoke made my eye tear. I let it tear. First, a low guttural sound came, then the words, "If you have compromised in any way this expedition I will leave you to die on that island. You can be sure of that."

I swallowed hard and murmured, "No… I mean… He said he was joking, right?"

She grunted one more time and a wave of smoke filled my lungs, but I didn't stir a hair. She then freed me and addressed the captain, "You! Old man! You better be the fool you pretend to be..." and left before finishing.

After she disappeared I turned to the captain, "Why are you doing all this?"

He put his hands to his waist and walked away looking about the ship as if surveying merchandise. I followed as he, ignoring me, was speaking to himself, "A bit unkempt, a bit rusty, otherwise a good ship she is. A fair barque, should she be quicker, but she'll fetch a good price that's fer sure."

More and more uneasy I was feeling about the fellow. "What are you talking about?"

There wasn't to be an answer. I heard Nikki's voice calling aloud, "Two boats are speeding—towards us! Two boats are coming towards us!"

"Two?" asked the captain somewhat disconcerted.

The sisters appeared on deck while I took out the eyepiece. They were still too far to make out the subjects on board.

"This is because you talked," Sigrid said to me.

I didn't answer, but I prayed she wasn't right.

They were getting closer by the minute. A mile out, as they came from starboard, they split and one of moved in a large circle with the clear intention of rounding to our port. By now I could make out people on board. There were five in each boat; most of them bust naked and wearing bandannas. They were carrying guns. Big guns.

In one of the boats, standing taller and wider than

everyone else, with a shiny scalp reflecting the sun and a smile so sincere it would make the envy of the snakiest hospice matron (yes, I'm talking about you, Rose), stood an old acquaintance, whom I had hoped never to see again. A rising discomfort in my groin, I directed the glass toward the other boat which was now just off our bow and to neither my surprise nor joy I saw Ruzban.

Sigrid, who saw it, too, dropped her glass and caught Ros Nir by the throat, "You brought them here, you work for them, you *hurensohn…*"

The captain tried to defend himself as best he could, but he wasn't strong enough to withstand the deadly grip. "On me honor," he groaned, "I don't know these lads."

"Leave eem alone!" yelled Marlene. "We 'ave more important seengs to do! Who are zhey?"

"They are the people who attacked us in Caracas," answered Sigrid, letting go of the captain's throat before not grunting in his ear, "I will kill you after I kill them. But if I find out you lied, I will kill you slowly."

He didn't answer, just massaged his throat and mumbling watched over the waters.

Marlene brought out the two shotguns.

The boats were now fifty yards out at both our port and starboard and I saw Ruzban bringing a bullhorn to his mouth, "My friends," his devilish voice screeched out, "we have unfinished business. I will come aboard."

There was a bit of a gale that morning and if not for it, maybe one of the two shots that followed would've hit him.

"I see there is no reasoning with you. I shall see you

soon then."

The two vessels took off and started circling around us at great speed one clockwise the other counter, shortening the distance between themselves and our boat with every tour.

"Aim for the one with the horn!" yelled Sigrid.

Shooting and cursing was what they were good at but only one man they hit and he was quickly thrown overboard by his mates. The wanted head stood untouched. They finished their munitions and sent me to bring more. I searched the place thoroughly, but found nothing and came back up bringing the news.

Like a wounded lion, cornered by a party of hunters, Sigrid roared to the skies, then she caught the unsuspected Ros Nir by the collar and dragged him away, "You, treacherous rat, to the cabins! Move!" Before she disappeared she turned around and, cried sarcastically to her sister, "Of course, you were more worried to refill your liquor cabinet that the munitions boxes, you drunken *Puffmutter*!"[7]

"I sot she take care of zhat," said Marlene looking disconcerted.

The boats were now yards from our hull.

Sigrid appeared and waved the gun at them, "He who dares set foot on my ship dies! *Für alle Hunde in der Hölle*, I'm going to take as many of you with me as I can!"

"Iz *my* ship! *Merde!*" cried Marlene from the other side of the deck. "And I will have zhe pleasure of kicking zee first uninvited *salopard*. Come and get it, you... you... *sauvages!*"

7 • *madame (of a brothel)*

The boats met shortly at the stern; I saw Ruzban giving some short orders and they split off again.

Resolved that this time the end had come I decided I would die fighting. So I got my hands on a metal bar, long as my arm and about two inches thick, and posted myself in front of the bridge. Inside frightened maids were clinging to their virtue, and I was planning to sell it as dearly as I had cheaply lost my own. If this doesn't pull a sigh out of you my beauties, then I don't know what!

Next, a mighty battle ensued! I wish you had been there! I watched in awe as two old women held back an army of pirates. As soon as the first one tried to board Marlene kept her word: she planted herself sturdily on her flesh foot and the crutch, turned slightly sideways, brought the metal pipe, that was substituting for her other leg, backwards and as soon as the man's head popped up at deck level she sent forward a kick that would've won medals in some sports. The second one got a mouthful of her peg and went right back after the first. To the starboard now: there was cursing and kicking and screaming and punching. That was our Sigrid! Here she punches one so hard that three fall; there she uses some poor chap as a bat and beats his own mates with him. Ha! What a fight! To the left and to the right and overboard, bodies flew like in some kind of pagan celebration. Yelling and grunting, and pushing and throwing and yelling some more, *Les Terribles* were magnificent! A battle your history books have most certainly missed, for no scribbler was present to record it. Ha! Your loss, not mine!

Inspired by my mistresses feats, I blasted every unfortunate pirate that came my way. Of course, it helped that most of them weren't there on purpose just wandering the deck with soft knees unsure of what world they were in. But I treated them to my rod with the conviction of a man who knew that he won't get a better chance. Bravery is in the eyes of the beholder my beauties. And I be the one holding the metal rod.

I don't know how long it lasted, ten minutes, an hour, the whole day? I couldn't tell. Marlene's exploits ended when she dropped her crutch and was tackled to the deck by four pirates. She screamed, she bellowed, she blasted. Her face reddened with fury and effort, but in the end she heaved hard one last time and gave up. Sigrid, on the other hand, was defeated by the only thing, man or beast, in a thousand mile radius that could have defeated her—Babar the eunuch. He came at her with his asinine smile and she did everything she could: punched him, kicked him, she even kneed him... Unaware he should hurt, he took the beating as something he deserved for what he was about to do. Following the kneeing, his lips quivered and the intensity of his smile diminished a few carats and paused for the time of passing a gulp, but then he grabbed Sigrid by the throat, lifted her off the deck and held her in the air with one hand until the butt of the cigar fell to the planks below and her head dropped over to the side. Then he lowered her to the deck and tied her hands together.

The battle was over. The war—lost.

CHAPTER 10

WHERE YOU CAN CALL ME HERO

Aye, the fight I yarned the other day…still in my mind. A mighty one! As I lay now in bed thinking of it, it comes to mind that it was the first one I ever experienced. Defeated and about to die I was. Now, I've lost a number of them battles over the years, some big, some small, some I wanted to lose, some I was too lazy to fight, some where I got my nose smashed in; but I must assure you that most I won, or I wouldn't be sitting here telling about it. I'm your hero in slacks and clogs, my beauties! Now, don't go laughing … Even as decrepit as I may be (and you should hear 'decrepit' as un-liquored, for that's what I mean by it), I'm worth twice your beaus. With their long hairs or shiny scalps (I don't know what the custom nowadays requires), with their scrupulous speeches and honeyed manners, yet feisty in absence of an opponent… most of them beaus I've met in my life were more bark than bite, more lips than teeth. You need a man, not a pair of lips, *ma belle*, and I'll let you know if yours qualifies. Ready to fight the whole world I am! But not ready to die… not now, not in a thousand years!

Well, at that time as I was lying on the deck, well

pounded and roped, ugly men turning the ship upside-down in search of a map, I told myself that I should
make ready, for there was where it ended. A damned man,
whether he wants it or not, in his last moments reminisces
through his life as a prospector through the sands of the
river for the littlest crumb that could bring him joy and
relief, and allow him escape. But I, surveying back through
my life, fell prey to a reverie of most philosophical nature,
and finding no trinkets of gold scattered through its sands,
came to a most painful conclusion—my life had been up-
settingly short.

Why hadn't I stayed home? I asked myself. I could've
gone back to school and become a thinker, or an artist, or
a writer of books, something bound for great fame and
money. Oh, school… How I missed it in that moment! …
Just let me go back, God, and you'll see what a good boy
I'll be! I was willing to try and do my chores now and then,
for not once in my school years had I done what I was
assigned. Not once. I had copied a few times from some
thick-glassed, big-eyed, school-bug, but not once did my
brain light up in benefit of knowledge. Not once. And what
did I gain by it? Who was the loser here? I was about to
walk the plank at the end of the world, while the school-
bug had likely ended-up in one of them smart universities
where the only real peril awaiting you is thicker glasses and
thinner hair. Ha!

Later, they brought the girls out to join us and my out-
look immediately changed. I am unfair in that way. Biased,
when it comes to beauties. Anna had been shoved down
next to me and I could feel the warmth of her body, the

sweetness of her breath. I was drowning in her being. That's the way to go! The only way I'd do it willingly.

Of course, she ignored me, but it didn't matter, for I didn't her and I was abusing her presence like a condemned man his last cigarette.

Sweating and empty handed, Ruzban got back on the deck. His men were moving about the ship, but I could see the hunger in their eyes when they looked at Anna and Nikki. Sigrid had regained her senses by now and heartily greeted the Jack-o'-Lantern with a set of words should I repeat them here, this tape would likely melt. He ignored her. "Now, I must have something to make me feel better," he declared leaning on the rails.

At his sign, Babar rolled us on our stomachs; then Ruzban yanked out a whip and arduously started having at us with such pleasure and delight that you could see the man had been wanting it for a while. Our screams, combined with the sisters' curses and the pirates' cheers, only further eased his hand and the whip cheerfully met our backs, at each strike the lead bits biting deep inside our flesh. He neither rushed nor did he seem stingy with the blows for he took his time behind each of us, giving us a proper thrashing the proper way, to remember him by. This being my first flogging (for many followed over the years, being as common in my world as paying bills in yours) my screams and cries surpassed those of our lovely girls who took their share and little complained.

When he tired, Ruzban asked for a towel and wiped the sweat off his four brows, then ordered Babar to roll us on our backs. This pulled from us even more cries. He listened to them, evidently proud of his work, and sighed with satisfaction as a man who at the end of the day has done his job and has no remorse in taking your money. "Ah! This is how a day should start," he groaned. "That's how my customers should feel about me. Now, I can work!"

Just then, Albert and Ros Nir appeared on the deck, pushed forward by some pirates. The captain, seeing the dame he fancied trounced as such, let rain a hail of curses, promising them death upon death. "Ya're no true pirates!" he cried at his captors. "Fer I know all the pirates in these waters and ya're not of them! Ya're jest a bunch of vile creatures for treating these good women in this fashion. God have mercy on yer souls when I'll get my hands around yer throats, fer I won't..."

Ruzban ignored him at first, but as the captain kept adding to his already long list, had Babar force him to assume the position and together with two other pirates hold him in it, and went on working onto his posterior the same way he had ours. The captain never gave in and followed each strike with his own verbal one and in the end it was the abuser who had to give up, for the sun was up and burning—scourging his bald head more adamantly than he the captain's back. He ordered the captain to be removed, adding that only the fact that he knew these waters was keeping him alive.

Ros Nir went below as vociferously as he had been above and then Ruzban turned to Albert and asked him if he too desired to give a complaint. Albert fitted even more of himself under his hump and only shook his head. He was thus spared.

The evil creature stepped before Sigrid and following a crack of the whip asked, "Are you ready to talk, old hag?"

Oddly, she kept silent, just watched him and biting on her lips, and I wondered if it was because such humiliation she had never received.

"Babar," he turned to the ever-smiling giant. "The map must be with them. Deprive each of them of their clothes and give them a full-body search. Start with these horrible creatures!"

The pirates applauded the first part of the speech, but I heard a collective cry of disappointment for the second. Their eyes were riveted on the two beautiful lasses. I began to yell at the sisters to tell him everything. As for Babar, he revoked his smile and looked at his master with a distressed face, which proved that even hormone-free, he still had some sensitivity left. Slowly, he directed himself to Marlene, the lesser of two critters, when Sigrid intervened. "Leave her alone!" she said calmly. "I will tell you where the map is."

"You will?" asked Ruzban, incredulously.

"Yes I will. Come closer, I want to say it in your ear."

"Very well," he took two steps in her direction and stopped. An unearthly smile split his face from ear to ear. "You thought I would fall again for your treachery, no? Ha, ha, ha! Babar, will you disarm her?" His laugh was difficult to watch; the purple, gnarled remains of his lips pulling around the small teeth, to the point that, wincing, you readied yourself for one of them to snap at any moment.

Babar smiled affirmatively and with immense relief, picked Sigrid up by the neck, propped her against the cockpit wall, then looked around as if searching for something; not finding it, he disappeared below deck. He came back a moment later carrying a wooden board from the galley which he set flat in Sigrid's face. Then with the lower part of his palm gave a short, brusque thrust to her right temple. I heard a familiar sound, like a burst of air and to everyone's amazement a dart, not longer than one of my nails, planted itself in the board. Her patch was now ripped in a star-shaped pattern. Ruzban took the board from Babar, unstuck the little projectile and examined it. The board, he threw into the water.

"Hum, that's how you had us... Old witch shooting bullets through her eye. Very ingenious! I should've guessed it a long time ago. What kind of tranquillizer do you use?"

"Just stick it in your ass and find out," replied Sigrid, fuming.

He grinned, then leaned over and lifted her patch. A dark cavity came into sight, but that was all that I could see. "Your launching mechanism... fine German craftsmanship, I am sure," he said as he was trying to examine it. "Babar could use one of those. Hum, Babar what do you say? With a weapon like this you will be truly invincible. You don't need both eyes."

The giant's face slowly altered and fear replaced smile. He looked around in distress as if searching for help. Ruzban laughed and said it was a joke. Babar laughed too, but his laugh resembled more that of a donkey's cough.

"Are you ready to talk now?" Ruzban asked Sigrid.

In answer, she recommended him to a place not very different from the one she had wished him the first time they met, only possibly darker and smellier.

He stood up, turned around and slapped his hands on

his legs. I could see that he was growing frustrated by the look of the scars on his face. They were purple now. "Ok, I need to find out where that damned map is, and someone is going to tell me. I don't have all day. Babar, throw somebody overboard! Start with…" and he moved his index in a circle a few times above us, "with… her!"

To my horror his finger was pointing at Anna. This while Babar, probably to make sure the secret of the eye mechanism stays forever unknown, had already lifted Sigrid over his head and was just about to cast her overboard.

"No, Not her! Not yet," cried his master. "She has to see people die. Throw the blonde!"

Reluctant, Babar dropped Sigrid and lifted Anna above his head, as if she were a twig.

A sudden madness came over me and I could see only red in front of my eyes. Squirming in my ropes, I inched across the deck like a caterpillar yelling as hard as I could, "Nooo!!! Leave her alone!"

My reaction was so unexpected that everyone including Babar froze. Ruzban spun on his hills, "Do I detect a romance on board? Haa! Love is… is…" and he stopped searching in vain for a word, "… is … anyway, is something. I myself knew it once, but it ended when she died. In my hands… and of them, too! Ha, ha, ha!"

"Drop her!" I cried. "She has nothing to do with this."

"She is here, isn't she?" he snarled back at me. "And so, to me, she is guilty…" and he flicked his wrist toward the sea.

"Throw me instead!" I yelled.

"And how is this going to help me? Is the witch going to tell me where the treasure is? You see my young brother, I will first kill people she cares about less and work my way up to the ones she cares for more. That is how it works, not the other way around. If she stays silent when there are no more people to kill, then I will torture her. Don't you think it is a good plan?" He tilted his head to the side and a crooked grin split his face. "Go ahead Babar, but before you do, free her hands so it will be more fun! Your turn my brother," he said in my direction, "is right before the cook."

The giant put Anna down and cut her ties, then, no more disturbed by her slaps and kicks than an ox by the bite of a fly, with one brusque movement flicked her over the rail.

Ah, in that moment, my beauties, your hero, he who draws a sigh out of your chest at night when you close your eyes and think of him, the champion you try to find in every sad failure you meet, was really born. Now you already have seen the weak, meek, little wimp that I was, but as you know—and if you don't, I'm telling you now—we are all born cowards and only our choices lift us above this state. Of course, my cowardice will surface at times, for it didn't die as a live thing would from a deadly blow, but lingered like an illness that needed time to cure. But, let me return to our story, for I consider it is quite barbaric to keep telling tales after leaving someone hanging between life and death as I have. Besides, I feel with so much detour and nonsense, you'll think me more of a storyteller than a dazzling warrior, and that would be the end of me.

What I was trying to say, and should have been saying, a phrase that would've made it easier for you to understand, for it is well used in your world, and which I feel would make the young gentlemen giggle, was that in that moment I instantly grew a pair of nice and heavy ones. As it happened, I glanced at Sigrid and saw that she was watching me intently with her lips tightened. She shook her head as if to forbid me, but I didn't care, for I was brave now. I knew I didn't have much time; I had to do something drastic, I had to shock. So, I inflated my lungs and yelled coolly and calmly and with all my power, "Give me the girl and I will give you the map!"

A deep silence fell upon the boat. You could hear Anna panting in the water.

Ruzban turned around and caught me by the throat, "What did you say!?"

"The girl," I managed.

"Tell me where the map is!"

"There is no map," I said.

His hand tightened his grip, "What are you talking about? I know there is a map."

"You're suffocating me... There is no map. It has been destroyed. All that remains is in my head. Let go."

"I'll kill you with my own hands!" Sigrid roared.

Ruzban's eyes darted between mine and Sigrid's; then they slowly squirmed into a grin. "That is the confirmation I need. You are full of surprises, my little friend," he hissed in my ear. "It seems that you finally fulfilled your mission. But why would she tell you? I know her, and it's not like her."

"She told me," I said, filling my burning lungs with air.

"Why?"

"In case something happens to her, she wanted me to know."

"Hum," he stared into my eyes, "So, that nose story worked, eh?" He stood up, "Babar take him below deck and hurt him until he's ready to tell everything."

As, I saw the giant stepping towards me, I felt a rise of panic, "I won't speak!" I shouted as loud as I could. "He can cut me in pieces, but I won't speak!!" As heroes often do when the time requires, I squirmed and struggled and almost burst into tears as he lifted me up, "Just give me the girl and I will tell you! You don't have anything to lose!"

I was under Babar's arm and he was setting for the stairs when Ruzban turned around and caught me by the chin. He stared in my eyes for a moment, and I swear to you my beauty, I would not have told him anything, even had the giant deprived me of the newly grown parts. "I might lose a lot of time with you," he said untying me. "Stand up! What do you want?"

"Pull the girl out first," I said.

He looked over the rail, "Why? She seems to like it, she is a good swimmer—she might get there before us."

I could hear Anna yelling off the port quarter, meaning that she was falling behind.

"The girl."

"No."

I remained silent trying my best to exude as much confidence as I could. "Eey, brother, brother... But I warn you... Babar..."

The giant cast out a rope and pulled Anna up.

"You see, safe and sound. A little wet that's all, but just as pretty."

He then made a sign and Babar gathered what remained of his people as far from us as possible, I guess because he didn't want them to hear what I was about say. "Now tell me where my gold is," he asked.

"Calbosa Island," I said while Sigrid was showering me with a torrent of blasphemes and death threats.

He rubbed his hands, brows shooting upwards, "Ah, good! Good! Where on Calbosa Island?"

"Somewhere in a cave. I'll take you there."

"Ah. *You* will take me, you weasel? *You* will take *me*? This is not our deal. You tell me now and I spare your little whore, that's our deal."

I knew this was an important moment. So, I stepped where the shivering Anna was squeezing water out of her clothes and with no warning I raised my arm and slapped her with all my might. Her head went sideway and she landed on the deck, half knocked out. I pointed my finger at her, "I told you whore that I'd make you pay for the humiliation you made me suffer! Now, it's my time!

"I barely know these people," I said turning to Ruzban. "I don't care about them. But I want both girls. You leave them on the island with me. Tied up, of course. And I'll tell you where the treasure is.

"And something else," I added quickly as he was preparing to reply. "You have to get rid of the hags. Now! Or I won't say anything!"

He looked at me, he looked at the girls, he looked at the sisters, he looked around. "Babar," he called, "throw him overboard!"

Well, now it was my turn to swim with the fishes. Mustache Dick, I thought, here is your opportunity. But he didn't come.

"So," Ruzban hailed, as I was trying to keep up with the moving ship, "nice day for a swim! Do you understand that I am the only one here who decides who dies and when? Good! Next time you advise me, I'll make you a girl as I should've once."

He let me swim some more and as I was beginning to tire and fall behind, he had me pulled out. The deck was free of my shipmates when I got there. I understood that I saved the day and everyone else, my beauty. And I dare you to find another way in which I could've done it better. Of course, I knew he was going to kill us anyway, I had seen it in his eyes, but as any of those useless philosophers you fancy so much could tell you—death in the future is better than death today.

CHAPTER 11

AN ISLAND WITH CHARACTER(S)

Rose I'll tell you so you know: I won't dance! Write it in your book! I won't dance! I am sure of that. As sure as a nose is the first thing I see when I open my eyes.

Did I tell you that they want me to dance? *Me. To dance.* Ha! Smoke me dry and cuss my name! I will sooner kill than be forced to move a leg anywhere than in front of the other. Dancing night! Here. Can you believe it? Yes, here! ... Unheard of! Going to shake my loose skin and disjoint my bones in a demeaning and molestful orgy? Not!!

At first, I thought they were joking, but they weren't. They want me to scramble feet with the ladies from the place. Said they don't have enough men. So what? They don't have *any real* men. Should I replace all of them?

Now, a couple of half-aged beauties dancing for me, as many a time has happened, I wouldn't mind enjoying; but for the heavens I wouldn't dance even with them. Why dance? What is dance anyway? Man is made to hunt, to fight. Isn't that enough movement? Women—I can't say for I'm not one. But since I'm more man than all of you men out there I can tell you: dancing is not for us. Leave it to them maids! And they shouldn't dance *with* us—only for us.

Phew, it makes me so angry, I wanna crush a skull and it will be your fault, Rose. How I miss the old days when the cure for a foul mood was to walk into a tavern, choose the most vile looking beast in there and drink to his mother's health. Ah, what a stress reliever! In pain for the next week, but happy as a juju fish. Nothing like an old fashioned beating. Given or taken—no matter.

That's it! If they want me to join in the humiliation, they'll have to fight me! All of them. I will take them all at once.

Phew, I'm so mad! I'll turn my mind to the story before I do something someone'll regret.

We were on our way to Calbosa Island, if I remember correctly. My home base.

You'd think people would be more grateful when you save their lives. I would. I would hug'em and I would kiss'em and if they're handsome I would double it. But, my old crew, no sir! Locked up in Marlene's quarters *Les Terribles* spent all their time drinking and cussing my name. You could hear Sigrid's damnations from anywhere on the ship. No place to hide. She was mostly singing solo, but her sister usually chimed in for the finale—by then the liquor had worked its magic. It was nice to see that hatred for me was helping them bond. But it wasn't their hugs and kisses I wanted.

When everything settled, our wounds properly licked,

and on our way to Calbosa, only the cook and I were allowed some freedom on the boat (the cook for cooking, I for serving). I then, filled with hope and hormones, entered the girls' cabin ready be hugged and kissed. Nikki approached me first. I held out my arms and puckered my lips, but she slapped me so hard that, briefly, it made me forget who I was or what. Oh, I forgot to tell you that one of her palms was worth both of mine in size.

"That's for my friend!" she explained. Then she doubled it with the other hand. "That's for myself."

"But I am a hero…" I moaned after I caught up with my mind.

I hadn't properly finished when I got it again. This time I was sure it wasn't Nikki. "That makes me feel much better," I heard as I was recovering.

This was a proper massacre! Imagine how mad I was, and even madder that I could do nothing about it. "Are you people crazy?" I yelled from an unreachable distance. "I saved everyone and that's how I get treated?"

"What if she had been eaten by your friend the shark?" Nikki scowled. "How would've you saved her then, huh?"

"I did my best," I replied. "Now, you better be nice to me. I own you." Luckily, I had lightning fast reflexes.

I'm telling you my young ones, lately I've been watching those moving pictures on that box in the rest hall and I've made my mind about how you civilized gents think you should act to get into a young maiden's graces. Let me describe the typical scene to you: There is a young and impetuous lad with the brain of a shrimp and heart of a whale. He's given it to a beautiful maid and would like to have hers in return. He treats her as a gentleman, he is respectful, speaks with words seemingly written by some loony poet on a deserted island, always looking his love in the eyes and nowhere else. His hands are either in his pocket or joined upon his heart and never go forward to pinch or squeeze one of the many meaty parts adorning his beloved. This young lad, they show, in the end gets the maid. That sir, I believe, is a fabrication! This is how I know it works: unless you speak the loudest, so she can hear you above the clamor of the tavern, tell her the naughtiest things you can do, try hard to measure her with your hand while she speaks about something not important, unless you do that, and much more—the more daring the better, like beating up two or three of your men whose hands eased by the liquor come to explore the territory you've already claimed—unless you do that, you sir, you don't stand a chance in the world with that chaste maid. 'Chaste' she calls herself, chaste I will too, for everyone is entitled to his opinion and if I want to call myself Peter, I do, and maybe I will, and who are you to tell me I am not Peter?—unless you've seen my papers, but even so, papers I had enough to be called a whole apostolate of Peters and Johns, and as I said, if she wants to call herself 'chaste,' this Peter doesn't mind it. And perhaps she is not as poised and as pretty as the one on the screen, and she might be in need of a few teeth, or a nail trimmer, or a shave, but I bet my horses that she is as worthy as any you'd ever want to pay. And I'm sure, in her modesty, she'd never ask for as much money as I am told the one from the screen demands to be with a lad she'd just met a few moments ago. In conclusion, if I can remember where I'm coming from and why I'm here, never pay the maid what she asks—be it money or manners or sentiments.

But, of course, I didn't know any of this good stuff at that age. It takes years of practice to become a ladies' man. All I knew was that I liked the girl, I wanted the girl, and exactly the opposite was happening. So I rubbed my crimson cheeks and did what every defeated general in the history has ever done: devised another plan. Divide and conquer, I thought. Together these wildcats are unbeatable, but alone Anna will be easy prey.

As for our other companion, Ros Nir, he was confined to a bunk in a room near our cabin. He stayed mostly drunk. By mostly I mean permanently. The dirty old scoundrel had me steal alcohol from Sigrid's cabin, which now was Ruzban's, under the menace that, being claustrophobic, he would sooner die fighting the pirates in a last mighty stand than remain in a room by himself and sober. His cure for claustrophobia being the spirits, I had to steal him a daily dose, which wasn't difficult seeing that neither Ruzban nor Babar were fond of liquor and I was the one cleaning their quarters. And, as the sisters, but in a lower voice, he was now singing constantly, all kinds of terrible sea-songs where the sailors perish at the hands, or mouths, of fearsome sea-monsters or at the fury of the sea itself.

By the third day, we had the island in sight. As the map indicated that it was more accessible from the northwest side, we set to go round it. It looked neither big nor small, shaped like a fat sausage, with dense vegetation, rocky shores, and a bay where a ship might anchor. As we approached it, I perceived further up the shore, under the green canopy, three small huts. Through the binoculars they seemed empty, and no boats were to be seen anywhere. I recalled the captain's stories about the dark creatures and my heart rushed with panic. Between Ruzban and Sigrid, I thought, I should've already met with what the world has most wicked to show, but what do I know? This planet is old and I young, and time to concoct something that would make our two frightening companions look new born kittens in comparison it had, all of it—all the time in the world.

I was meditating upon these things when Ruzban called and his men had everyone board two inflatable dinghies. *Les Terribles* fought against every step they were forced to take, while blaspheming of free will. Gallantly, I helped Marlene onto her boat. Contrary to her sibling, she seemed fresher that day. She smiled, then winked, and I understood that she approved of what I had done. It cheered me enormously to see that finally someone was on my side—that is, until Sigrid, looking more like a desperate old lioness than...than...I don't know what, something less harrowing and desperate, took a swing at me that I barely dodged. As for the captain, they dragged him out of the cabin yelling or singing, I couldn't tell, something about a terrible punishment to be bestowed on those daring to set foot on that island. With a bottle of rum in one hand and a bottle of gin in the other, he was finally lowered onto the small rowboat. During the short trip he managed to empty both of them and no sooner had we landed, than he fell into unconsciousness uttering a last cry towards the island. We pulled the boats up the beach and left him there.

The sun was slowly melting into the waters, dyeing the world before us in a surreal reddish light. Our small army moved cautiously through the sands on the verge of the tree line, our shadows vanishing inside the dark mass of vegetation. Prepared to conquer three small huts they were, while I, prepared to put my feet behind my back at the slightest sign of anything unholy, was.

A feeble candle-like light was illuminating the window of one of the huts. Surprised, we stopped and looked at each other. I was ready to make a run for it, but Ruzban searched for me and flicked his head toward the light, "*You,* you said the place was deserted. You go and see!"

I swallowed a big knot and tried to protest, but one of his men hit me with the barrel of his gun between the ribs and took my air away. I gave up and very cautiously approached the door. My heart was racing. I knocked. Nothing. I knocked again, harder.

"Come in!" spoke a voice. It was heavy. You could feel in it tobacco, alcohol, and age. It took me thirty seconds of slow breathing and fast praying to push the door open. I held my breath and looked inside. At first I could see nothing. Then, in the yellow light of a candle, a ghastly picture painted itself before my eyes. The blood in my veins froze and my heart stopped, too scared to stir. The hut comprised one room, of which the opposite side was crowded by a stone-slab table. Huddled over its sides were two completely dark beings. The light flickered as I opened the door and their uncertain bodies seemed to momentarily disintegrate, then disperse and fuse with the surrounding shadows. When my vision cleared I saw that they were sitting on bare tree trunks and only their slow motions above the top of the slab indicated that they lay claim to some form of life.

I remembered Ros Nir's tales and spun ready to run, but the naked torso of the giant Babar stopped me. As usual, he was smiling wholeheartedly. Ruzban followed pushing the girls in front of him.

They didn't look anything human; just two blobs of black paint on the lighter décor. The candle was between us and them and once my eyes adapted I could discern arm-like extensions moving about their bodies, which they used to alternatively release some stones on the slab. Soon, I could see familiar forms and I realized that every member of their bodies all the way to the ground, even their fingers, was wrapped in cloth. Black cloth. A hood of the same color covered their heads. Oh, a grimmer image you've never seen, I'm sure! They were grunting and emitting sounds which my imagination resolved were unnatural and extremely terrifying.

As we watched in amazement, none, including Ruzban, dared to utter a sound. I thought they were spirits from another world and we were all going to die. 'Ripped to pieces' came to my mind, and as I lifted my eyes to ask God's forgiveness—as one should do before dying a horrible death—my eyes fell upon the undisturbed, worriless Babar, whose visage looked as pure and innocent as if he was watching mass in some cathedral.

Patiently, awaiting our destiny we stood. I don't know for how long, it could've been minutes or hours. Finally, grumbling Sigrid and Marlene pushed their way in and broke the spell. Unnaturally, coming upon the sight, they fell quiet. I, being at the forefront, got pushed even closer to the beings as they continued their game with no acknowledgment whatsoever of our presence. It felt as though they were on another realm playing our very own souls and any moment they'd finish and come to take possession of those they had won. Then, suddenly, with a few grunts of discontent from one side and a nod of satisfaction from the other, the game was over. Slowly the hooded heads turned to us.

I gasped and tried to withdraw as much as I could, for there was darkness inside them. I cannot explain it now but it felt empty and dark as a dreamless sleep. As in a dance, they both raised simultaneously an arm and pulled down the hoods. The feeble light, as their partner, dimmed then brighten and when it did revealed two heads covered also in layers of black cloth. On the front of each lodged two small slits: one about where the eyes should be, the other toward the mouth.

The voice, though coming from the one on the left, sounded like it had crawled in from the other side of life, "No man has set foot on this island in ages, my lords," it said. "And, since that time we've seen no human, so, we've hard to remember how it is a human looks. I see beautiful ladies and I see young men. If your ship landed in misfortune, I and my friend will make the most of our desire to help you, though much, as you see, we haven't got."

Ruzban pushed us aside and advanced with an arrogant step. One hand on his hip, he waved his gun with the other and replied, "I wish to say the pleasure was also mine, but I cannot see if you are man or devil. You speak, so man comes to mind; but devil I see in front of me, and I am puzzled if I should shoot the devil I see or listen to the man that talks."

A deep silence sank in the room as the creatures mulled

over the words. Then the same one answered, "My lord, I never said 'the pleasure was mine,' for no man having his reason about him would enjoy being seen like this; I have only said that people are scarce in these parts and, for our condition, if we could help it, we'd keep it that way. As for the gun, not much damage it can do to our bodies and even less to our souls, they being dead for many years."

"Who are you?" Sigrid bellowed.

"We are people whom mankind rejected, my noble lady. We are the society of the most unwanted, for none even recognize our existence. We call ourselves men, you will probably call us monsters, yet as monsters we poorly limn the word since we hurt none, but are punished by all."

You could see that Ruzban's patience was running short as his head was bobbing left and right and he was tapping with his foot on the wooden floor. "What are these things, these words, you tell me?" he suddenly burst out. "I don't understand half of them, though we speak the same language. I want to see who you are! And your partner? Why doesn't he speak?"

Indeed, so far no sound had escaped from the other individual, but his partner continued like he had a story to tell, "The man you see next to me, my lord, was once amongst the world's most famous orators. In his time, or should I say, in his other life, he was a prominent lawyer who used speech to defend and set free many horrible men, criminals, and murderers. (God may have punished him for now he lives like one.) As a man with fame and money his only weaknesses were, naturally, liquor and women. Furthermore, because he could, he enjoyed them in large numbers as his depravation knew no limits. How he got his present affliction, I not know for he never spoke of it, but I can tell you my lord, the man loved to argue; the man loved talk. Oh, how he loved it! Beautiful women and fancy parties and gallant adventures, this man had it all. He spoke with such pleasure and delight that I had my suspicion he was living them again right here as he was telling them. And wondrous stories they were! It made our life easier, for entertainment, as you see, is short around these parts. Alas, at some point he lost his tongue. (I wonder now if the lad was really meant for sainthood for every time he has the littlest of pleasures it is taken away from him.) Since that time, I have done most of the talking and he is only good as a partner in games. Though, as it happened recently, I haven't had the time to get used to it and at times the silence overcomes my discipline and I set for those rocks on the coast line and scream, my lord, and let it all out for Our Father in Heaven to hear of his servant who suffers the pains of Hell ere Hell. But I'm straying. As for my friend and companion, this is his story, my lord, the one I just told you.

"You see now, without a tongue it would be hard for him to answer your question himself. And he would, my lord. Oh, how he would!"

"Wait," Ruzban grinned, "what happened with his tongue? Somebody cut it out? Who else is on the island?"

"To respond to your three questions with two answers, my lord: it fell and nobody," replied the voice.

"It fell… what?"

"Just like that! Without warning. I just saw it on the ground. And what a fabulous discourse we were having!

You see, I, myself am a man of God, a priest. I never yielded to the life my mate here was advocating. The sermon in question (because when he could speak he was the one keeping them), was about the advantages, or as he called it, the benefits (and I declare it now as well as I did then, a blasphemy) of having more wives than one. Of course he didn't call them wives, he called them women and he didn't say more he said many, but, as a Christian I take it as it should be: a woman—a wife, one—not many. Anyhow, as I was saying, he was in the middle of enumerating the so called 'benefits' of the said sin, I wasn't paying much attention for I knew the matter was more important to him than to me, and that he was arguing just for the sake of reviving old days, in fact the only pinch of attention I granted it was counting the sins in that unholy lifestyle, when… silence. I naturally stopped my counting (for silence is not a sin but a blessing) and waited. As nothing followed, I turned to my companion and there on the floor, just about where you are standing miss, his tongue lay, as if by some kind of divine intervention. Since…"

Just then, bang! A deafening detonation, not far from my ear, made me jump beside my pants. Except for the two men who were still seated, everyone was startled. The gun in Ruzban's hand had gone off. "This is the end of my patience! If I don't find out in the next ten seconds why his tongue fell!" he cried with his voice shaking. "I don't care if your soul is dead or not, I will blow up that thing there, which looks like your head!"

Without hurry, the man answered in one word, "Leprosy."

"Leprosy?"

Everyone instinctively took a step back.

"You see my lord, you are now in what is left of one of the last leper colonies in the world. And we are, on this island and on another few surrounding us, its last survivors. The reason we cover our bodies and our heads is because we might be missing some of the appendages attached to them, and even on some of the ones we still have the fortune of possessing the skin is peeling away like the shell of an unduly ripened fruit. My friend here just lost his tongue; I, myself, lost an ear two months ago. We are so hideous, unclean—as the Bible calls us—that we prefer to stay covered at all times, not to be reminded with the sight of each other of our own curse."

"Leper colony... I never heard of such a thing", said Ruzban.

"There are a few around these parts. These islands forgotten by the world are our last resort."

"I don't believe you. Show me your face! If you have lied, you'll regret you weren't a leper."

"As you wish..."

He pulled down the hood and began unwrapping the black cloth covering his skull. When he was almost done, he held the cloth over half of his face and showed us the other half. Or at least what was left, for most of it was missing. There was a large hole where the cheek should've been; you could see part of the mandible bone with the teeth and everything. The ear was also missing with some of the scalp. A quiver went through our group. Lepers—could they be Ros Nir's creatures?

"You see, my lord," continued the man, as he was wrapping back his head, "years ago, I came to bring the word of God to these dark parts of the world and got this as barter. If it doesn't guarantee me a place in heaven, I don't know what else could. But be not afraid, we aren't contagious for our malediction is in the dry stage. We lose portions of our body that are too dry to recover (which makes me suspect God's hand in what happened to my friend here, since not only was his tongue not dry, but by the use he made of it, most likely the most lubricated organ he still owned). Although, no one exiled us here, no one wants us either; in a way you could say that we were forced to remain here by choice."

Ruzban pointed his gun at him, "Perhaps I should kill you right now. Just to make sure you tell the truth. Keep the world cleaner."

The man seemed unimpressed, "You are to do as you please, my lord. I can see that you're not stranger to pain yourself. But I must tell you, leprosy is not as easy to catch as one might think. Besides, you could use our help in this place; as I understand not chance or misfortune brought your party to this island."

"Indeed my brother, indeed I know pain. And I know revenge," groaned Ruzban, thoughtful. "I've come on your island with business and you could help. Just stay your distance from me at all times and you might survive my passage. What is your name?"

"I am father Grant and this, my accomplice, is Rudolph."

"Well, father Grant, I am Ruzban and this big man here is Babar. You don't need to know the others, but you can inquire with them what Babar will do to you if you try anything."

Slowly the two lepers arose and instinctively, we all took a step back. Rudolph was taller than the priest and his shoulders were broad. He took an extra step in our direction and seemed to scrutinize us carefully. Through the slit, I could see two penetrating blue eyes dissecting every inch of my body.

"His sight is weak," added father Grant quickly, seeing that his friend's gaze rendered me uncomfortable.

We soon learned that they were the only habitants on the island; that every few months they received a visit from some Christian mission which brought supplies from one of the larger islands to the north and that their diet consisted mainly of fish. Ruzban found it strange that they did not raise any animals, but his question went lost when Sigrid, not used to playing the docile hostage, tried to grab the gun from a guard's hands. Fortunately (I say fortunately, because I am sure I would've been her first victim) this one had the strap around his neck, for she would've succeeded as she had knocked him cold with her fist. But before she could pull it free Babar was upon her, lifted her off the ground by the throat with one hand and took her outside.

Ruzban had another fit and threaten to kill everybody, but in the end calmed down and sent us to sleep in one of the huts, with a guard outside in case we were to grow legs. As my luck knows no limits, I was put in the same hut with my former mates. Even though I didn't mind the younger half of them, I protested saying that I would be killed and that much preferred to sleep with the lepers. He snorted, cocked his head and added that I had better be alive in the morning, if I wanted everyone else to live. Which made no sense to me, but that's what he said.

Now, before I go off for my siesta (a cursed nap, it's what it is), I must tell you something. As the leper said, and as is the habit on any island, fishing was one of their main sources of food. Well now, to fish you need, if not a boat, since you can do it from atop some cliffs or even from the beach, at least some fishing gear. Nothing fancy but some sort of tackle or some line and a stick to throw into the water. And when you have fished for many years, you find such stuff spread all over the place. But as I glanced around the hut, and later on the outside, I saw no sign of it. Not the smallest bit of scrapped line, or a broken rod, or anything at all. And when you fish, and what you catch is part of your diet, there is a certain odor about the place you live, from the fish you clean, from the fish that goes bad, from the fish you cook, and so on...

But, this place held no fish odor whatsoever. And if that doesn't smell fishy to you, I don't know why I am not saving my breath.

CHAPTER 12

LIKE A SEA IN THE FISH

A bottle of rum washed up on the shore,
    Yo, ho, with the rum below!
Where I'd been marooned 'ore three days before,
    Yo, ho with the rum below!
But nought hundred be
Pint o' comfort to me
As back on the open sea,
As back on the open sea,
    Yo, ho with the rum below!

Hick! Hee! Ahhh. *Hick!*

If men o' spirit we are still
    then drink and fight is all we know,
And for a bottle you can kill
    no matter friend or foe

But when a bonny comes in sight
with favors up 'n down,
Yet is there reason more to fight
and slaughter the whole town.

Ah! Good old times!

Hick! Hee! No more of their rotten medicine! I've got
my medicine now. I told you I'd get it! The best in the
world. Strong enough to start a fire, strong enough to put
out one. Strong enough to burn your insides while healing
your soul! A miracle. I didn't say it saves your soul, it just
heals it. If you want saving, come to me, meet my stick and
let the saving begin. Hah ha! *Hick!* I've missed you me lass!
Let me give you a kiss … and another…

Heh, heh, I'm having my yarn with you here. And with
Rose. Rooose! Where are ya? Where are ya? I'll take ya
with me Rose! I take ya… Just wait… Just let me finish my
business I'm here to…

Where was I? These buttons… so little… Curse on
those who made them!

"…didn't even smell like fish."

…

Well, I tell ya—it stank. It stank like your chopped head
on a pike for a week, or like a whorehouse at drought time,
I tell ya!

Sweet the gin is, sweet the brandy,
but the rum is sweeter,

I'd give lasses, gold I'd give'em,
for a keg or for a liter...

Hick! Hee! And I grab her by the neck, And I turn her upside-down...

This... my best friend here, nobody going to separate us ever. Ever I tell ya, ever! I'm going to hold on to it. Just like that, on the table here... next to my head...

Ok...

...

Ah...

...

...

...closed my eyes for a blink there and the time has passed... Oh...Have I lost the habit? Never!... a sip from my old friend here... Ah! It oils the mechanisms! God bless you, for a moment there I thought I'd have to kill to get me some of it. Liquor for the sailor is like the wind which blows a sail: it keeps her moving, and never should stop. Never!

Good! Good! Where was I? Aha, it comes to me... I was to spend the night and possibly lose my life... *Which was it to be?* you ask. Aha! I'll tell you right now... Nothing! I mean neither! None!

This part, as in any decent story you find out there, should be about love. I don't give a rat's tail if you like it or not: just skip ahead if you don't, as I do when I think of you. Ah, love! Love is beautiful let me tell ya. Love is magnificent, timeless just like *I* should be. I'm young enough to love—I should be young enough to live. To hell with death. *I* will choose *my* death before death, any death, chooses me.

Love and fighting—the two things I love. And liquor. I do love the stuff! And women. Ah, I do looove women! Give me gin and show me a beautiful maiden and I will fight anyone to the death. As we sailors say: One for the head, one for the heart, and one for the body. That's what a sailor needs. And all harmoniously combined. Too much of one and the sailor be doomed. That's why the sailor is only safe at sea. There he lacks them all: the wenches stay behind, the liquor soon runs out and the fighting, well, with no temptations around it is unnecessary to fight. We're not barbarians.

So, in spite of my protests, I found myself locked in the hut with those wretches. All right, since I'm in a good mood I'll call them maids. Ladies, that what I should call them! Well, I couldn't call *all* of them that, no. Not for, or before, or after all the liquor in the world would Sigrid fit this breed of nature I so love. Stronger than a man, horrid as the worst nightmare, more wicked than ten unrepentant nuns she was. And now she had an eye on me (ha! made a joke there!). She proved it as soon as the door was shut when with a strong arm she caught the back of my shirt and practically lifted me off the ground and into the corner. Her face was only inches from my ear. The good thing was that I couldn't see it, the bad—I could feel her breath, and I tell you, it was clear that she hadn't had a drink in quite a long time (which reminds me... Woof! That's good!). She obviously and unnecessarily wanted to kill me. Me, of all people! The pinnacle of creation, the summit of nature's art, the delicious navel of humanity!

"Listen to me you little vermin," she growled, "I'm going to break your neck like a chicken and then pull out your tongue and rip it off. I knew I couldn't trust you!"

"But we're not dead," I moaned, a galaxy of beautiful stars encircling my head.

"I don't care. I want what I came to get and I don't care if I have to kill you *all* for it."

If Marlene had not intervened, the abominable creature would've choked me to death. "Leave zhe boy!" She interjected with a firm voice.

"You stay out of this. It's between me and him," the mad one snarled, tightening her grip.

I could see on the dirt floor as Marlene's silhouette approached. She set her crutch against the wall, leaned over me to the point that my face was inside her buxomly bosoms, and with a force I didn't think she possessed, unclenched Sigrid's hands from my shirt. Happy to be free, I immediately slid down and out of there, for another kind of asphyxiation was waiting for me.

"No," she declared, "iz between all of us. You are *juste* a bitch zhat would kill 'er own sister for 'er own benefit. Ee did what I should've done, ee saved my girl and ee saved us."

There was silence as Sigrid mulled over the spoken words. "I'm telling you to stay out of it," she said at last. "I need to know."

"Oh, *au diable* weez you, I need to know

moi-aussi why I walk weez a stick, but I don't kill people for zhis."

"Oh, you go to hell, you crippled whore…" etc., etc.

And they continued on this note, complimenting each other's handicaps and other physical and moral virtues, as I wandered around with my blanket and looked for a place where I could close two eyes. Everyone had taken to the sides and I was left with the center. The thought of getting close to Anna came to me, of course, as I could have used some comfort, but she had read my mind and squeezed herself between Nikki and Albert and, aside from hovering like a bumblebee atop a flower, there was no way I could reach her. I gave up and said a prayer, for the next day I knew I could use some help. Later, I fell asleep to the unmerciful sounds of the two sisters, who had finished with each other and now were taking the fight to the walls of the hut, testing for resistance and durability with their mighty snores, snorts, and grunts.

So this part is not about love, are you happy now? Of course you are, you little scoundrel. I wish you were here. I'd show you love. But as I lack you less than you lack my teachings, and in want should be the one who lacks more, I shall keep to my friend here, gin, a sweet and old friend, its soul as clear as the crystal sea, and to the story, for today the mood is high and I feel a glorious ending for you and I.

In the morning I regretted not trying harder to have a moment with my girl, and, as you will see, I knew I was right as soon as I was kidnapped. Yes, kidnapped. I thought I was at the end of my adventure, but the adventure proved to be just starting. For that night, I disappeared.

How this came to happen? Well, let me tell you that sometimes during the night I have needs. Now more than then, but then I had them too. Usually at times of stress. And if you don't know yet how anxious that night I was, stop listening and go jump overboard before I make you do it!

As I was saying, about the time when the first smirks of the morning peeked from under the darkness's skirt, with a bladder as large as a cow's evening udder, I stepped carefully over my roommates' sleeping bodies, opened the hut's door and received with opened arms the also-sleeping-and-not-at-all-guarding carcass of our guard. Apparently, he was guarding us more with it than with his wits. He jumped back surprised and if not for Heaven's interest in my story and his sleepy said-wits, which made him forget that the gun had a safety and the safety was on, I would've taken a bullet straight through the region were my bladder was located (and still is, thank God!). This would've helped relieve me of everything. As he desperately pulled the trigger, I caught the gun by the barrel and shoving it away desperately tried to reassure him: "Ok, ok, pee, pee!" The idiot finally understood what I was trying to say and stopped struggling to shoot me. Upset, he nervously motioned me toward a nearby tree. I went, and let out a river. Wah hou! Sweet relief! (Now, if you think I spend too much time talking about this activity just wait 'til you come of age.)

Standing at ease, my ears caught a thump, but I didn't pay attention for I was quite content with the world at the moment. I finished, shook vigorously, as my habit ever was, and zipped (which, I wished I could say is also a habit). I turned around and promptly received a blow straight in the center of my super-contented countenance, blow probably destined for the back of my head. Nonetheless, I went to sleep immediately before having time to change my point of view.

Nighty-night!

I came to my senses with the sun burning my body and in terrible pain. As I lay on my back, I opened my eyes and the first thing I noticed was my nose. Being the furthest thing from my head, it had received the best of the blow and had acquired fabulous proportions. Like a giant mushroom sheltering my face from the sun, it allowed a view of nothing but itself.

I moved my head trying to adjust my eyes, when a large creature en-shadowed me and I heard a familiar voice saying:

"Ya aren't dead are ya? Good. Yer mind is still with ya? Fer I've no need fer ya with a wasted head."

I sat myself with difficulty and raised my eyes to the dark figure, "Ros Nir? Captain Ros Nir?"

"Aye, me boy. I see ya're all there. Bless yer poker fer I sometime don't know me own brawn."

I got up and looked at him. He still had his black eye courtesy of Marlene. "Why did you hit me? Where are we now?"

I was long to come to myself. My nose felt heavier than my head and was painful to touch. There was dried blood on my face.

"Ya're with me and we're going to get rich," said the crazy man in a cheerful voice.

I asked what he meant.

He explained that he had saved me from 'the hairless creature' and was expecting to share the treasure with me. "With me and me old crew. Curse them! They should've been here long ago."

"What crew?"

"Me own crew. Pleasure to represent meself: Captain Ros Nir, the most feared pirate of these waters."

"You are a pirate?" I asked, and in spite of the pain almost betrayed a chuckle.

"Aye. In me own right."

"So, you are a thief?"

"Ay mate, mind what ya let out. There are pirates and there are thieves. I am not a thief fer a thief takes it and run, away; me, I ask fer it, ya give it to me then *ya* run away."

"You can't be serious," I said. "There aren't any pirates in the world today. They're only stories now. They all disappeared long ago."

"They disappeared in yer world, but not in this one, lad, not here. These parts are as wild as the rest of the world two hundred years back. Here *we* make the law. If ya want to use these waters ya have to pay yer dues. Nothing less, nothing more. I tax ya fer yer safe passage on me territory. And if I like yer ship I might take it, that's all. Nothing less, nothing more. Don't upset the bigger forces, is what I say. Nobody cares fer the little guy that has lost his barque or didn't come back. The forces... ya have to be smart junior," and he tapped his temple with the index finger.

I looked around. I was on a strange beach with no huts

and no *La Baveuse*. "Where are we? Ouch! And you hit me…"

"Time was a needing it junior. It was fer yer own good. I saved ya from those mad-men and now we are going to be rich."

Suddenly, I remembered what was going to happen to those people, if I wasn't there the next morning. Then I realized that now was the next morning. "I have to go back!" I cried. "They will be killed without me."

"Less for us to deal with. Ya can't go back lad, ya are me prisoner."

I demanded he tell me the way to the camp, but he refused. I then proceeded to threaten him, to which he didn't respond. Then I jumped on him, but that must've looked like a bug tying to jump a horse. He pulled me down without much effort and slapped me one that sent me sprawling back to the dirt.

"What's with ya?" he asked. "They treat ya bad anyway. Nobody likes ya back there."

I jumped back up and cried from the bottom of my groins, "If you don't let me go, I will kill you I swear!"

"Eh!" he dismissed me with a wave of his hand.

Irate, I charged like a madman, and this time he responded, taking my feet out from under me and pinning me to the ground, one arm behind my back, face in the sand. "No listen, junior," he said into my ear, "Don't move or I'll have to break yer arm, and I would'na prefer to do that. But I will. It's no use struglin'…"

"If Ruzban didn't show up, were you going to kill us?

You were going to kill us," I cried, struggling to lift my face. He jerked up on my arm, and a jolt of pain shot through my shoulder.

"No, junior," he continued, rising a little, but keeping his grip, "I would've just taken everything ya had on yer barque; herself, I don't know, not fast enough… But the moment ya said Calbosa ya sealed yer fate. Yerself, I would've let live, because ya fed me—it's me rule. Still, ya have to join me crew. As fer yer own crew… better sorry now than sorry later." Then he shook his head like he'd just recalled some good memory: "That buxom beauty, what a lass! A lady I tell ya, I can tell! She stroked me with such fierce passion… I'd wish to meet more of her and keep her for me lady, treat her like a queen…"

"Let me go!" I begged. "You don't understand. They are innocent. You can't let them die like that. Marlene will be killed, too."

"This is the real world mate. Innocent people die all the time. Jest last year twenty thousand people died in a typhoon, most of them innocent.

"Ah, but the treasure…I heard about it long ago. I believed it a myth, a legend. Now, I have ya and ya'll give it to me. Ha, ha, the old fart is going to blow his spigot, ha, ha! …" He clenched my arm suddenly and growled in my ear, his beard scrapping on my neck, "But, if he shows about, we're going to war, I tell ya. We're going to war!"

"The old fart?" I said, scattering sand with every breath.

"The second best pirate of these waters," he said, standing and placing one foot on my arm, which was pressed against my spine. One move would've popped it out of joint. "Scalding hell, where are those cursed men? Stick's going to meet the Sharpie, I swear, if he got drunk again and forgot his mission…

"Aye, the old canker, a worthy adversary, I tell ya… He's sought the treasure fer years; he believes in it. I didn't, and now it's going to be mine. Heh, heh. Ya, old bane… I got ya this time! I'd still like to kill ya all the same…"

We sat thus for a while, he musing and watching the trees and I inhaling a dune's worth of sand, until a crash in the woods sent him whirling around in search of its origin. "Keep yer eyes open me lad, if he shows we're going to war… Hey, where are ya? Where yer think ya going?"

Profiting from his distraction I'd silently gotten up and begun scoring space between us. I figured going anywhere was better than staying there. All the while I had been wondering what was Anna thinking now? Knowing how much faith she had in me, you can answer that yourself.

I began galloping towards the jungle where, once inside, I could disappear, I figured. I was about to make it, with ten yards to go, when I heard a whoosh and from nowhere felt something binding about my throat. Time to see a thin rope with two balls attached at the extremities rounding my neck I had, before one of those balls bluntly hit me… you guessed it, in the nose. From the weight and feeling of it I guessed it was metal, but I failed to gather more details. The pain was so intense that for a second there I thought I was going to explode in a million pieces and I quickly passed out.

Voices woke me: "…lucky boy. The stone can kill you if it catches your temple," said some unknown voice.

Well, it wasn't metal, you'll forgive me, it was stone, but in the mood to feel cheated I wasn't.

Then the same voice continued, "Say Cap'n, what happened to your eye?"

"Curse you Stick!" I heard the captain say. "Me eye it's not yer business, but yer skin is mine. I told ya to stay close. Ya want to get me killed, don't ya?"

"I'll be damned if I do Cap'n," answered the same voice, "we followed you, but then two boats with armed men passed us and I decided to slow down not to get in trouble and we lost you. Luckily you told us where you were going."

"Ya'll be the end of me Stick, I tell ya. Ya're a pirate, ya're made of trouble. But I guess it's better to get them here. They're fewer. But I tell ya, ya'll get me killed one of these days."

"Sorry Cap'n, last time this happens. I see the boy came to himself. Ooh, that's a healthy sniffer he's got there."

If gigantic is healthy, then it was true. I tell you, now my nose was so large I could see east and west at once.

I stood up and discovered that I was surrounded by a group of strange and colorful men. Scarred, crispy faces, with sharp eyes and sneered mouths, they were leering at me like a flock of starving vultures might eye a chicken lost in their territory. There wasn't hate in their eyes, no; only mockery and hunger. Something like you'd be looked at if you dropped on to my ship in the middle of nowhere, you tender rump. Next to theirs, the beard-hidden but familiar face of Captain Ros Nir was standing out like a gentle Santa in the middle of… well, a heap of blood thirsty pirates. How well I know such faces! I've lived with them for more than what feels like all my life, but at the time I was scared out of my pants. Imagine yourself opening your eyes in the morning to the scariest, ugliest, craziest, roughest faces anywhere in the world, or even in your dreams: there a marked cheek, over there missing fingers, bad teeth grinding at you... Oh, how I missed the quiet life I had shunned in my country! But was I wrong my worthless friend?! Quiet life births quiet destinies.

"Ha, now ya tell me boy, where is the cursed treasure on this cursed island? Be swift 'cause we don't have much time," said the captain taking me by the shoulders.

I glanced around at a crowd of bulging eyes, drooling with expectation, their ears dressed to catch my every word, greed wringing their mouths. My shoulder ached and my nose was pouring blood. Ros Nir clenched the long neck of the open bottled in his hand, and furrowed his brow. I took a step back and I gave them my answer:

"Never in a million years."

CHAPTER 13

MY FIRST TORTURE

Let's drink!
Forget the sorrows, keep the laugh!
Let's drink!
By the mouthful, by the cup!
And if the sea of liquor be,
I'd sink the ship with you and me
and drink the sea from bottom up.

Ah! But such joy, such delight to the gullet, dare to the reason, light behind the eyes, this ambrosia of honest qualities and miraculous proprieties gifts upon its user! I sang to you my friend for high is my humor as the sky is on a bright day. Let there be a time to sing and a time to weep and if you mistake them, it is at no cost for though sorrowful death is and joyful the birth, more hurtful and dire than birth nothing to the breathing creature is. And you my unworthy friend, you've already been birthed. Reason to sing now—yet no birth or death inspires me but just this nectar of fruit and grain—I have, for I'm spinning a yarn while lifting a bottle and what more a man that lives could want or need? Another bottle, I tell you, and that should be it.

Now, that we drank and sang, let's turn our ear back to my adventures for noon is almost upon us and past it I am expecting the arrival of yet another round of this bottled wonder.

I wish I could say that I spat in their faces and stood my ground as they charged at me, but alas, I simply ducked and anticipated the blows with closed eyes. Instead of murder, however, they started laughing as if I'd just finished one of those jokes that, though no one understands, all laugh even louder and more heartily than necessary to make up for their stupidity. The captain patted me on the back and rubbed my shoulder and even squeezed a lonely tear, but I'm not sure if it mightn't been that a grain of sand scratched his eye. So I repeated:

"Never in a million years!"

The laughter stopped abruptly and their greedy expressions turned to confusion and bewilderment. The man called Stick asked, "Are you serious mate?"

With a resolve only the crazy or the ignorant possesses, I tighten my half-moons and my lips, and nodded. He sighed and turned to the captain and shrugged widely, "He's serious boss. Let us question him our way." As he said this his mates began woofing and barking like a clique of dogs at a passing cat.

Ros Nir calmed them down and pulled me aside, "I thought we were friends, junior. I like ya. Ya're full of spirit and a few years under me command, ya'll be a round sailor. But, ya have to tell us the location mate. Ya have to."

"But I don't want to be a sailor, captain. I've had enough of this! Let me go home," I answered, unnerved as I was.

He faced me, "I'll be honest with ya junior," he said. "Ya can't go home; alive or dead. Alive, ya can't because ya know about the treasure; dead, nobody will take ya—ya'll stink the place, ha, ha! Tell me where it is and I'll take ya with me and make ya rich."

"No," I said, pulling away and pulling myself straight, "what good is it to be rich if I can't go where I please?"

"But ya'll have plenty of women… and things… and ya'll drink the best liquor ya can find…"

"That's good and well for you captain not for me. But, this is not the reason I'm not telling you…"

"Ya'll have to tell me mate…" he interrupted.

I swallowed, "My friends are dead because of you. Never in a million years."

I know, from what I have told you that it is hard to believe I would be as brave. I couldn't believe it myself as the words came spilling from my mouth. But that day I was in a worse state than I'd ever been so far in my short life. Every square inch of my body was in pain. My nose was throbbing and pulsating like it had grown a heart of its own. My eyes were practically kissing my ears and my spirits were so low you could say they were swimming at the bottom of the sea. I had caused the death of my friends, I was stranded at the end of the world with a band of bloodthirsty characters you should only find in some poor wimp's fairy tale. I decided for myself that I'd better die now before I suffer too much.

The later thoughts I shared with the captain. "You better kill me now, you savages," I said, "because I'm not going to tell you anything."

With pity he looked at me, "I don't want to kill ya junior, I like ya. I'm sorry ya think we are jest a bunch of savages with no worldly manners, but Stick will have to extract the location from ya anyway, so I suppose ya might be right about his manners."

Without much ceremony he passed me to said Stick whose men opened their arms, each with hands holding bottles, and warmly received me, spun me around, studied my nose and wondered at the wounds from the other day's flogging. Then they pushed me toward the trees.

Now, I have the marks to prove that I've been through this a number of times in my life. I've been harmed in more ways than you can think of: fingers broken, nails pulled, feet roasted, hanged upside-down, etc., but I can tell you it gets better with time. Not that you start to like it, no, but in time, you get to a point when you know right away if you are going to talk or not. The rest is a game of endurance. If they stop before you get to your limit, you win, if no, you talk. If you think it's easier to be on the other side of the knife, or whip, or fire, you are wrong. I have done that too, and to be sincere, there were times when I would've preferred to be at the receiving end.

But this time was my first and I was riddled with nerves. So nervous I was that I half-fainted and they had to drag me. I say half because my legs literally gave up from under me and I took the occasion to close my eyes. They didn't need to throw water on me, no. That's just in books. In my world when someone goes soft, unless it's a lady of course, you just kick him until he wakes up, and eventually he does, believe me.

That's what happened and since I wasn't really unconscious I got up faster than a sailor to the smell of gin. They didn't seem upset, as they kicked and slapped me around and shared me brotherly-like, neither stingy with the slaps and the kicks nor greedy with the time I passed with each of them. So humiliated few have ever been. After long minutes of healthy beating, where I defended my nose as well as I could, Stick asked again if I'd talk. I didn't answer because, sincerely, I didn't know where I was, nor why was I there. I was listening to him like a man in a dream and couldn't figure what he was mumbling about. Then, more pleased with my silence than anything else, they produced some rope and attached my body to a tree. My spirit they couldn't. My spirit was left free to roam the plains. Unfortunately it had some kind of relation to the aforementioned body and didn't get too far. I was slowly regaining it when I felt the first cut searing lengthwise down my chest. It sped up the acquisition, and upon making eyes I realized that they had broken their empty liquor bottles and were using them to slice me up. They seemed to enjoy this activity as much as the first, for not once did they ask a question. I would've gladly told them anything I knew and more.

Being cut with broken glass has different effects on different parts of the body. When a finger is slit, the pain feels deeply and suddenly, like a stab to the brain. The chest by nature isn't endowed with the same sensibility and the pain delays its stinging like a teasing lover its first kiss. Myself, I was just the same; I saw the blood pushing it way through my shirt, but couldn't feel much. It was like cheating. Many have died this way, thinking they cheat pain when pain is the one cheating them.

In my case the boys, God bless them, were professionals and after eleven cuts (I know because I later counted) stopped the chopping. They untied me, wrapped my torso with a cloth and hung me upside-down by one foot, for a change. The blood remembered I had a nose as big as a harbor and began freely vacating the body, filling both of my eyes. Fortunately, my ears weren't affected and I heard when Stick said that he would cut my knee tendons if I didn't decide to move my mouth for any other purpose than bawling. I was not to walk ever again on that leg. I yelled as loud as I could that I would tell them everything, just please spare my leg. My mates were dead by now, anyway. Why should I die, too? I'm young, I must live! For them! Ugh! Judas! They should've killed me on spot, just for those thoughts.

But instead, they cut me down and dragged me in front of the captain who, sitting on a large rock on the beach, was kissing a bottle. He expressed his joy that I had changed my mind by offering me a dribble of his drink. I accepted for I was in much pain and the alcohol is known to help. What I wasn't thinking was that my nose might be in the way. Which it was. The bottle, thick with a short neck, my nose, a parasol sheltering my mouth, kept me from enjoying the smallest dram, but managed to spill a good quantity on my fresh wounds. The bray I released, a wounded jackass, or even a happy one, could never equal, froze everyone.

I pushed down two pirates who were in my way, ran and jumped in the water. I then repeated the musical performance, for the salt water didn't help. By the time I ripped out the cloth of my shirt, two pirates caught me and held me down under water until the pain faded away. "Take it like a man mate, you got off easy," said one of them with a sneer that brought the long, deep scar on his cheek to his mouth, giving the impression that on one side it ran to his ear.

Ros Nir and the others were having a good laugh at my expense, "Yer comedy is most worthy," he said, "but I'll ask ya again where the treasure be."

I told him.

"The treasure is on the south-west hand aye? We shall leave now and cross the jungle in two days, aye.

"Stick, take the lads and bring weapons and supplies! And hide the barque."

"Wouldn't be better, Cap'n, to send a man around with it? In case we find the gold, we need to load it," said Stick.

"Nay, the old romper has many eyes in many places. I can smell him close by. Let's not tell him where to wait for us. Need be to fight we shall use all hands and if God blesses us with the treasure (here he signed a cross over his chest and spit to the side) we'll send a man or two to bring the barque around."

"Yes Cap'n," said Stick and took off across the beach.

"Now junior," said Ros Nir turning to me, "ya're with us till the end. Ya want it or not, yer life has changed course and it steers this way. When I was yer age I was told like

I'm telling ya now, 'Better a pirate than dead!' The circumstances were different fer all that, fer I was swimming with the fishes at the hour. I didn't have much choice, but I don't regret a second of it, not a second... Better a pirate than anything else, I tell ya that. I dreamt once of becoming a moving picture star, junior, an actor, how yer sort call it. But this is freedom mate, this is freedom! No laws, no king, no president, no mother to tell ya what not to do. I am the actor and director at once. This is me play," he declared majestically lifting his arms and gesturing around him. "And in me picture ya play how I tell ya to."

The old dog, how true he spoke! Of my life I don't regret a moment. Only time itself. Cursed time! I was fortunate to be powerless over things that happened in that episode of my life, otherwise, who knows what I would be telling you now? Sometimes you have to accept that the show runs how someone else directs it, not how you would have it go. Your way is not always the better, even if you believe it with all your heart. I'm glad it wasn't my way, but at the time despair had weighed me down and I felt as though the end had come. I cared for nothing any longer for I was sure they would kill me: treasure—dead men can't enjoy it; love—dead men can't feel; fame—maybe, but others will enjoy its fruits. Or, should I survive and join them, I won't last long in that lifestyle, I told myself—I was a city boy. And for what purpose? Far from everything I knew... forgotten... We define our lives par rapport to others and I was never to see my others again. Who was I to be then? Better dead than nonexistent, I say. Of course, then I was too ignorant to know that. As for gold and diamonds you have to dig deep beneath the earth; for pearls, dive to the bottom of the ocean, for fame too, you have to suffer and sacrifice and sweat blood sometimes. But if you can rob a person of his gold and diamonds and pearls, you can never take his fame away. Fame is the hardest of the three to acquire, my callow friend, because it is everlasting. It is the only thing that five hundred years later will still bear your name.

And since I treat myself to have a talk with you, let me tell you something now: Don't give yourself a hard time—it's alright to be young and stupid. There is no other way. Except that you youngsters nowadays think the opposite: the world is an oyster and you its pearl. The old, experienced people, disagree with you? Because it's them who are stupid you say. We humans make most of our mistakes and do things we later regret, as old people, don't we not? Thus you go through life proud of yourself and your feats, which would be less than one if your parents hadn't pushed you from behind with a shovel, until one day—and mark you my word—you find yourself aged and stupid and looking upon the youngsters that so treat you, and feel an itch on the backside of your palm and know that that scruffy beard and unruly hair hanging on that fresh cheek would scratch it just fine. Just as I feel now about you...

Eh, what for? Just a waste of backhand.

CHAPTER 14

THE END.

Can't say if I'm going to finish this story. I don't feel like it. I got my pipe, I got my liquor, I don't feel the need to talk to the stupid machine any longer… And I don't think you are quite worth it anyway.

You know I am still alive—alive, but not living I tell you!—what more do you need? You listen to a story for the ending no? Well, you know the ending. I am here drinking and blowing smoke. The rest doesn't matter; regardless of what happened in between, everyone is dead by now. (Should be anyway, but then with Sigrid you never know…) Time has only me as its memory of that moment at that place. But time doesn't care. It will wipe me out, as it has wiped out countless people that you don't know lived and had a life just like you have one now. And why would you care? You're ignorant. We've established that. You're not even conscious of your own "aliveness," much less anyone else's. And stories, tales, why do you like them anyway? They make you feel like a hero? Or do you look for the artistic aspect in everything you spend your time on? …Hum?… I salute the former and bewail the later, dreamless, forlorn creatures! I used to close my eyes and dream

I was fighting those villains. *I* was kissing the girl. *I* would kneel before the king and become a knight... Ha! Good times! Good for you dreamers! To the others, the analytical bastards, I pity you! Deprived by nature of its most sublime gifts, in the tree of life you grow towards the ground not the sun, reach for dirt not light, see the pebbles not the stars... You're a lost cause, you sad souls wallowing in the mud of your eternal grief.

I couldn't possibly hurt anyone by ending my saga here. The dreamers can dream the rest of it; the artsidiots shall like it, for unfinished crap is not crap but art these days it seems.

So here I stop and drink. Let it be known that I lived, I drank and fought... and I aimed to be an artist in the end.

CHAPTER 15

I GET TO KNOW ROS NIR BETTER

...

Rose said if I don't finish my story, she'd throw me out in the street. Well, she was more descriptive than that, but there's no need for raunchy words as I am narrating for the whole family here. It seems my glorious future as an artist is undermining her own cravings. You greedy wench! She said she'll take my pipe and I can't allow that. My liquor... you should've seen the scene she made, and the names she called me, the huss! She is a tyrant, I tell you. Liquor and smoke—food for the soul, and she wants me to starve. Though she hasn't a clue how I got the drink or where it is... Rooose! You thief, I know you can hear me out there, stay away from my stash, or I'll have you killed! You hear me? ... It wouldn't take much...

And she had the nerve to ask why I'm here. Do you ask yourself that? *What is he doing in that wretched place?* Do you? *He's an old man, godforsaken and worn-out,* you probably think, *retired and waiting for the end in a place where they wipe your behind when you can't do it for yourself.* Well, I can still wipe my own butt, you thickhead! I'll die before I let anyone else wipe it for me. Do you think that I *need* to be here? Do you think that the sea can't take care of me? She has for so long! And I have riches enough to buy this country and throw your sorry-ass out if I want! I don't need to be here. But I must. Why that is, I can't tell you. Not now anyhow. You hear, Rose? I might just tell you later if you stop badgering me.

So, where was I? …

I left with captain Ros Nir and his crew, did I? We found the treasure and became rich, did we? Simple, no? Oh, but it wasn't that simple…

I was tired, cut, beaten up, and disfigured. My brain had stopped functioning and I was following the trail as puppet pulled by a string. The jungle proved to be, for the first part of the trip, dense, and the terrain not the friendliest. When I fell behind, not because I was tired but because I simply hadn't the will, the pirate behind me gently gave me a push between the ribs with the stock of his rifle, which momentarily woke me and gave sprint to my brainless legs.

Let me give you a few geographical references to help you sort things out. Of course, at the time, I didn't know them, but I shouldn't deprive you because I was so. Just imagine a plump mid-sized sausage. Now, don't eat it, but turn it vertically with the curved part to the east. This was our island—Calbosa, shaped like a juicy German bratwurst. The treasure lay at the southernmost tip, but the beach we touched land on was to the northwestern side. The place the captain had brought me lay to the north north-east. I know that I said there was only one safe place to shore a boat, but leave it to the pirates to find another on the opposite side of the sausage. We were to cross the entire length of the island to get to the treasure. Two days walk through the jungle.

If you've ever been in a jungle in a hot day, you know that humidity makes the air almost irrespirable. Add to that the bugs, the vegetation slapping your face at every step, slapping the wounds… it was like a march through hell. But I didn't care; I could've marched through Satan's bowels without feeling much discomfort. I was marching in pain and hatred and those two can take you a very long way.

It must've been about midafternoon when we stopped. Hardtack and dry fish, pushed down with liquor, or water, or both, filled up their stomachs. Mine accepted a biscuit and some water. Seeing my grief the captain got closer and offered me a small canteen he had at his belt.

"Ya look like ya need this junior," he said. "Just don't abuse it, it will turn ya over."

"What is this?" I asked smelling the inside.

"Secret recipe. I mix it meself. I use it fer the ladies," he answered, winking at me, "but I think it might help ya now."

"Thank you," I said to him, holding back the bottle, "but I don't think *that* is what I need now."

"Ya little urchin," he said laughing and lightly slapped my head, "ya think the admiral gives me grief? No worries there… Take it! Just a sip. It'll spry yer mind and yer body… Aye… good aye? Ya'll tell me…"

The concoction tasted like rum with something else in it, something I never found out with certainty what was, but today, after sampling many unchristian things throughout my unchristian life, I strongly believe that what I had then was one of those things. For the next thirty-three seconds I still felt like spinach, then I became Popeye, the fellow with big forearms and a lot of strength. A new life was breathed over me, like someone had removed my pains with his naked hand.

I walked the rest of that day through the jungle as Little Red Riding Hood did through the forest before she met the big bad wolf. I could feel no pain, no fatigue; I didn't care how I looked.... At the same time I kept a driveling eye on the captain's magic bottle. A little bit more that's all I needed. At nightfall we cleared up a spot on the side of the trail and made camp under the trees.

"Ya better prepare yerself 'cause tomorrow we meet trouble," the captain said dryly sitting next to me.

I asked why he thought that.

"I can feel it in me bones. I always feel the plight beforehand." He took the cork out of a bottle, not the one of my interest, and put it to his moth.

"Ayee! It's good, ya want?" he asked and offered it to me.

"No, no, but I would like the other one," I pointed to the one at his belt.

"Are ya crazy junior? Ya won't close an eye tonight, and tomorrow we'll have a hard day."

"But... I need it."

"Stop it, or I'll smack ya one!"

He sounded like he would make good on it, so I stopped. He sat down next to me.

"Aye, it's been a long time…"

I waited. But as I could feel the sandman tempting my eyes, and the answer wasn't coming I asked him what.

"Since I was yer age… They say time flies, but to me it seems time jest happens. It didn't feel like flying from when I remember meself 'till now. Before ya'll have time to ask why ya'll be like me. If ya stay alive, of course."

"I don't want to be like you," I said and I believed it.

"Not now junior, not now, but when ya'll be like me ya'll want it and ya'll be glad ya're," he answered, and he was right.

"Do you think there's a treasure?" I asked.

"There has to be, junior. I've heard word about it long ago. Where ya see sails there's a ship, ya hear shooting there's a gun, that's fer sure. Tomorrow we'll know if it's but a legend. I jest hope the old fart doesn't show up. He must be around, he wouldn't miss it."

"What about Ruzban?"

"If we see him it will be me pleasure to send him back to hell. What a cruel fellow. Not a fine pirate fer sure."

I lay back on my bed of leaves. I could see a few stars through the dark mass of vegetation above us. I thought about the people I'd spent the last few months with, whom I considered now something like friends. Were they alive? Whom had Ruzban killed to make the sisters talk? All of them? Or only…

"You know Ruzban works for somebody. Maybe it's your 'old fart.'"

"No. Captain Jim Brrow wants to find the stuff himself. Twenty years he's been looking fer it."

"Captain Jim Brrow???"

"He must be Canadian, the old canker. In this business nobody knows yer true name. Ya choose it yerself or they give it to ya."

I smiled to myself thinking that I already had a pirate's name, not one I had chosen myself, but not a bad one either.

"What's between you two?" I asked. "Why do you hate him?"

"He's been on me tail fer years now," he said and took a healthy gulp. "He was once me captain."

"He was your captain?"

"Aye. He started me in this business. Fore, I was just a simple fisherman."

As I waited for him to continue, I closed my eyes and relaxed my muscles. *Better enjoy life while I can*, I thought. The air was cool but still humid, my cuts stung only slightly, and for the first time in a long time I felt good. Really better, I should say, for good is too strong a word. Strangely enough, I was more comfortable around the captain, whom I regarded as thief and a killer, than around my boat mates.

"Go on," I said, when nothing followed. "Tell me your story. How did you meet him?"

He emptied the bottle, set it aside and told me his story same as I tell you mine now:

"Much I forgot of me cursed life, but I remember the

day I met Jim Brrow … I was a fisherman, or, to be truthful I should say, on me way to become a fisherman as ya're in yer way to becoming a pirate. He cast anchor in our island's little bay, not far from this place; when I think about it, the most handsome barque to ever stop there. Fer a week I didn't see him and I was asking meself what a fellow with a barque like that could find on our small island, when, one afternoon I found him standing on our deck. He was older than me, still a young man, but he had that air about him like a man that knows what he wants. Me father had that. As I always lived with him and obeyed him, it was some-thing I was missing, but I admired those who had it. He asked fer the owner and I answered that he'd gone home and I was left there to clean the boat, as his son. He spun to leave, but then he turned back, approached and, half-laugh-ing, asked me if I knew of a ship that had sailed in these parts and never sailed back. I answered no, and he again turned to leave. 'Although', I said with a cursed inspiration, 'I've heard a story from an old man about a German ship, years back, but I think it's a legend…'

"He stopped right on his feet and, again, faced me. 'And how can I find this old man, my friend?' he asked.

'He died two years ago.' I answered.

'Any kin?'

'None', I said. 'I was the one who took care of him.'

'Who else knows this story? Your father?'

'No, I answered. Just a myth. Old man was crazy. He said that he saved a German sailor from that ship and that the German told him that it was right full o' gold. He was delirious. I wouldn't bother me father with it.'

"In fact me father knew about it, but something came over me and I wanted to look more important to the man. Probably saved his life at the time.

'So, you are the only one who knows this story?' he asked again.

'Yes,' I answered, proud of meself. 'I was the only one to take care of the old Rake and the only person he ever talked to.'

'The old Rake, huh?' said the man.

"He gazed at me with a strange eye and left. And two hours down the road they took me."

"You were kidnapped??"

"Yes, jest like ya. Somebody stoned me head and I awoke on his deck."

"That's how you became a pirate?"

"That's how ya become a dead man, junior. A pirate, takes time."

"I don't understand," I said.

"I didn't understand either, but then he explained that he was specifically looking fer the treasure from that ship and he couldn't afford word to get out and that he regretted that he had to get rid of me."

"And what happened?" I impatiently sat up for I could see the resemblance to my case. "They cut you, too?"

"Easy junior, the night is still young. They didn't cut me fer they didn't ask any questions. They jest threw me overboard. Ya see how lucky ya're?"

"I see." I said and felt my bandages which, in short,

were made of a pirate's old shirt; blood stained and never washed. Luckily, the fellow named Stick had applied in between it and my cuts some potion he swore could set straight a disemboweled man. The unexpected result was that I was feeling much better.

"I guess it wasn't me time that day," continued the captain. "I was pulled back on the deck and the captain—fer the strange lad was the ship's captain—captain Jim Brrow, he presented himself, asked me were the treasure be. I answered that I hadn't the faintest idea fer the old man never told me, fer I never listened to his story to the end, fer I judged it jest senilities of his old age. He offered me the deck, never to see me family again, or to take my chances back in the sea. I chose the deck, as anybody would. We looked fer the cursed treasure fer years. That's how we became pirates. First, a ship now and then to survive, next, ya know, it became a trade. Our trade."

"You never saw your family again?"

"Me mother died in grief soon after I disappeared. Me father died in captivity."

"In captivity?" I asked.

"Aye… in that of captain Jim Brrow."

"He killed your father?"

"Nay, he perished of sickness I believe. But as a captive on Jim Brrow's ship. Yet, I reckon him at fault."

"How did that happen?" I asked, yawning big. My eyes were growing heavy and it was hard to keep them open.

"Eh, I'll tell ya another time, junior, now jest spell yerself fer the night. Tomorrow we fight."

"No, no, please I want to know," I said yawning again with a mouth big enough to swallow a whale.

"He took me father captive because I took his place and his barque. Na, now ya know everything. Close yer eye and let yerself rest!" Saying this he stood up.

I wanted to know so much more but my eyelids were heavy with bucketfuls of sand, so, "Ros Nir," I said. He glanced down at me and I asked, "Are you sure we're going win?"

"Aye junior, we have something he doesn't have."

He left before I could ask what.

I fell asleep wondering who Jim Brrow was and how Ros Nir had come to take his place and his ship.

...

Smoke me dry and cuss my name! The clod! The dog! The wretched woman! I will not stand for this! I will do something as soon as I think of something! I will think of something as soon I drink something! Any man would be dead by now! A thousand times dead! You don't steal the Captain's liquor! You don't take the bottle from a pirate's hand! You die if you try! I am the pirate here! I confiscate things! The vile woman! I promised her riches...

I was followed! I was spied on! I was betrayed! Caught in the fact! In *flagrante delicto*, as you schooled folks say. Red-handed like the cat with the bird in its mouth. You name it! My vengeance shall be terrible! Rose, your name will be forever forgotten! I'll take you out of my story right now! As soon as I figure out how to work this machine.

Damn it! Those tapes are so small... I need a blade...Where do you make the cuts? How do you erase? Damn the machine! ...

That cursed Mrs. Schultz, she's sold me out! The century-old death rag was the only one to know I was getting a delivery. I refused to share with her and she sold me out. Let her get her liquor herself. I take, I don't give! And I share only with the crew. Nobody else gets anything they didn't work for! And my source is safe, you dried up mummy! Safe and ready to provide. Ah, these women! Too bad you can treat them like men!

CHAPTER 16

WHERE I COULD BE LYING

Tonight is a new day. I'm going out on a mission, a mission I mastered at sea: come hell or high water, I'm going to replenish my stock. Land is no different and danger is danger, thus my dagger, here. No matter where, it cuts the same. Nothing will stand in my way, I tell you!

Ros Nir, the old dog, bless his memory, used to say: 'A clear head is an empty head!' So, I'll cut short the talk, granted it is only morning, for my head is clear and just as empty and my throat itches with impatience to be put to better use than wasting itself on the likes of you!

...

......

Mission successful! At the sight of my dagger, the poor bastard lowered his price next to nothing. Now, that's a fair trade! "Call me crazy but give me cheap liquor!" said somebody important, I've forgotten who. Probably Caesar... Or Ros Nir.

Ehe! Life looks different through the bottom of an empty bottle—I feel like telling stories now. Where were we? Ah! Lying flat on my back in the jungle, wounds stinging my flesh, a long day behind, a longer one ahead, and little but sleep on my mind, except for the occasional pinch about the ones I'd left behind in the huts. Yes. So, now, how shall I say…

Well, now, this is my story, we've established that. But as I became separated from my party and there was no one left to make known what happened to my mates, I suppose I must leave myself in my wounds, surrendered to a hard-gained rest, and go back to the camp where they lay and, obviously, things were not to stay the same. Let me just unlock my treasure here… Aaah! Good! Here we go…

This is what I later learned, or at least how I understand it to have been…

Just let me appraise one more time my loot. For inspiration that is…Ah… Let no one say I can't spin a yarn, I'll enjoy myself:

Let us begin on the same small beach where we first arrived and where the last rays of the sun were slowly drowning into the sea allowing the darkness to creep in. A lost firefly landed in the unkempt beard of a man sprawled face up inside a small boat on the shore and began preparing its belly for the night. Mating season. The man's beard twitched once, then again, before a heavy hand landed on the place from where an instant earlier the cautious firefly had just taken off.

"Damn bugs!" he grunted, pulling himself right. "There are no bugs at sea! Well if ya don't count the fleas and the lice. And the cockroaches. Hum, what do ya know? There *are* bugs at sea. At least not the flying kind. Them's the worst."

He got out of the boat and unfolded himself straight from the hips with a grunt.

"Ahhh, the years are catching up to me. Time is a bug, I tell ya. Ya don't feel its pinch, but ya see its bite. Oh!"

And grumbling and groaning he stumbled inside the jungle and walked straight ahead with an ever swifter step until he arrived at a small beach on the other side of the island. There he put his hands to his mouth and released a bird-call of some kind. An educated man could tell you that it wasn't indigenous to that particular island, but as there wasn't any education to offer its criticism (as it so often delights to do), it didn't matter. He stopped, waited, and called out once more.

"Hum, not here yet. Better not be late, or I'm going to have Stick flogged."

And he sat himself down on a rock close to the sea, away from the trees and bugs and he might as well have been asleep for he didn't move an inch for many a wave. When the night was well on its way, he sat up, looked around and cursed, and returned to the forest, mumbling that it is not easy to find your way through the jungle at night. He certainly underestimated himself, for he was moving through the forest as easy as a younger man in daylight.

Arriving at the opposite side once more, he didn't go on the beach, but turned left and kept walking towards what, if you could see in the low moonlight, looked like three small huts. Approaching the first one he crouched down.

Seeing no movement, he turned to the second. There stood a guard weapon on shoulder, cigarette in one hand and a busy bottle in the other. Salivating, the seaman studied him a few minutes more, but seeing that the bottle was getting dangerously empty, he sprang into action.

He waited until the lad's back was turned and slipped in from behind. As the bottle tipped up to offer its goods, a large, healthy hand, rolled into a fist dropped on top of the guard's head, sending the unsuspecting gentleman to a land of many stars. The priority was to save the bottle, which the visible arm of the fellow in the shadows caught perhaps even a moment before his fist met the guard's skull. Bottle in hand, his stomach and chest provided a sling for the witless body to fall against before sliding to the ground. Then he aimed the bottle high and long, for too little there was for sipping and his parched throat begged. With ease, while spending the booty, he pulled the body away from the huts, inside some bushes where he set it carefully down, together with the empty container.

At the third hut he ran into some trouble: a guard leaning on the door, slumping and sound asleep. As he was devising a new plan, fate smiled on him again: the door opened, the frightened guard spun to greet with the barrel of his gun a devilishly handsome young man who wanted to exit. Wild negotiations of flailing hands and harsh rifle jabs finally resulted in the young man stepping some yards away to relieve himself. Without hesitation our hero applied the fist treatment to the guard, but without time to dispose of the body and at the sound of the zipper, he forced desperately the distance to the handsome young man and with a formidable punch aimed at the back of the

head, got the youngster as he turned, in full frontal nose.
I think I've already told you how much that cheered me.
Then he picked up my body, for this was the purpose of his
campaign, and disappeared into the night.

Now, the lepers, as most lepers you know have fine ears
and keen senses, witnessed in silence the captain's feats.
Their moist and functioning brains had decided on a most
splendid *coup d'état* before the captain even left the picture.
They patiently waited for Ros Nir to disappear, then, without a word, slipped out of their hut and into the clearing.
Moving like shadows they approached the place where,
under the stars, three drunken guards lay sleeping and
without hesitation and nary a sound, three necks snapped
in the silent night.

As Rudolph was pulling their bodies away, father Grant
proceeded to where the first guard, the one Ros Nir put to
sleep, lay. Applying the same treatment, he took the man's
weapon and moved along to the second. He pulled this one
away from the hut. Only just finishing, he turned to look
for the man's weapon when a hard, probably cold piece
of metal stuck to his veiled neck and a deep, manly voice
scraped out into the night:

"If you want to meet your maker holding a gun, then
don't give it to me."

With clerical resignation, the father handed back his
gun. Sigrid took it, slung it on her back, and pushed the
man towards his hut. Inside, Rudolph, with his back to
the entrance, was checking on the weapons. Surprised, he
released a guttural growl, but guessing more than seeing

the determination on the eye of Miss Cyclops, didn't put up a fight.

"Good," she said, "you've saved me the trouble."

She pushed unceremoniously the two prisoners to her hut, where their entrance woke the three other captives. "These two," she said, "just killed our lovely guards."

They didn't believe it. Some even laughed, as if it was a joke.

"If I tell you they killed the guards, they killed the guards," growled Sigrid, waving the gun at them. "I'm not in the mood for joking; they snapped their necks as if they were birds."

Four pairs of eyes stared in disbelief at the dark shadows before them.

"What kind of lepers are you?" asked Anna.

"What kind of priest are *you*?" said Nikki.

"Vhere iz zhe boy?" Marlene questioned her sister.

"I don't know," answered Sigrid. "Somebody else came up before, knocked out two of the guards and the boy disappeared."

Another exclamation.

"Shh! Shh!" bellowed Sigrid. "We still have those two over in the first hut. I don't know what happened with the boy. Unless you killed him?" she asked the lepers.

They shook their heads.

"Then I don't know what happened to him. Maybe he ran away, I knew I couldn't trust him."

"You know you can't trust zhis and zhat, every time,"

snapped Marlene. "Zhe boy wouldn't run away. And on zhe island, *de plus*. Ee iz a nice boy."

"I don't care if he is a nice boy, and I don't care if he ran away. We have more important things to do now. *Scheisse*," she turned to the two men, "I knew everything you said back there was a bunch of lies. Who are you?"

Rudolph grunted nervously while father Grant answered, "We are just two forgotten people, my lady. We have been invaded and we defended ourselves. We knew you were prisoners to that mad man, we would not have hurt you."

"Forgotten people my *arsch*. You snapped five necks in less than two minutes. It takes practice to do that. But you made my job easier and I will deal with you later. Now, I have to get my hands on my old friend and his brute so I can get some answers."

She handed everyone a weapon, and left the lepers in Nikki's watchful care. Albert protested that, "Zees iz madness. Ruzban vill kill all ov us," and something else in German, but Sigrid gave him the look and his complaints died away.

Passing the lepers' hut, they stopped fifteen yards from Ruzban's. Sigrid pulled everyone together and exposed the plan of action. They were to split in two teams and while one covered the back she would force the door and surprise the sleeping babies. Then, she positioned herself in front of the entrance, lifted her foot and with a terrible cry leveled the fragile door. Yelling, she bolted inside. The place was empty. She heard the cock of a gun and when she turned around she found herself facing Ruzban. Out of the gloom his cuts burned with fiery venom. Behind him, Babar appeared holding up the rest of her crew.

"I would have been disappointed if you didn't try anything," Ruzban said. "Don't make any problems now! Give me the gun!"

"You should rethink your strategy, pig," she growled, stepping back. "I will bore a dozen holes in your worthless body, before you can even reach out to touch me."

"Then your sister and your people will die, too."

"Yes, but you will be also dead, so why do you care?"

"Not if I shoot first…"

They faced each other, fingers tensed upon the triggers, ready to shoot at any moment. Then father Grant's voice was heard, "Master Ruzban, put the gun down! You have lost." He moved closer, holding a rifle on Ruzban. "You see, my lady that we are on your side," he said to Sigrid as Rudolph disarmed Babar. "Never let a girl babysit grown men."

Behind them Nikki just shrugged her shoulders.

"You see, your grace," repeated father Grant, "we don't like this fellow, he is a very bad man, and we would appreciate if you let us take care of him, then everyone can follow his own path away from our island."

With an agility that I've already mentioned to you, but no one in attendance could've guessed she was capable, Sigrid leaped behind him and stuck the gun in his back.

"No one is going to take this gun from me!" she grunted. "I appreciate the help, but I don't trust you. The pig is mine, and after I interrogate him, you can have them. As for my path, it runs through your island and there is nothing you can do to stop me."

"You are badly mistaken, my lady. There is nothing on this island you need," said the father calmly.

"True. But there is something on this island I want and that belongs to me. And it's not you who's going to stop me." She then handed a sleek-barreled weapon to Albert who was standing by. "Sit on those two chairs in the corner and don't move a rag," she ordered, then she turned to Ruzban and Babar, "You two, on your knees!"

As they didn't move she went around and with the butt of her charge delivered a blow to Babar's scruff. He grunted and fell heavily to his knees. Ruzban followed before she could get to him. She propped the barrel against his neck and roared, "Now, it's time you talk, you scarecrow. Who sent you? You have five seconds, I swear. This time I will skip cutting you up."

"I don't think you'll kill me," he began with a smirk.

"One."

"If you kill me you'll never find out…"

"I'll just tell myself I never met you. Two."

"I don't know him, I've never seen him."

"Three."

"It doesn't matter; it's someone you don't know."

"Four."

Her index curled up on the trigger.

"I can't…"

"Now you die. Five. "

"Ok, ok!" he yelled, "I will tell you! I will tell you, but I need your word that you will spare us and you won't allow the two profanities back there to touch us."

"You'll be spared long enough to talk," replied Sigrid. "This is the only thing I promise you. Now talk or be dead!"

"The person who sent me is…" began Ruzban, stringing the words out into the darkness.

"Who, who?!" cried Sigrid, on the verge of shooting the man in the back of the neck.

He paused, then the remaining of his lips curled in a hideous smile. "Gunther," he hissed, with obvious pleasure.

And the sound of the name produced a small ado amongst the spectators: Marlene released a surprised *Quoi?* Rudolph a painful moan… As for Sigrid, she just lowered her gun and leaned on the hut's wall.

"Gunther?" she murmured. "All this time it was Gunther?"

"Eee iz lying," replied Marlene. "Gunther iz dead, many years ago. You read zhe *rapport* yourself."

"No sister, I'm not lying. Your husband…"

"Not my husband!" groaned Sigrid.

Still on his knees, Ruzban turned his head slightly to the side and, eyes glistening, allowed a slow smirk to spread over his face.

"Not your husband… Orlin," he said, the name slipping out slowly into the air. He continued, "At his death, you were supposed to receive two envelopes. Gunther intercepted the second and since, he has been trying to get his hands on the first one. Of course, at one point, you could say, he faked his own death to get rid of those who were chasing him…"

"No. Eee iz dead," Marlene insisted.

"But why? Didn't he hide it himself? I don't understand…" Sigrid muttered.

Ruzban looked up, letting his answer linger. His eyes flickered in the dim light, catching Sigrid's attention. She struck his back with the hilt of her gun, knocking a burst of air out of his lungs.

"Talk! I'm not just having fun here," she ordered.

Taking a deep breath, he began once again. "Once the treasure was unloaded and hidden Gunther killed everyone aboard that ship. At least he tried. Orlin escaped, badly hurt, but he escaped with life and as his revenge, moved the treasure to another location. For years Gunther hunted him. Of course, he caught up to him. That's how Orlin died, but with him died the new hiding place, not a clue left behind except his scrap of a will. It mentioned an executor, a man named Rada Magat or Mada Ragat—I don't remember—who had an envelope, which he was to deliver personally to you upon his death. Before Gunther could get to him, Orlin's death made the news and the lawyer set out. With a bit of luck, he intercepted the man in Germany, killed him and took it. Unfortunately, it contained only half of the map. Many years later, about to lose all hope, he found out that there had been two lawyers, both named Rada Magat—or Mada Ragat—each with an envelope to deliver. That's how you got your half…"

Marlene clicked her tongue. "Zhis iz all very nice, Mr.

Ruzban. But, I seenk iz *too* nice. I knew Herr Gunther. Tell me, why didn't he come to *ask* for the map?"

"I don't know his exact reasoning. But I know he believes the treasure to be all his and that it would easy taking. Obviously, he was wrong…" he murmured the last part between his lips.

Sigrid stared down at him, "Were you there when I lost my eye?"

"And *moi*? *mon pied*?" Marlene hopped to where he was and lifted her crutch above his head, *"Réponds miserable, ou je vais te casser la tête avec ma cane!"*[8]

"I told you everything I knew. I don't know what you are talking about," he answered, scrunching his head between his shoulders.

"Were you there that night or no?" repeated Sigrid.

"I wasn't there. I don't know when that happened."

"Ee iz a liar, don't believe him," cried Marlene, "zhis *histoire* about Gunther iz a lie. Gunther iz dead, I know it."

"You can have him now," said Sigrid to the lepers. "I hope you make him suffer."

Ruzban struggled to get up but she held him down with the gun.

"Wait! Wait, you promised!" he cried.

"I promised I would spare you long enough for you to talk. And you talked."

"You dirty b…"

Rudolph was quicker: he hit Ruzban in the face before he could finish. Then he dragged him outside while Sigrid struggled with Babar pushing the barrel of the gun into his neck as the giant grunted and twisted, seeming to want to force his way up.

Outside, with a last effort, Ruzban pulled away from Rudolph and shouted, "I can give you Gunther!"

Sigrid whirled her head to the door. "Wait!" she cried, but as the mad giant was still forcing his way up she knocked him out with the gunstock. He fell loudly with a thump as she rushed to the door.

Not far from there, Rudolph, who had dropped Ruzban with a stomach punch and was now standing above him holding his head in the dirt, raised his dagger and was about to strike when a strong hand caught his arm.

"Not yet," snarled Sigrid.

He grunted and tried to force the blow but her grip was strong. "Not yet!"

He growled like a cornered wolf and for a second their eyes locked. Neither was giving up, but Sigrid was firmly planted on her feet and atop of him. "I said not yet!" she wrestled and pushed him aside.

Visibly unpleased he planted the knife in the ground and used it as a prop to get up, then pulled it out and left for the hut.

"You'll give me Gunther?" Sigrid asked while Ruzban was pulling himself up.

"I'll give him to you, if you keep that beast away from me," he answered.

"Where is he?"

"He has men watching this place. I am supposed to meet him not far from here, on another island after I find out where the gold is and get rid of you."

She watched the horizon; where the sea touched the sky you could make up the outline of another island. "Then I will give him the surprise of his life. But first I will finish what I've come to do. Get back inside, now!"

Marlene met her as she entered the hut, "You don't believe eem! Ee iz lying. Gunther iz dead, I know."

Sigrid looked at her under one eyebrow, "Why are you so insistent on this? Gunther was your friend, he sent you the other half of the letter, he never bothered you…"

"*Au nom du Dieu,* I lost my leg! Are you zhat crazy to insinuate I am in *clique* weez zhem? Ee iz playing weez your head." She was outraged and turning rounds on her peg.

"You lost your leg. I've lost my eye and two men and much more. No one wanted to lose anything. It's not like a sacrifice of good faith was demanded. But I don't believe you are in clique with them. You are my sister after all. I don't think even you could lower yourself that much.

"One thing I can't explain though, and neither can you: if Gunther is dead, how does this piece of junk here know so much about him? But I will find out. There is nothing to lose at this point."

Marlene, ignoring the last part of Sigrid's speech, stopped and pointed the crutch at her, "Good! Because I go home right now, if you suspect me." She went and sat down on a chair, "Now what we are doing weez zhe two bandits?"

"They will have to stay here, guarded by somebody. Too

bad the boy disappeared; I don't have anybody else…" Sigrid answered. She looked around, but before she could say anything Ruzban intervened, "Let us come with you. Babar can carry your supplies."

Sigrid turned to him, lowered her face one inch from his, and said between her teeth, "I wouldn't take you with us even if I have to tie you to a tree and leave you there until we return, vermin." She got even closer, her eye slowly piercing his one by one. "And if you lied," she growled, "I'll sail to the center of this ocean and drop you out there with no food, no water, no clothes! Did you lie to me?"

He shook his head. A shadow passed through his perfidious eyes and where a casual observer would read just the usual hatred, a keener eye could've seen, for the first time, the flicker that fear gives out.

But Sigrid was already facing Albert, "I'm sorry old friend, there is no one else I can ask… I can't ask them…" she motioned to the lepers. "I promise I will make it up to you."

Albert, at first didn't understand, but when he did, his eyes grew twice their normal size and his moustache dropped a few degrees, "I must stay and guard zhem?" he asked with incredulity.

"I can't force you, but I would appreciate it," answered Sigrid. She approached him and put a hand on his shoulder, "It won't be long, I promise, the island is small, two days at max. They will be tied up and chained to a tree. Don't take your eyes off them and if you feel threatened in any way just shoot them. I won't hold it against you."

From under his hump Albert shrugged his shoulders,

defeated, "Iv I must stay... but I don't know zee guns very vell..."

"Just aim and press the trigger," replied Sigrid. "And thank you!" Then she went to the men in black, "I need your word that you won't stay in my way, otherwise you won't come with us and I don't know what else to do with you!"

Four eyes looked long and deep at her. Only from under two did words filter out, "Sometimes, my lady, the dead should stay dead and the buried, buried. I know you won't listen to me. You've crossed half the world to find out what you've just heard and I feel there is something that keeps pushing you further. I know my lady that you won't leave here before you get to the bottom of it, but I can tell you now that you might regret it. I don't know for sure, but there is a good chance that you might regret it."

"Better live with regrets than ignorant at this point, old man," replied Sigrid between her teeth. "Now, I won't ask you why you said what you've just said, because, as you said I will find it out by myself, but I need to know if you are with me."

But the father continued, "...It must be duty, I guess. You feel it's your duty to finish this chapter of your life. And from what I've just learned, what a long chapter it was! I admire your courage my lady, I will help you even if it's against *my duty* to do so," he said with his head lifted and his voice raised.

At his words, Rudolph grunted and jabbed him between the ribs.

"Forgive him, my lady, he doesn't understand yet how

important this is for you. He's been a selfish bastard all his life and now his paying for it by rotting up alive. But I was trained to feel my people's pain, and I can feel yours, as our Lord felt ours on the cross."

Rudolph grunted again, then got up, ignored the gun directed at him and left through the door.

Sigrid distributed weapons to Anna, Nikki and Albert and commanded, "They move you shoot!" Then with one hand she caught father Grant's arm with the other Marlene's and pulled them out of the hut despite their protestations. "Who are you people and what are you doing here?" she then asked.

"I see no reason not to tell you my lady, now that I've promised to help you…"

"Well?"

"We are the guardians, my lady."

"Zee *gardiens* of what?" asked Marlene.

"Of what we are looking for, stupid," Sigrid jarred at her.

"You are *stupide*," replied Marlene.

"Never mind this," said Sigrid to the father, "I want to know more, why are you here, the history of it… Orlin left you here?"

The father paused and looked at them, then answered, "I don't know the man you call Orlin and I can tell you nothing more my ladies. People who know more have the bad habit of dying." He then paused again, "You see," he said lowering his voice to a mystical depth, "I am a man of God, but my friend isn't," his head pointed in the direction where Rudolph had disappeared, "he is a damned rogue and very dedicated. From now on you should stay close to me at all times because I can't vouch for his actions."

"Let him try," grunted Sigrid.

"No my lady, do not let him try, pray to God that he doesn't try, because if he does, it won't take much for him to succeed. I have seen him countless times and he has never failed. To tell you the truth, I am a bit afraid myself; since he lost his speech I don't know what he thinks anymore—because as you know, a man is as good as his word. I can't read him like before: I can't see him, I can't hear him, sometimes he does things of which I don't approve—the Lord doesn't approve—and I don't find out until it's too late."

"Then I will kill him before he kills me," decided Sigrid, readying her gun.

Marlene hit her on the shoulder with her free arm, while the father looked at her with indignation and said in coarse tone, "He is my friend, my lady, *he is* my best friend, and I will happily die at any time for him. Don't make me regret what I so readily promised you."

"Forgive her, *mon père*," said Marlene, "she iz *stupide*, she doesn't mean it."

With a grunt of discontentment and a movement of impatience, Sigrid jerked the rifle back on her shoulder. "Ok, old man," she said rashly, "I will trust you for now, not because you are a priest, but because back there you could've fought me and you didn't; and also, because I don't have time for anything else right now. I will allow you to come with us since I don't have anyone else to guard you, but I'm warning you: if he tries something against any of my crew here, I will blow his head faster than you can say 'Amen!' Understood?"

"Thank you my lady," answered simply the priest.

"Then go take care of those you killed. We leave right away."

Chapter 17

Where I find blood

A nurse (a young one, not you Rose!) approached me today and asked, in confidence mind you, when I will finish my journal. Damn you people, this is not a journal! Is this a journal? What am I, a little girl writing about the things that broke her tender heart? Woe unto you, unfaithful soul, if you had asked me that, for my wrath is only limited by my patience!

But she—one of those, tender bodies and souls dedicated to saving the world and all its beasts—being a fair one, I graciously composed myself and with most pitiful countenance I charged my sufferings—for what but pain would send a man as myself to pen and paper? (she wasn't aware that I, I don't scribble, I yarn)—to loneliness and to the cruelty of my peers who confined me to a world of solitude where but words I have for friends. You should've seen the tears washing down her fine cheeks when I confessed that I yearned for human touch, a warm hug and other crap I've already forgotten, and how she promised to visit and hug me daily. Once, she said. Five times, I beseeched—for the sake of my spirit and the health of my aching soul. Ha! Careful, you maidens, I'm back! Of course, I've promised her a story or two between hugs for I have told you: words I have enough to sink a ship but maidens, pleasing to the eye, sirens—as I call them, for you've seen the way they walk— are scarce in these waters. The forecast: sunny and warm with no storm in sight. Scattered hugs on the horizon, yet fierce I hope, and from there, may the wind be with us for it is a good time to yarn!

Four women or so, a leper, and a priest or so, left a few hours later to find a treasure. Ruzban and Babar were each attached to a different tree with chains just long enough to allow them some movement. Just as a precaution, need was to use two chains on Babar, who had recovered his peaceful and innocent smile, and let himself be handled with the serenity of a faithful nun after a vision or two. A so untroubled and blissful creature, yet so powerful, being the instrument of a sadistic torturer was an unusual thing, but as they say, the sin goes to the hand that holds the dagger, not to the dagger that cuts. To this day, Babar remains one of the characters that amazed me most. To see him and his master side by side, one healthy and radiant and full of life, the other, dark and scrawny and rotten as the breath of Death, was as striking as watching night and day walking down one road.

"You need not worry about him," said Sigrid to Albert once they were ready to leave. "He won't go anywhere without his master. Him, on the other hand, you don't let his mouth open even once. His tongue is more poisonous than any snake in this jungle and if he doesn't want to keep it shut shoot him. First in the leg, than in the head if he complains."

This was said close enough for Ruzban's ear to hear, which he did and his answer was a sneer filled with hate and murder.

"I am glad to have taken you with me," continued Sigrid. "I hesitated at first, but now I'm glad."

With big eyes and no words, Albert saw them leaving. He then clutched tighter his weapon and turned to the prisoners.

Limping and swearing and in silence they traveled through the jungle. Harder on Marlene it was, but she didn't complain; just the occasional blasphemes in a language that sounded like sweet music to father Grant's ears. Rudolph and the two girls were carrying the supplies while Sigrid, stub in corner mouth, stick in one hand, marched in front as a conqueror would march through his new territory. It so happened that there was a trail running in the same direction and she just followed it with no need to cut the dense vegetation now walling the sides and forming an impenetrable barrier. For the night they stopped and as they had no machetes, set camp directly on the track. A guard was set to be changed every few hours, but when the sun's first rays grazed their faces they woke up and discovered that Rudolph was missing.

Father Grant was accused, threatened, then interrogated by the butcher of Cigarville. He had slept between Sigrid and Marlene, closer to the last one because she had complained of the air being cooler and more poignant at night than during the day.

"You planned this, didn't you?" Sigrid accused, watching him suspiciously through a cloud of smoke.

"We did not, my lady, and you have to believe me," answered the priest.

"Well, I don't. I don't trust anyone—especially a so called man of God on a deserted island. I think nothing you've told me is true…"

"Where do you seenk ee went?" interrupted Marlene.

"What worries me most is that I haven't the faintest idea," he answered, "but as I told you, he is capable of anything and we should be on our way as soon as possible."

"Do you think he will attack us?" asked Nikki, nervously trying to peer through the vegetation.

"I hope not, young lady, for there won't be much we could do to stop him."

"Let him try," growled Sigrid, "I was right when I said I should've got rid of him back at the camp."

"Maybe he went to find our handsome missing boy," I'd like to think Anna's dreamy voice said, but, it was never confirmed.

Back at the huts, Ruzban watched as Albert approached, dragging his leg. He had dropped the weapon and was coming now empty handed. Slowly, a remarkable transformation took place in the old man as he walked. With every step, his humbling hump inched farther inside his chest until it was no more, giving way to a pair of broad shoulders as aligned as any man's who never carried anything but clothes and luck on his back. His limp, too, disappeared and when he erected his head Ruzban could see a pair of piercing eyes that looked at him not with fear, but contempt. When he got closer, Albert was a head taller than the cook he used to be. Only the moustache stood witness to the old hunchback, now as firm and proud looking as its owner.

"Good to talk to you again, master," grinned Ruzban.

"You've failed me twice Ruzban," answered a resounding voice. "No one has ever failed as much and lived."

"I didn't fail you, sir. We aren't even delayed. They are on their way to find it right now."

"And I, here babying you, when I should be with them!" rose the voice. "After years slaving for that viper, and now it's so close... What should I do with you Ruzban?"

Ruzban stopped grinning; his head wobbled a few more times and came to rest in a somewhat vertical position. "Just a minor setback, sir. We are going to get it," he said.

"Yes, I am," shouted the man, pointing in the direction Sigrid had left, "but for that I must be there with them. I told you to wait for my sign to show up. Again you have failed me."

"I saw the old pirate get on board and as my contacts had informed me that he was a dangerous man, I decided to capture you all before he could do so himself."

"I guess you weren't wrong there," muttered the man. "Nonetheless, I expect that they are on the island now. Yet more trouble..."

"You see master, you still have me. And Babar. On my order he will crush them like bugs. This time I won't hesitate, I promise you."

The former cook didn't say a word, just shook his head as a man who had heard the same words before. Then he went back inside, picked up the bag he had brought from the ship, pulled out a long blade, returned to where Babar, half confused, half amused, was sitting, lifted the weapon and struck the first blow.

Now, as I have you heated and properly confused, the time is fit to get back to your humble hero, who is also mine.

The next morning I woke up fresh and ready to live, more so than any of you who had been tortured and drugged in the same day ever did or will do. In fact, it was a boot to my ribs that awoke me, for I was sleeping like the dead and, of course, someone had to make sure I wasn't. Indeed, that being true I roused to my feet sorry to be there and not in my dream, in which I was eating some kind of pie made by my mother, which pie tasted like Ros Nir's concoction.

I was given a biscuit and some water and the men set out as soon as I took the first bite. Things were pretty uneventful for the duration of my eating that biscuit—a good ten minutes, for my teeth were painful and my lips still inflated. I was just thinking to ask the captain for his special remedy when, as we entered a clearing, the men froze, glued into place.

I made my way to the front. There, twenty yards ahead, on the other side of the lea stood a man. Someone I could not have mistaken for I had seen only two of them so far and this one was the taller, with broader shoulders.

As dark as a stormy, moonless night, there stood Rudolph the leper, feet squarely planted on the ground, his left arm lifted above his head. It looked like a signal of some sort, his arm hanging there, except no one else appeared. The pirates on my side split off and let the captain come forward. He appeared with,"ya idiots…better have good cause…" but stopped at the sight of the black shadow ahead. For a moment he hesitated, glanced at his men, then took a step forward and called out:

"Aye! Ya over there, ya're in me way."

As no answer came, he turned to Stick who was closest to him, "Why did ya stop? I say ya keep going and I say when ya stop!"

Stick looked at him but didn't say anything.

"Well? Fer God's thunder Stick, it's jest an old mummy, ya know as well as meself the stories of the black creatures they're jest stories."

Stick shook his head in silent negation.

The captain cursed and spit on the ground then addressed his crew, "What is wrong with ya lads? Ya don't wanna move? Ya're up to mutiny now? I'll peel off yer skin and cut out yer ears as soon as I'm finished with that creature over there!"

Still nobody moved.

"He's a leper who lives on the island," I piped up.

"Didn't you know? And he's mute."

He looked at me as my teachers used to when I interrupted their monologue to ask for the bathroom, "Mute leper? There is no mutes here and there is no lepers."

I shrugged and turned my eyes back to Rudolph. With firm steps he was now approaching. He stopped ten feet from our group. Then he spoke. And his voice was the kind that stays with you forever. It sent shivers down my spine.

"Aye Ros Nir. It's been a while."

"Mother of Jehoshaphat! But it's Jim Brrow," sneered the captain in surprise. "I hear yer voice, but don't see yer face. I was expecting ya today. Ya're dressed like a mummy all set for the burial."

"I see you haven't forgotten your captain," the voice thundered, this time in a cheerful tone. "The attire is to protect my island—scare away the weaker spirits. But I see now the past is catching up to me and it seems I can't stop it."

"Yer island? It's God's island fer he made it. As fer yer past, I hope it strikes ya down like ya struck mine."

"All signs show that it may happen," replied with majesty the voice behind the veil. "And this island, you know it's mine. You've stayed away from it. Until now, I see."

Saying this, the man in black reached up and slowly unfurled the rags that were covering his face. Strike me dead! What I saw first nigh made my heart stop! In the middle of his face, there was a protuberance very much alike the one I had watched over the years in the mirror. This protrusion—I would call nose, but many, often, called it trunk—

this thing, was indeed identical to mine. By the time he had finished unveiling, we stood before a strong, powerfully built, well-aged man, but still not aged enough for even a fool to miss that he was the man from Sigrid's wall, the man who had left so many years ago with an invaluable treasure on a rickety old ship. He was none other than Orlin von Lindgren himself. That nose couldn't lie.

"Until now," Ros Nir jeered and stretched an arm out behind catching me by the neck and bringing me forward. "When I saw the young lad, I knew time had come fer us to have a talk." He then turned to me and said, "Ya see now junior why I think ya're very precious to me? It's unthinkable that yer not his blood; yer nose there, big as it is, is my witness."

"Orlin?" I said, wrestling in Ros Nir's iron grip.

The man smiled, "That name died long ago, son." He lifted his head and looked off in the distance, "It's Captain Jim Brrow now, the owner of these seas," and he turned his head back in Ros Nir's direction, "and of this island. We will talk our resemblance at a later time for it surprises me as much. Now I have to deal with the fool in front of me." He turned to the man who was holding my neck and continued, "I waited long to have a talk with you—since you stole my ship and my men, Ros Nir."

"Ya killed me father, I consider that a bigger offense that taking yer ship. And I didn't steal yer ship, ya left without word and I judged it mine after some time."

"I had reason to leave, you old fool. As for your father, I wasn't what killed him. He died of old age in his bed in his house. If you weren't the fool that you are, you could've been there. Have you ever once visited his grave?"

I was watching him as he spoke. Playing games in the mild breeze, his light hair ran down his sunburned, leathery neck which was holding a proud head with fierce eyes the color of the sea whose son he was; his salient muscles raced down in strides underneath his browned skin, disappearing beneath the light colored shirt he now stood in. He was watching Ros Nir with neither hate, nor disdain, but with sadness. I admired that man right then and there and I wished that he were indeed of my blood, or that I was of his. I have since striven to be proud and memorable as he. Not that my father wasn't a good model, but he was the model of a different sort, the quiet, honest worker that gave up life and hope of a future to raise his three boys. Had I chosen to be of the working class too, there isn't another man I'd like to resemble. But the man standing before me was the man of the wild open sea, where strong winds blow and the glowering sun burns and you're bound only to encounter the thrill of another being in countless hard fights. What young man could resist that, I ask you?

"What's this you say?" Ros Nir muttered, his eyes squinting in question, as he eased his grip on my neck.

"And he said to tell you," continued the Captain, "that he enjoyed his stay with me on the sea. By heaven Ros Nir, you never thought to bring him with you even once?"

"He had no need to know what I've became."

"Eh, well he found out anyway. He learned to accept it after some time. Just a job like any other. What he couldn't understand was you wouldn't give me back my ship."

"I jest did what ya taught me—steal," exploded Ros

Nir. "Na, now ya're happy? And ya wicked man, ya set him against me. He died hating his own son."

"Neither is true. He just wished you were there, that's all."

Ros Nir released me and it looked like he was about to wipe a tear from one of his eyes. But, as he never lifted his arm and since his beard began right under his eyes, I'll never be able to tell you for sure. Somewhere, in the forest of scraggly white strands, amidst food remnants and dust and pollen and animalcules may lay the memory of a single tear, and I tell you now, that would've been a special tear for I never saw that man tearing again, not even ten years later when I had to cut his both legs from under him with no aid of medicine whatsoever. But I'm getting ahead of myself... Seeing a grown pirate cry... Sometime that might be the rarest fish in the sea...

"Where is yer crew?" he asked twitching his nose. "Don't tell me ya came to find a treasure all by yerself."

"This is my island, remember? And my crew stands behind you."

Ros Nir looked back and saw but his men.

"What d'ya mean?"

"Your men are my men, Ros Nir. All this time you've been working for me and you didn't even know it."

"What do ya mean?" mumbled the captain. Then he understood with a terrible grin and turned to his men, "Ya bunch of treacherous dogs. Ya're *his* bunch?"

"Don't blame them," said Jim Brrow. "After you stole my ship I wanted to find and kill you. But as I thought it better,

I realized that I could only gain if I had some competition out there. I then caught all of the men one by one—they used to be mine, remember—and persuaded them that if they wanted to live they'd have to work for me. I didn't required much, just to keep me informed about your activities. As nobody dislikes living, and in addition getting paid twice, they all agreed."

Stick's voice along with a few other voices piped up, "Sorry Cap'n."

"Ya shut up, ya dogs!" cried the captain, "I will deal with ya as soon as I'm done with his majesty the king over here. His majesty the king of this place. Ehe, ya got me there old dog. I thought meself an honest pirate trying to make me living, but what do ya know, I was jest a puppet, ha?! Now what do ya propose? Tell yer dogs to cut me dead? I'd have this young lad's neck slit before they'd laid hand on me, but I took a liking to him and I don't think I could do it."

Orlin, or Jim Brrow if you like, looked at him with the same sad eyes, "You're a good man, Ros Nir and a good captain. I regret what I did to you so long ago; I should've let you become a fisherman like your father…"

"Eh, I don't regret. The sky above me head, the water below it is all I need. But it seems it has to end now."

Jim Brrow looked at him, "I want you to work for me Ros Nir. Nothing will change; you'll still be the captain you were…"

"Aye, except now I'll know. Not if ya kill me, this is me answer! I'm me own man!" Saying this he pulled a dagger from his belt, pushed me back and stepped aside, lifted his head high and roared to the skies, "I'm ready fer ya, ya dirty mongrels! I die today but many of ya won't see the sun set tonight!"

No one moved, except Jim Brrow, who ignored the blade and planted himself a foot from Ros Nir's face. The Captain was half a head taller, but Ros Nir was thicker, and both men stood measuring each other eye-to-eye, neither giving up even a blink.

"You know I can't let you go?"

"I know," answered Ros Nir. "I wouldn't allow meself go free."

"Then what do you propose?" asked Jim Brrow. "How do we resolve this situation without one of us dying today?"

"There is no way!" the captain answered fiercely. "Ya have yer jackals to do yer job fer ya. Ya're a lucky man I tell ya; there is still honor in this old pirate otherwise I would've planted me knife long time ago in yer heart."

"I know," answered the Captain without moving. "And, I don't want to kill you. Men like you are rare."

"We would never attack you Cap'n," said Stick.

Ros Nir grunted in their direction, but didn't bother to look.

"I would've never asked that of you," said Jim Brrow. "Ros Nir, these men need a captain."

"Then ya fight me like a man. If I kill ya I take yer place. If ya kill me, ya kill me. That'll be it!"

"If you kill me you kill me. That'll be it," repeated the Captain. "If I defeat you I'll have right to choose what becomes of you. Agreed?"

"Agreed," answered Ros Nir after a pause. Then he took a step back, swung his dagger up-high and cried, "Prepare now to meet yer maker Jim Brrow. Yer bill is long overdue. These waters can't suffer the two of us, one must die today!"

Jim Brrow didn't say anything. He just took a few steps back and from inside his covering pulled a long beautiful knife with an encrusted blade and gilt leather hilt, leaned forward until his left hand sat on his knee and waited.

Ros Nir froze, his eyes on the knife, "How...? That knife was in me family forever."

"Your father gave it to me to give back to you. But you stole my ship... It's up to you now to take it back," answered the Captain waiting.

"And have it back I shall!" roared Ros Nir as he swung forward.

Jim Brrow dodged the blade by fencing back and to the left, but the bearded man was quicker than his stature let on and at the same time stepped to the right and turned with incredible speed. I heard his dagger cut through the Captain's shirt at the abdomen. He groaned slightly, his hand searched through to the cut and came out bloodied.

"By heaven, I think you just cut me Ros Nir," he said simply.

"And I shall keep cutting ya!" cried Ros Nir. "This time deeper!" and he attacked again.

He fenced, the Captain fended off the blade, but Ros Nir's free arm formed into a fist and hit the Captain in the full jaw knocking him off his legs. He jumped back up quickly as though he had expected it and shook his head.

They faced again.

I can close my eyes and see them battle as if it was yesterday. There stood two titans fighting for the right to rule their world and I shall say that I later learned it was a world worth fighting for. They continued swinging their blades and grunting and panting as I watched my first life-death fight in amazement not knowing than soon my hand would be one of those sparring a dagger. The Captain, though bleeding, stood proud and cold-blooded and had a dignity I never could equal. Ros Nir, after the initial success, started to be less careful in his rush to finish the game. I saw him make a few risky moves and on one occasion he had his back completely offered to the Captain's knife, who ignored it, and waited until they faced again.

At one point, as their blades collided, Jim Brrow's was yanked out of his hand, under the force of the impact. Or so it appeared. A small victorious grin began to draw on his opponent's face, but didn't last long, for the Captain swung his other arm and caught Ros Nir's knife-branding hand at the joint. Ros Nir, losing no time, tried again to punch at the Captain's face. But deftly, Jim Brrow ducked and stepped forward catching Ros Nir under the arm with his shoulder and with a powerful cry lifted him up and fell on top of him to the ground. There, with superhuman strength, because you needed superhuman strength to overcome that arm, he forced Ros Nir's joint backwards until his own dagger pointed at his own hairy throat. Ros Nir grunted and struggled like a buffalo caught by the neck in the jaws of a tiger, but the tip of the blade pushed deeper into the soft below his Adam's apple.

"I couldn't kill you with your family's knife," said the

Captain grunting. "But I could do it with yours. If you don't mind."

"It's jest a common knife," groaned Ros Nir, eyes on the blade.

"And now my blood stands on it and yours will too, if you don't give up the fight," said the Captain. "Do you agree that I have right of life and death over you?"

Eyes bulged, face reddened, Ros Nir struggled more, but the iron claw did not release its grip and the dagger was now drawing blood.

"Agreed," he grunted and sighed in the same breath.

"It's good then," said the Captain pulling himself up. "Here is your family's inheritance; back to its rightful owner," and he picked up the encrusted dagger and planted it next to Ros Nir's head.

"From now on I am your captain," he said, carefully removing his clothes to inspect the wound. The cut was long and grisly, but not deep. "You, Ros Nir, keep command of your men and your ship, but you are all mine. As you see, not much has changed."

The men cheered and I with them.

Ros Nir stood up and ceremoniously cleaned his dagger against his clothes. Then he raised it and looked at it in the light, kissed it at the hilt, and put it on his belt.

If you have never seen a pirate's belt, allow me to describe it to you, for it was then that I saw my first. A pirate's belt, this thing, is made of strong, thick sturdy leather and it is double lined. Every few inches the two linings are sewn together to form an empty opening between them, never equal for they have to fit blades of different sizes and shapes. The inside of the openings is lined with metal so the respective blades don't cut through the belt. It's a glorious thing, I tell you, heavy and sturdy, ready to protect its owner in a fight. Mine, which I keep right here next to me, burns with desire to do you a favor and scratch that itch on your backside should you ever neighbor it.

"Ya're me captain, that's right," said Ros Nir. "It's yer right as ya have defeated me in honest combat. Here and now I give up me claim on the booty we both search."

"Good," said the Captain. He told the men to advance a hundred yards and wait there, which they did, glad to sit down and bask in the sun, the excitement now gone with no loss of any of their captains. Once they were out of spoken word's reach, he turned to Ros Nir and said: "I have the treasure."

Ros Nir, who was prepared to follow the men, stopped in his tracks, "Ya have it? Ya found it?"

"It's been always mine," replied the Captain, "I am the one who brought it here. I am the one that almost died for it. I am the one who defended it for years."

Ros Nir weighed the words coming to him, "Then why search fer it? Why kidnap me as a young lad?"

"To defend it, I told you. The best way to guard something is to pretend you are looking for it yourself."

"Aye," said the captain scratching his head, "then ya did a good job fer sure. Then those crazy women and that maniac, what do they want?"

"That is a long story," answered the Captain with a sigh.

He then stepped over to where I was standing and studied me for a good while, "I see from his nose that you treated the boy well."

"Well… I thought he was yer blood. And he didn't want to speak… at first. But not to worry I have his cure right here." He held out the canteen.

I grabbed it and drank. Oh, sweet concoction!

"You know where is it?" asked the Captain, his piercing eyes on me.

As I was still swallowing, I only nodded.

"Welcome to your new world," he replied.

I had finished drinking, but still could say nothing.

"What are we to do now Captain?" Ros Nir asked with an itch in his voice.

"You take the men and go meet those women. They're heading for the Southern Point. You tell them the treasure was moved and we shall meet back at the huts. The boy comes with me, he needs to be baptized."

"What about that scarred bastard?" Ros Nir asked. "I hold a great debt to him and I yearn to make it right."

"We will take care of him. Me and the boy," answered the Captain gazing direct in my eyes.

"Aye, Captain. It's yers then," said Ros Nir and, motioning to the men, disappeared into the jungle.

As for me, what else was there to do but keep swallowing big empty knots?

CHAPTER 18

FOR ONCE, I'M GIVEN THE CHOICE

It's gone! It's gone! All my liquor's gone! Rose, now you listen to me! My patience is up! Give me back my medicine, you hear? It's my medicine, Rose! May the legions of dogs in hell have no pity on your soul! What is she doing with it? What's her business? What kind of person would do that? What kind of people are out there? There was once a time when only the fittest, the strongest could survive. Now everybody does. The weak, the misfit, the sick, the whiniest—they survive, they rule the world! People like you, Rose! Give it back, I say! It works for me, and cures my brand of ills. Ah, this world is going to hell, I tell you! You'll miss me, Rose, when I am gone! What am I doing here? Ah! How I hate you all!

One of these days I must finish my story and be out of here for immortality is taking a heavy toll.

As I was saying before, when this place betided happier times, side by side or, trailing each other on occasion, two noses, of a quite different age, and—mine now being almost as wide as long—of different proportions, set out to bring justice and repair injustice. Their bodies simply chased from behind.

Not yet come to terms with what my role would be in the next episode, I kept silent for a while, but as I was anxious to find out about my former mates, dreading the answer as much as the question, I finally inquired with a simple, "…the others?"

"They're fine," the Captain answered.

I breathed out a long puff of relief and followed with a question about Anna in particular.

"Which one is she?" he asked.

I described her at length with enthusiasm and far more words than necessary. He stopped and turned around and measured me like an adult measures the kid that grew up too fast since he last saw him and said that she was as fine as she could be and a bit more, now that I had gone to such lengths to portray her. I reddened all over, except at my nose which being already in that very state had no choice but to blanch, and mumbled something about my duty to protect the fair sex and that she was like a sister to me, so on, so on… It was quite a monologue. He listened for at first, but as I was getting loquacious turned around once more and resumed the walk. I continued mumbling even as he had gained distance and couldn't have heard, for I wanted to prove to myself that I wasn't interested in the girl.

Later, once the blood had regained its proper place—away from my cheeks and ears and into my nose—he asked about my origins. At the name of my country he stopped and hesitated. "What is your grandmother name?" he asked.

"Katerina," I answered.

"Katerina..." he muttered, and seemed lost somewhere in a thought. "She had brown eyes the color of ripe chestnuts, intense black hair like pure charcoal, lips you could eat like freshly picked berries... Is that your Katerina?" he asked.

My turn to measure him the way he did me. "No," I said hesitantly. "...I don't think so. My grandmother had white hair and I don't remember the color of her eyes."

But he wasn't listening, "Katerina..." he whispered. He spun and caught me by the shoulders, "She used to squeeze her lips when she was mad until they became blue and played with a strand of her hair on the right side of her head to help her think... Do you remember any of this?"

Oh, and how I remembered! For how many a frown had she birthed raising the little devil that I was? And those blue squeezed lips her mouth now permanently flaunted? Do you think she was born with them? And indeed, she use to play with her hair when thoughtful. So, I nodded.

"Then, by heaven you're my grandson!" he exclaimed. "No doubt about it. I was stationed in your country as a young soldier. We were going to get married. Then I was sent to the front, and a few months later I received a letter from her mother saying that Katerina was killed by a stray bullet while working as a nurse in a field hospital. It devastated me. I went home and married Sigrid, I hoped I would forget. Later I started drinking..." He let go of me, "Now, I find out I've destroyed two lives instead of one..."

"It wasn't your fault," I said, but he had started walking again and was deep in his thoughts.

With such small talk and great findings we arrived at the huts.

"They've escaped!" cried the Captain at first sight of the naked trees and cut chains.

"Who?" I asked.

"That ugly lad and his gorilla. But I don't see the old man's body…"

"Who?" I asked again.

"The old hunchback she left to guard…"

"She left Albert to guard Ruzban?" I asked incredulously.

"There wasn't much choice. Better than the girls."

Ah, the girls! "We have to find them. They are in danger!" I cried and turned toward the trees, ready to sprint like a bullet from a loaded gun.

"They have Grant, and Ros Nir is on his way," he said after a moment. "God protect them! We would arrive too late as it is, and anyway, I want to take this time to show you something."

"But if we rush," I insisted for I could see Ruzban's evil smile in front of my eyes.

"They have all the help they need. We can't make it today. They'll be fine," he said with a voice that left no space for anything else. "I brought you here with a purpose."

Angry, already mad at my new kin, I demanded to know what.

"Let's go, it's not far. The time is good now," he said with no other explanation.

I followed him mechanically. My thoughts were somewhere to the south of the island and had the scent of light perfume and blond hair. She was in danger and I was powerless, again. And how would she react when she found out I was alive? Did she even care that I had vanished? I asked the Captain if he had seen Anna crying, or if she was at least red eyed for a moment or two.

"Not that I've seen," he answered, squinting at me.

Hum, I thought, *now that I am the grandson of a pirate maybe she will consider me in a different light.* I didn't have it then, but here is some of my wisdom: To some lasses, power and money on a man, is what light, or garbage, are to a fly. Have power or money, or both, and you appear to them as a beacon of light; or a can of garbage—whichever you're more worthy of and pleases you more. I had neither, but I had the protection of one and the mystery of the second. Most of them dames don't need to see it. It's enough if they smell it. Look at Ms. Schultz, up on the third floor—I can't get the old hag off my back!—the wreck, she should've raised the flag long ago, but I'm sure the smell of my gold won't let her. Look at my young and innocent hug-a-nurse. God bless her, for a bit of good she does me! And for what? I tell her a story or two, for as I said words I have plentiful—enough to hug the whole world. Eh! Had I had this wisdom at your age… but as many men out there, I acquired it just in time to be unable to enjoy it. Young and wise, it seems, is against nature.

Young I was, and impetuous, and to top it off worried and furious for I felt so powerless against the man walking in front of me. I wished I could catch him by the neck, lift him up, and say to him: "Listen, I know you're the big man here and grandfather and all, but I don't care! There is a young girl back there that needs help. Now let's go or I'll do something we'll both regret!" It feels good to be brave, if at least in a speech inside of your head, so I spent the next while giving myself a treat.

Belligerent as such, I didn't even realize when we had left the trees and exited on the reef, at the edge of the water. The reef was composed of an agglomeration of immense rocks which stood there on top of each other like fallen giants. I looked around and saw no other rock formation beside this group, the rest of the shore being either the white sandy beach or the higher land edging the sea. It looked as if small pebbles had slipped through God's fingers when he created the world and landed here. Pebbles for God, giants for us.

"What is this?" I asked grumpily.

"What you came here to find," he said, ignoring my tone.

"But… but it's at the Southern Point. The map said…"

"When I found out the second letter didn't reach Sigrid I moved the whole lot. As a precaution."

He lowered himself through the rocks to the shore. "There are only two people alive who know this location," he said once I joined him. "The other is my friend Grant, you know him."

"Yes, but what happened to his…?" I asked pointing to my head.

"He lost half his face, I kept my life. I wouldn't be here without him. Sometimes it comes in handy when you need lepers. Everybody is afraid of lepers. Now, you will be only the third person ever to know the location. Do you know what that implies?" he asked.

I looked up at him. His great stature towered over me like those boulders dominated the waves. "Does it imply anything?" I asked.

"Of course, it does. You can't see what you're about to see and then go about your life as if nothing happened. Now, I ask you again, are you ready to suffer the consequences?"

"What are those?" I asked fearfully.

"You will become one of us, that's all."

You see, he gave me a choice. For the first time since my adventure began, I was able to choose. I could say "no" as easily as "yes." But, I ask you to put yourself in my place at that moment: a legendary man stands in front of you in all his grandeur, a man who has fought hundreds of battles, cheated Death more than once, seen the world and lived the life—as some say, a man wanting to show you the possession he had guarded with his life for decades, a man who in the end was my grandfather. What would you have done?

Yet, giddy with the liberation and not ready to hand it back, still I asked "What happens if I say no?"

He sighed deeply, like a man who never knew he had a son, like a man who'd been lonely for decades, "Then you'll leave here forever and forget I exist."

I couldn't let this man down. "Okay," I said and too, let out a sigh.

He smiled and patted my shoulder, "I'm proud of you, son. You know what this means?"

"That I am now a pirate?" I asked with heavy heart.

"You are a pirate with treasure, son. It makes a big difference." His voice, raised to cover the waves, sounded like thunder, "Do you swear to guard it and protect it with your life?"

"I do." I said somewhat cowed. I still had some questions but was afraid to say anything else.

"Don't let anyone know what you know, my son. And never betray it. A betrayed treasure is a cursed treasure."

I nodded. As I often do when I don't understand something.

"But I must tell you," he cried over the waves, advancing to one of slabs, "that your oath is not valid until you kill a man."

As he had spoken with his face to the sea, I thought I must've heard wrong. I stopped.

"What?" I yelled.

He pointed towards the rock, "Many people have died for this gold. Some of them didn't have a choice, but some had and they chose to die. You must kill to become one of us. It's my rule. You must learn to survive. Life in these parts of the world is not worth much, unless it is yours, you will see."

I couldn't believe my own ears. What a thing for a grandfather to require of his own grandson! "I can't kill anyone!" I cried. "I don't want to, but I know I couldn't even if I did. Why didn't you tell me this before I agreed? You could've just let me go home."

His eyes froze the blood cold in me, "Now, you already gave me your word, son. My word is sacred and yours is too from this moment on. You have already crossed the line. I didn't bring you here, you came. Sooner or later you will have to kill to survive. When you have a secret such as the one I have given you, the opportunity arises very quickly. It's better you know and are prepared before the day comes when it's you or the other. For you, it begins now."

He tricked me! The son of a gun tricked me! Was all I could think. I felt like I was starting to hate him all over again.

"Begins what?"

"Life. Real life," he said and smiled. "The life that you, yourself, chose."

Sigrid brought me here, I didn't come of my own will. I don't want to kill anyone. I don't want anyone to want to kill me. I don't want to know that I might even be in the slightest of dangers. I don't like to feel insecure. I have problems sleeping as it is, just imagine if I knew someone was after me? I want peace and quiet and good Christians around me. Those were some of the thoughts that came in my mind at that moment. I can think pretty fast when I'm scared. But how can you say no to something when it's already too late? My problem was that I was only meeting people I couldn't say no to. None of you out there could have done any better. Do you think you can say no to Sigrid? Ha! And, do you think I could've said no to the man standing before me? Some things just aren't possible, and this was one of them. It would've been like saying no to… to… the wind for example. Just go ahead and say no to the wind. The wind just happens anyway. It carries you along or blows you away. Looking back now, I see the two choices I had clearer than I saw them then: be dashed all to pieces, or unfurl my sails and learn to command the breeze as well as a seaman can.

I mustered all my forces and said, "I don't want to kill anyone," one more time, as a record to God, for Judgment Day.

"Blasted hell! Then you'll probably die," he said, giving me a severe look and turning his back on me.

He went to the rock he had pointed out before and removed a large boulder in front of it. It would've been impossible for a human to push away such a rock but upon closer inspection I saw that it was set on some kind of underground rails.

"I dug out this cave inch by inch with my own two hands," he said as we entered.

Along the walls hung gas lanterns, but the sunlight was strong enough to cast its glow most way back. The cave, which looked as natural as any I'd ever seen was rather large and cut upwards in such a way that at high tide the boulder at the entrance would have been half submerged, while the last half of the cave remained dry. The inside was damp and cool, the sound of the waves hitting the rocks outside reverberated around the walls, creating a low, rhythmic throb.

In the back, scattered everywhere, lay several dozen large chests.

"This is it," he said and lifted two of the covers. "Here is gold, and some jewelry… the same here, here… aaah … gold… this, the small one inside holds the diamonds…"

I could've fit everything I owned inside of the small one.

I am not a man easily impressed by shiny metals. Gold, jewelry, precious stones don't tickle anything in me. As a young man I cared even less. Just metal and glass. Even so, the sight my eyes were feasting upon… words can't begin to describe. There were coins, any jewel you could want in every setting available, multicolored diamonds, thousands of them smashing the few dim rays entering the cave into millions of twinkles so powerful your eyes couldn't withstand them. It was the greatest sight ever seen by a man, I tell you, and for some time I stared at it speechless. And I was only looking inside only two of the chests.

"There she lies," he finally said. "Twelve people were massacred because of this lot." He leaned on one of the boxes and put his head to his chest. "I was the thirteenth. Lucky thirteen, I guess. Half dead, but alive."

I stopped running my hands through the diamonds. "How?" I asked, excited as I was.

"It's a long story… many years long," he said.

"We have time, as you said," I insisted. "Sigrid told me part of it some time ago."

"Well," he replied, "Tell me what you know first, if you don't mind."

I told him the story Sigrid had given me. The one you've heard in the beginning.

"By heaven, she seems to have gone through the gauntlet," he granted musingly, "and she didn't even know why. Soon, I'm going to make things right."

"She is very angry," I said. "She might even kill you when she finds out you're alive."

"She probably knows by now," he said.

"But how did you come into possession of all this?" I pulled him back to what interested me most.

He was thoughtful. I watched his profile against the lighted entrance and his nose seemed to grow in its own shadow.

"Gunther," he finally said.

"But Gunther… Ruzban said he was the one…"

He lifted his head and his eyes flickered like the beacon of a lighthouse in a moonless night, "Gunther has been dead for many years. I caught him; I was the judge; I was the executioner."

I lowered the cover on one of the chests and sat next to him. There, like a goose nestling a golden egg, I listen to the second part of the story that changed my life.

"Who do you think has been trying to get Sigrid's map for so many years?"

"Ruzban lied." he said. "I don't know why, but it wasn't easy standing there watching him do it. It was a rehearsed lie though, of that I am sure, as if he had been coached to cover for someone. But who? I would've intervened if I wasn't still hoping she would leave this place and let things be as they were. It's been so long… we're strangers now."

"But who do you think gave her the map?" I quickly asked, determined to know the whole tale before he decided to leave.

"I did," he answered. "Gunther and I, we were both hunting each other. We both knew where it was and also knew one had to die before the other could have it. He had left me for dead a few years before, when he killed the rest of the crew. I was pulled from the waves by a fisherman from Ros Nir's island. He saved my life. Some papers on the big islands reported the rescue and Gunther inevitably heard. Then I began searching for him all over the world. When I caught him he had in his possession part of the map. Not knowing what happened to the other half I became obsessed with the cargo. I was sure there were others who knew about it. And I was right, a while later I realized that I was the one who was hunted. So I faked my own death and sent Sigrid two envelopes. One included Gunter's partial map, the other a letter asking her to come to a certain location if she wanted to find out more. I went to meet her as planned and was almost killed."

"How?" I asked

"I was attacked, it was night. I didn't see him, but I think he wanted me alive. There was a fight. If Grant had not intervened I wouldn't be here now. He didn't even know me at the time and he was shot in my place. A shotgun to the face. A real man of God. The fiend thought he killed me and left. Grant and I, we've been friends ever since.

"After that, I concluded somebody had intercepted the letters, so I got back and moved the gold here and decided the best way to guard it and protect myself was to take control of these waters and their hundreds of islands. A pirate will do. A pirate I became." He smiled, "Grant fought against it every step of the way, but he helped me nonetheless. The years flew by, filled with glory and battle…"

"But why didn't you go back to Sigrid?"

He sighed, "To protect her. If I was thought dead, maybe she'd be left alone. I didn't know the first letter had made it. I thought they were both intercepted, and since the treasure had been moved I thought it safer for everyone if I never reappeared."

He got up. "The past is catching up to me. Remember this son: the past always catches up to you." He motioned towards the chests, "Have you had enough of this?"

I looked at them. Enough to buy a country, but somehow it didn't feel right. "Yes. Just trinkets," I said, bravely.

"That's good son. It's easy to become obsessed. Believe me."

We exited and pushed back the boulder.

On the way back I asked why he had showed it to me.

"Who could you trust if not your grandson, huh? I wish I had known I had a son. Things would've probably been different. Now I'm old and, where I'm going, I can't take it with me. What am I going to do with it?"

"Give it to poor people?" I suggested.

He laughed. "You will soon see, it's hard to let it go. Some of it has gone to people in need; there were 25 cases to begin with...It is hard to break from it, you'll see."

He then put his arm around my shoulders.

Something my father had never done.

CHAPTER 19

WHERE I KILL SOMEONE

Now, there were things happening on the other side of the island.

Sigrid and her gang had reached the Southern Point and were preparing to look for the cave. The verdant jungle had died abruptly in a conglomerate of rocks over whose still bodies the zealous ocean waves were breaking noisily, fifty feet below. The map claimed the location lay between a three-rock formation and Anna and Nikki were sent to scout the terrain.

"You know where we're going, don't you?" Sigrid asked the priest.

"Yes, I do my lady," he answered. "But you'll have to find it for yourself."

"I will, don't you worry, I will," replied the stout woman and stepped to the edge of the cliff. "Your friend didn't show up, I see."

"It's not too late, my lady, it's not too late," replied the veiled voice.

"Let him come," muttered Sigrid clutching her gun. "I should've put a bullet in him back there. There was something about him; couldn't put my finger on it..."

"Iz said to look for shree big stones," interrupted Marlene.

Sigrid opened her arms and gestured to each side, "There is one to the left, one to the right and we are standing on the middle one. This is it. Where are those girls now? You can't trust them with anything. Let's climb down! You help my sister!" Ordering that, she remitted her cigar to the corner of her mouth and began the descent.

The girls finally returned and Sigrid motioned Anna behind to stand guard. Father Grant took Marlene's crutch and helped her get an arm around his neck. If she had any, she showed no fear of touching him. The cliff was steep and chunks of rocks broke under their feet. When they finally arrived at the base, Sigrid had already entered the cavernous rock. The tide was low and the passage free.

Slowly, they advanced inside a large cave, which cave, this time a natural one, was set deep inside the earth. Finally, they stopped. At the far end, Sigrid, arms hanging down at her sides, stood defeated. The cave, as you know, was empty.

"Nothing..." she moaned. "There is nothing here."

Marlene took back her crutch from the Father and pushed him away. She advanced alone, "Zher iz nossing?"

Head low, cigar resting at her feet, Sigrid rumbled, "I've been a fool to think I would find something here. A fool to think I'd resolve anything. A fool to hold onto that map for so long... Now what?"

"Vhere iz zhe treasure?" Marlene yelled at the priest.

He shrugged, "I said that you might regret it. If I had told you this grotto was empty, would you have believed me?"

Finally overwhelmed, Sigrid sat on a stone and caught her head in her hands. Marlene, however, wasn't ready to give up, "*Misérable*," she exclaimed, "you tricked us. Mon Dieu, what are we going to do, two old women in zhis jungle? I left my buzinez… Do you know where it iz?" She rushed to him and was menacing him with her prop. "You must know where it iz…"

"Marlene! Marlene, leave him alone," called Sigrid. "Don't you see that's how they planned it? Is not him, is the other one. *Gottverdammt,*[9] I knew it was the other one! He's probably going to show up now and finish the job…"

The priest crossed his hands in a characteristic clergyman's posture and stepped toward her, "The job is done now, my lady. Don't despair, everything is not lost."

"Everything is not lost…" repeated Sigrid in a trance. "I've lost the damn boy, two husbands, an unborn child and an eye, the years of my life, she lost a leg… and you say 'Everything is not lost'? Can you give back to me even one of the things I've just counted?"

"They're not mine to give, my lady, they're God's." The priest lowered his hand above her head but didn't touch her. "I know He has brought you here to set all things right, so have faith my lady."

Sigrid tried to respond, but was interrupted by the clatter of a group entering the cave. Anna led them, followed by Ros Nir's pirates and Albert. He was limping, the hump

9 • *God damn it*

back in its place. They were nudged on by Ruzban and Babar both armed to the teeth, pushing in front of them the captain who was struggling and growling like a mad mangy dog.

"Ya just wait ya limp fishbone, ya just wait, fer ya got lucky jest now, but yer time is not a far-off…" He then saw the ladies, "Well, me beauties, we meet again…"

Ruzban pushed everyone up to the wall, only Sigrid ignored his gun and lifted a disgusted eye his way.

"Where is it?" he yelled.

"I ate it," she answered, distant, "and I'm digesting it right now." She burped, "If you want to wait…?"

"Damn you woman, you're filthy!"

"Go to hell!"

He then threatened Nikki, "Where is it?"

"How should I know?" she cried.

"Ha, ha, mate," laughed Ros Nir. "It looks like yer trouble was fer nothing at all. Now ya're stuck with us."

A slow burning madness was coming over Ruzban. It began in his eyes. Even his teetering head had stopped moving.

"Someone tell me what is happening here!" The words crept gradually out of his lipless mouth and all present could feel the danger in his voice.

"Zhe treasure az disappeared," answered Marlene. "We don't know where it iz."

"Then this is over?" he asked. "No one knows where it is?"

Most of them shook their heads, Father Grant kept silent.

Ruzban backed up a few steps and without warning his gun barked in a short volley. Two of the pirates crumpled, dead. A terrified murmur rose from the group.

"It's gone? Nobody knows where? Huh?" he snarled, "I guess then I don't need you, ha? I don't need any of you. I've waited quite some time for this. Better you then me. You, you should be first, you devil of a woman." He pointed the gun at Sigrid and fired.

"NO! Wait!" Father Grant who was closest to her jumped in front of the weapon. Instead of reaching Sigrid's head as intended, the bullet hit Father Grant in the lower part of the chest. He gasped, then wheezed slowly, and fell to the ground.

The silence that followed was broken by Marlene's cry. She ignored the gun and rushed to the fallen man yelling a stream of words like "*Mon Dieu!*" and "*Pourquoi?*" which few of them understood. Father Grant glanced at Sigrid who had gotten up and was leaning over him.

"Is not finished," he whispered. "Have faith…" then his eyes turned to Marlene and even though his face was covered, she could see them smile as his hand squeezed hers. Crying she held his head with one hand, with the other unraveled the cloth covering his face. Indeed he was smiling.

"You see," he murmured, "I am not what it seemed. Nothing is what it seems."

"I don't care," her tears were falling over his face, "you are a *parfait gentilhomme*. Please don't die! *Mon Dieu!*"

The priest smiled again, "God wants me indeed to meet Him…" he heavily breathed. "I'm scared now because I think myself unworthy… May He bless you noble dame!" His eyes closed as his head fell to the side.

Like a giant rising from beneath the ground, Sigrid raised her body from atop the dead priest. There was no fear, there was no hesitation in her eye. This was the Sigrid you know! The Sigrid that had a company of dead bodies in her orchard. The Sigrid that had crossed the seas to find an answer. The Sigrid that was a Force of Nature.

Ruzban shrank under the majesty of the terrible warrior that stood before him. Trembling, he raised his gun to meet the gaze of her almighty eye and took aim. Before he could pull the trigger a painful and confused expression seized his face. He grunted and with supreme effort tried again to squeeze the trigger, but the strength had flowed out of him and the gun slid on the rocks. Dragging his feet he slowly turned around. His eyes grew wide as he groaned, "You… you…" before falling face forward. A knife was resting in his back.

Behind him Albert's hands were shaking, "I couldn't allow it, Madame," he said in an apologetic voice.

Sigrid moved as to meet him, but from the back a moan like that of a wounded animal echoed through the walls. Without looking Albert reached down and picked up Ruzban's gun. He then turned with great agility at mid-level and sprayed with bullets the position where the sound came from. Babar jumped to the side and ducked, but the man was huge and a few made it through his shoulder. He dropped his weapon and for a second just stood there. Fear and hate were now plowing deep furrows in his once happy face through which tears streamed. Bewilderment also washed over his brow, as— probably for the first time he could remember—there wasn't an order to follow. His hesitation gave Albert enough time to pull the trigger again, but this time the clip was empty. With another moan Babar raised his gigantic arms and made a step towards the hunchback, but seeing Sigrid bending to pick up his former master's weapon, cried once more and with a great leap disappeared through the cave's entrance. Albert got rid of his weapon, picked up another one and ran after him, but the giant was gone. He curled his spine and made his way back.

You must understand that everything which required me so many words to tell, took in real time not more than a minute to occur. Some of the witnesses were still wondering what was happening long after it ended.

When Albert arrived before Sigrid he spoke to her in German: "I don't know Madame. I don't know what happened. I think fear compelled me to act fast."

Sigrid replied also in German: "What happened is that you saved my life and theirs. Thank you, old friend. I won't forget this."

"But this man who ran away... I had better go after him."

"You stand no chance old man. He is an injured beast. Leave him be, he will probably die of his wounds." Reticently, Albert lowered his head. "As you say, Madame."

Sigrid leaned on Ruzban's corpse and pulled out the knife. She wiped it against his clothes and looked at it.

Not far from there, Ros Nir was giving his men orders about the dead pirates. "Antonio and Sanju—good men...

Pick'em up lads and give them a decent burial."

"Why are you here?" asked Sigrid advancing. She was still menacing and hadn't lost an ounce of her grandeur.

Ros Nir scratched his beard, "On orders from me Captain, ma'am." Then he continued thoughtfully, "Fer now it seems I, captain Ros Nir, have a captain of me own. I am not me own captain no more, so it seems. But I would be dead right now, otherwise should be. Jest glad I am alive… jest glad… Anyways, I was ordered to bring ya back to the huts."

"Who ordered you?"

"Me captain."

"Who is your captain?"

"Captain Jim Brrow, the chief pirate in these parts… it seems."

"Never heard of him. Why should I follow you?"

"I don't know ma'am. There are strange affairs at work. He himself was strangely dressed like this dead fellow here when I saw him. He left with the boy."

"Rudolph," muttered Sigrid. "What's his role in all this?"

"He's known by many a name, ma'am," answered Ros Nir. "Captain Jim Brrow is just one." She turned away and so he added, "Also, it seems he has something you want."

She froze. "So then… it's not finished after all, is it?" she growled turning to glance at the priest's corpse. "Take me to your captain!"

Ros Nir ordered Ruzban and the priest's bodies be left in place for the Captain to deal with. Marlene followed them, tears running down her face. Anna had found out that I was alive and I'd like to think she was happy about it. She wasn't showing it, though. A woman in pain goes a long way in her hatred. Take it from me, I should know.

CHAPTER 20

WHERE I COULD'VE BEEN A HERO

There was a small estuary hidden between the rocks not far from where the treasure lay and there under camouflage were hidden a few boats. How many, I couldn't see because the Captain uncovered only one, a small speed boat which he said we were going to use.

I felt more important now that I was with him. Felt I wasn't alone at the end of the world, felt like I counted for something. Entourage is quite important, I tell you. It can decide your entire future.

We must not have arrived long after the others had left. The waters had risen enough and it was possible to pull the boat inside the cave. I saw the two bodies and I knew right away who they were. The blood was still wet on Ruzban. The Captain ignored the corpse and kneeled near his friend. Jaws tight as granite, his visage as impenetrable as a shut door—he was suffering his way.

"I've had many people die on me," he whispered. "But I never thought you would be one of them, old friend. Farewell."

That was all he said.

He then lifted the man in his arms as if he weighed nothing and brought him to the boat. He didn't even glanced at Ruzban's body. We left it there and his bones lie there still.

The trip back was a longer one. Or so it seemed because not one word was said. I kept silent and let the misty wind wash my face. The Captain was steering with no expression in his eyes.

He unloaded the body himself and buried it in the trees. It was dark when he came back. I waited in the hut and when he returned we went to sleep without words.

I had a strange dream that night. I dreamt that I was sleeping and that as I awoke I saw a pair of enormous feet. I lifted my sight and met two vast, dark eyes. They were only inches from mine and watching me. I tried to shout but a gigantic hand covered my mouth. There was pain in the eyes, endless pain. The hand pushed my head back to the ground and I felt pressure behind both my ears and I could remember no more. Strangely in the morning I could still feel the pressure in the very same spots.

When I got out the Captain said his surgical kit had disappeared. He knew because there was only one and it hung above his head in the hut where we had slept.

"Where is he?"

I was shoveling dirt on top of some dead pirates we'd found piled up not far from the huts. They were the ones that had accompanied Ruzban when we arrived. I had a hunch the Captain had something to do with it, but I didn't say anything. I found them because of the smell and the Captain came and dug a deep grave. His second in as many days. Then he pulled them in and let me cover them while he went to wash himself. I was amazed at how little I was now impressed with the sight of them lying there. There was a time when a corpse would've given me nightmares. At the moment I stood burying several, piled on top of each other like sardines in a can and hardly had a gag.

Sigrid was standing behind me. I hadn't heard her coming.

"Where is he?" she asked again.

The others stood behind her and I started to go and greet them.

She caught me by the collar, "I asked you, where is he?"

"Who?"

"Rudolph."

"I am here," said a voice just behind her.

Sigrid froze. "That voice…" she mumbled.

Marlene released a cry and fell down in a faint. The girls rushed to help her. The others were watching not knowing what had happened.

Sigrid turned slowly. Painfully slowly. She raised her hand to the patched eye as if she didn't know what to do with it. As if she would've liked to hide it.

"Hello Sigrid," said the Captain smiling.

"You…" she muttered.

He got closer. "Yes me."

"You…" she repeated.

"Me," he repeated.

"You were dead. You had to be dead…"

"I did everything to protect you. I told the boy," he said rashly, as if in apology.

"…otherwise you would've come back."

"I did it to protect you, woman! I didn't know you were in trouble. I thought if I disappeared forever, the past would go with me."

"The past *has* disappeared. The future was torturing me. And yet here you are!"

"I am sorry," said the Captain.

"Sorry for what? Sorry for my eye? Sorry for her leg? Sorry for years of torment? Sorry for the loss of a child? Sorry for all of the dead? If you died right now," her voice had risen gradually to the last sentence when the emotion broke through as a dry sob, "you still wouldn't be sorry enough!"

The Captain lowered his head under the weight of her words and did not see her coming. I told you a long time ago that she was fast, but I never saw her as fast as that. In a blink she was near him and her fist hit him square in the jaw.

"That's the least you can do to be sorry," she said. And she walked away.

The Captain didn't hear, for he was out before he touched the ground.

And days passed…

Long, lazy days of relaxing and bathing in the sun and waiting. I didn't know what was going to happen. I think no one did. We were just waiting and wondering. What were Sigrid and Marlene waiting for?

I don't know much about what the others did. The Captain was trying to get in Sigrid's good graces. Ros Nir in Marlene's. And me in Anna's. Everyone was chasing their own game. Even Nikki had made friends with Stick. In fact, they were alone in their friendship. We, the others, fought on.

One beautiful morning, I sat up and saw a new man coming out of the huts. It surprised me because there was no way somebody could've gotten by unseen or unreported.

"What ya're gawking at?" he asked, and only then did I realize that it was Ros Nir.

He looked nothing like the man he had been hours before. His head was two times reduced and his lower lip much wider than the upper, once covered in hair, making him look like he was holding an invisible pipe in his mouth. He had done it for Marlene. The shaving, not the pipe. The pipe was imaginary. He was trying to be a *gentilhomme*. Nonetheless, before could apply for that privilege he had to chase and curse out a few of his men who could do nothing but laugh and fall to the ground as he approached.

Me, I had my own problems, and was hard at work to win back my darling. How do you do it? I don't think I have ever answered this question. There is no formula, I tell you.

You bring her flowers? I couldn't. I judged no flowers available met the standard set by her beauty. Maybe a fish, as I was now an accomplished fisherman. I contemplated it, but what would she do with a fish? Never send a fish as a gift to a woman. It might send the message that you want her to cook it for you.

You talk to her? I tried. The first time, I received a slap that made me spit the straw I was chewing. The second time I remembered the first and avoided her, so there was really no second time.

You sing to her? I couldn't do such a horrible thing to the woman I loved. To anyone else but her.

Hum, so how to approach a woman who hates you? And, why did she hate me at all? I couldn't even remember. She should've been happy I was alive, the ungrateful. Why? Because I say so.

I tried to surprise her on the beach, I sneaked up on her in the forest, I splashed her in the water; nothing worked. God, what do I have to cut off to make her forgive me? I, often, was asking these questions aloud, in my solitary promenades, and at one point he heard me. Not God, the Captain.

"Don't be embarrassed," he said, seeing that I was trying to scurry away. "I have the same problem."

I realized that yes, he did. Though, I liked my problem better, I admit.

"Just give her time," he continued, talking more to himself than to me. "Time is all they need. Be around her, but don't be with her. She will come to you when she is ready."

Why can't males and females be ready at the same time? It's the wenches fault, I tell you. They never seem to be ready. There is always something in their way: you didn't say this the way you should, you smiled when you shouldn't have, your tear wasn't big enough, neither your gift, you are too insistent, you are not insistent enough, you seem too good to be true, so on, and so on… What is this? I was, am, and forever will be, ready all the time. Any minute of day or night. Just give a sign and I materialize myself at once, like the genie from the lamp. That's how you do it!

"My son," he continued with his wisdom (I respected the Captain, except, sincerely I couldn't see then where his knowledge came from. Obviously, I didn't know his life, but his humble abode looked like no comely feet had ever stepped on it. He was living with a priest for goodness sake! Later, I found out that I was wrong, but this is not that story), "a woman and a ship have many things in common. No wonder we seamen call our boats a 'she' for it takes an experienced man to understand her and if you lose control the whole thing is doomed to wreck on the rocks."

"But what should I do, sir?" I asked, for I dare not call him grandfather at the time. "I've tried everything; I don't know what else there is."

"Have patience my son. Let your patience match that of the sea that incessantly beats the rock claiming what it thinks is hers. Sooner or later it will win, you know, and so should their hardened hearts chip away and fall into our hands like the bits of rock that fall as sand into the sea."

Asking a young lad like myself to have patience… you might as well ask a pirate to give up liquor. I nodded politely, but a thousand plans for quick results were bustling in my head. And easy outcomes where time could be measured on fingers, not waves or grains of sand.

"You'll learn as you become a man, my son," he smiled reading my mind, "that the young heart's cross is impetuosity; for everything comes at a price, and the young one with time on his side is cursed to waste that which gives him the edge, while his elder uses the bit he has left like a sailor would his last drop of clean water when lost at sea. He knows that whereas he floats on a sea of it, he can't sip but what little is left in his canteen. It's called wisdom, my son, and I shan't ask it of you, but I wish it nonetheless."

Thus spoke my elder; and a wiser man I've never met, nor will, even though I ask the cursed mirror each day to show me one.

Anyway, all this is to say that my efforts with Anna were quiet fruitless.

Through the whole of this though, I felt I was watched. I couldn't understand it, but there were eyes on me and because everyone was busy with someone, and no one seemed worried about anything, I didn't find out about Babar until it was too late.

Albert spent most of his time on the anchored boat. He had, at times, the company of some of the pirates, who seemed to have taken a liking to his cooking. I could often see him from the shore observing us through his binoculars, but I thought nothing of it.

In fact, it's because I took pity and wanted to propose him a fishing trip with myself and Ros Nir that I discovered his secret.

I told you we were sharing the same cabin. I had promised God the previous day that if he helped me get Anna back I would dispose of my collection of private magazines. Every boy has one of those I know, and God's mercy is not for sale, but I was not above trying every trick in the book. So, with that in mind, I went back to the cabin with the intent of collecting the sinful papers and selling off them to the pirates. It would've been an even bigger sin not to. Do you know how much time a pirate spends at sea? Well, not that much, but a magazine can be enjoyed even on dry land.

I amassed them in one place and climbed into my bunk. One last examination would help me part easier with them, I thought. There under the covers, amidst clothes from my undone laundry, I sat flipping through some of my favorites when Albert entered the cabin. He was talking to himself, mostly in German. He didn't see me. At first I wanted to greet him and make him aware that I was there, but something stopped me.

His back was straight and he was agile. His hump had entirely disappeared.

Feeling that something was not right I sank my head under some sweaty t-shirts and listened closely. I could understand some German and what I gleaned from what he was saying went something like this:

"...damn woman... I will not leave here without it...I should've let him kill her... can't fail now, I am so close... need a plan, or she will just leave and all will be finished... curses on you woman!... he has it and she knows it... why she doesn't she just ask to see it?... By the pits of Gehenna, I will kill them all!..." And he continued thus while rummaging through his things.

I lay a few centimeters above his head, holding my breath, and it was a miracle he didn't see my weight sagging the upper berth. This story would've remained untold.

Finally, an eye out from under the cloth, I saw him in front of the door; slowly, his shoulders pulled forward, his neck lowered a few degrees and his back pushed out until, amazingly, a hump grew out of the center. With a grunt of discontentment, he opened the door and exited that way while I popped my head out. The first thought I had was that I badly needed to do the laundry, the second that I must tell the Captain. The former seemed improbable so I reset my priorities. It wasn't the first time I had delayed the laundry, as the mountain of clothes on top of me witnessed. How would I get out though? I swallowed deeply and prayed he wouldn't take notice of the small lifeboat I had used to get there, which was now hanging off *La Baveuse*. Fortunately, while the starboard was facing the shore I had tightened it at the port for it was in the shade and my buns like a cool seat, when they can have it.

Slowly as the dusk crept in, I caught my heart in my teeth and opened the door. I couldn't wait much longer for he would have soon come to bed. I slid through the insides of the ship quieter than an unspoken word. From the deck I slipped over the railing and into my dinghy. I pushed lightly away from the boat, going around it at an angle—not to be directly placed between it and the shore—and when I reached a comfortable distance, I rowed like crazy towards the lights on the beach.

Imagine my surprise when I arrived, running and out of breath, and saw everyone around a large bench and Albert serving food. The table was set between two of the huts lit by torches placed around it. There was a secondary one, smaller, holding a few pots and wine bottles.

"Where you go?" Marlene asked. "Albert iz cooking good food. Iz iz birzday."

The birthday boy watched me suspiciously, "Yes, vhere you go, yung man? I fas vondering about you?" he asked.

"I… I was fishing," I answered swallowing a big knot.

"And… no fish?" His eyes flickered in the light of the fire giving him a look I hadn't seen before. A look that chilled me to my bones.

Out of ideas, I shook my head.

"Sit down, yung man! Food iz ready. Special day today."

"Ah," I said, pushing Nikki aside and sitting down close to Anna. She gave me a murderous look. "Your birthday?"

"Not today. Tomorrow," he answered. "But today ve celebrate."

"Ah…" I said.

I looked around the table while he was serving us. The Captain and Sigrid were sitting side by side on the opposite corner; Marlene faced Sigrid, then Anna, Nikki and I, all on the same side. The first entrée was some kind of broth. It was good.

"Where are Ros Nir and his men?" I asked.

"They went to bring supplies," Nikki answered. "Apparently we're out."

Now I was sure he was going to try something. This time Anna had to listen to me. I elbowed her. She scorned me, but I elbowed her again. Harder.

She looked at me sideways, with deadly eyes, "If you don't stop, I will make you eat the spoon you're holding," she said.

"I have to talk to you," I whispered.

"No, you don't," she retorted.

"Yes I do."

"No, you don't."

(You see what I was up against?)

"It's very important."

She ignored me.

"Life and death."

Silent.

"Albert is planning to kill us all," I whispered again.

Now, I had her attention. "Are you crazy?" she asked.

"It's true, I swear. I heard him on the ship. He is not hunchbacked."

Albert came behind us and asked if we needed anything. I shoved some food in my mouth and shook my head. He filled my glass just in time as the Captain stood up and lifted his:

"Since you people landed here," he started, "I have lost two of my men, and my best friend and protector. I have spent more time with that man than many of you, at this table, have had to live; he was more than a brother to me, and though he was a man of the cloth—and in God's company I hope he spends eternity—not once did he ask to hear my confession. He knew what I was doing, though he never quite understood why, and the same for me—I couldn't understand what he found in my friendship that made him stay. Maybe he thought it his mission, maybe he was tired of the world, I don't know; he died before I could find out, and more importantly, before I could thank him. I took him for granted and for that I will forever repent." He lowered his head and paused for a few seconds, then lifted his glass even higher, "Here's to you Grant, an unknown but faithful comrade. I promise you as soon as I set foot on civilized land I will go to confessional. For you old friend!" He emptied the wine on the ground next to him, then filled it up again. "Now, his departure has made possible for me to reunite with my past. I was a fool to think it forgotten and I atone for that. There are still issues to be worked out," he glanced toward Sigrid, but she was looking straight forward and her face gave away nothing, "but I am confident that we will have a happy ending now that the past is repaired and everything made right. To a happy ending for every one of us!" he said and emptied his glass, this time in his mouth.

Anna turned her head toward me and I glanced at her raising my eyebrows in an irresistibly seductive fashion; no woman escapes it with her heart intact. She sighed and emptied her glass, and I followed along with the others.

"Albert," the Captain called once he sat down, "what is the second course? I haven't eaten a soup so good in decades. I hope the rest can match it."

"Even better, mein Herr! Even better!" answered Albert rubbing his hands together. "Even better."

"You have to listen to me," I said for the speech had made me forget why I was there, "he is preparing something. He wants the treasure. Please believe me! I'm not playing games this time!"

'Games' wasn't the most appropriate word I could've used. She reminded me with a certain look I can't describe here. I pushed my eyes together and tried to acquire the most pitiful countenance since man was made, "Pleeease!"

"Your nose is big enough already," she said, and dismissed me.

That was hitting under the belt, but this time I didn't care, "I have to find a way to tell the Captain," I said.

She stopped and observed Albert carefully, "If what you say is true," she said, "I wouldn't try it now."

"Why?"

"Albert has a gun."

"He has a gun?" my whisper was almost a yell.

"I saw it on his belt, under the coat, when he was serving us. I thought it was for self-defense, you know with Babar in the woods?"

Boy, oh boy! I was in more trouble than I thought. "Babar is in the woods?"

This time it was a cry I had released. Fortunately Albert was busy with his pots and didn't hear. Anna turned her head and watched me like she was seeing me for the first time. "You know, you can be pretty stupid."

You can't argue with that. "I know," I said.

"If you weren't that stupid, I might've liked you," she continued.

Good, now *she is ready to talk*, I said to myself looking hopelessly around.

"We have to do something. I bet he is cooking up something tonight."

"My preceding affirmation stands," she replied laughing. "A cook cooking something, huh… and you say this tonight while you eat his food, huh?"

I wanted to respond with something smart—I can't remember what—but the Captain was speaking again.

"Say, Albert, I'm ready for what's next. I hope I can't make it through… it's either the wine or I am very tired."

Indeed, I was feeling very tired myself and I wasn't even drinking much.

"There is no second course," Albert said without a trace of accent in his speech.

A heavy silence fell as hands stopped moving and with them the cutlery.

"What?" the Captain said.

Slowly, Albert went around the table. As he was moving, his back stretched, his hump disappeared and his leg straightened.

"You see," I told Anna with satisfaction while Albert positioned himself in front of the Captain.

He was now standing tall and straight and had he not had the famous moustache I wouldn't have recognized him. Venom, his eyes were spitting. "I'm sorry," he grinned, "but the happy ending you've mentioned, it is *my* happy ending. Yours, just an end. An ordinary end. This is your last supper, Orlin!" His voice was ten times as powerful as before.

I saw the Captain feeling himself for a weapon, and

then trying unsuccessfully to stand. "Who are you?" he grunted.

"Don't bother," retorted Albert. "I am but one, so I gave you something to even the odds. You liked the soup?"

My limbs and my head were getting heavier by the minute and as I looked around I saw that everyone looked very drowsy. Everyone except Sigrid.

"It's him!" she said.

"Who?" asked the Captain.

"The *Schweinehund*[10] I've been looking so long to find. He was under my nose all this time. *Für alle Hunde in der Hölle,* how blind could I be! And, I had my doubts!" she said pulling out the knife that had killed Ruzban. She planted it in the soft wood of the table in front of her, but she didn't get up. Just watched Albert as a tigress would its prey.

"Why didn't you tell me?" the Captain groaned and tried again to move but caught his stomach with his hand and fell back to the seat. I thought his wound was still bothering him and he hadn't recovered completely.

"It's the same type of blade some of my attackers used on me," Sigrid said. "I wasn't sure when I saw it, but now I am."

Albert put his hands on the table and leaned over until his face was a foot from Sigrid's, "Yes, it's me," he hissed. "You think you had it rough? Imagine having to disjoint your shoulders and spend years as an infirm and in pain, as your servant ordered around and humiliated, unable to just cut your throat. But, I'll have to thank you, for it was that pain which kept me alive, the pain of watching in the

10 • *bastard, swine*

mirror the man that I became."

"Why?" she asked.

"Because it's mine. It has been mine since the day my father bequeathed it to me. My name is," he straightened himself, for all to see him declare it, "Korb von Eichmann. I am Gunther's son."

The silence that followed spoke more about the way each of us dealt with that declaration than words themselves. There was only one face that stood carved as of rock, only one pair of eyebrows that didn't rise. Sigrid's. She was of stone. And death.

"I didn't know Gunther aad a son," Marlene broke the spell. Her lips were moving with difficulty. "I told you it wasn't Gunter," she mumbled.

"Gunther was a murderer," added the Captain.

"My father followed his orders!" cried Albert (now Korb). "You know it well. A German soldier follows his orders to the end. You should've followed yours and died."

"He was a killer. Cold blooded killer. He took twelve lives like it was nothing..."

"And you had to survive, didn't you? To ruin all of his plans. If you had just died, none of this would've happened. She would've lived a long happy life, I would've been rich long ago, no one here would die ... *You* are the cause of all this! More people have died to keep you alive, than if you had died. The hog you call wife was right."

The Captain thought for a second. I saw sadness on his face. "You are right," he said with resignation and lowered his head.

Now, it was Sigrid's turn to speak. "Before I kill you," she roared, "tell me why you didn't come to me for the map?"

"Because it's mine! It was my father's and he left it to me. We thought him dead then one day this map arrives accompanied by letter asking me to meet him. When I got to him he was dying. One word! He left me with one word: Orlin."

"Your fazher was a pig," declared Marlene suddenly lifting her head from the table. I saw her trying to grab the crutch, but she couldn't reach it. "You moved it, you *fils de pute!*" she cried.

But he paid no attention to her. He turned to the Captain, "It was all I needed. I knew you killed him, I knew you had the other half of the map. I hunted you for years and almost had you a few times. When I heard of your death, I knew you were plotting something, but I couldn't have known that you had sent out two letters at once. I got one of them and came to meet you. I thought I killed you. Oh, how happy I was! Half of my plan was accomplished and now I knew who had the second map. I thought it would to be easy, but oh, was I wrong?! ... So much time... So much time wasted on you two..."

"Oh, Grant," groaned Orlin. "He saved me..."

"And me," said Sigrid. "But, Uber? You haven't mentioned him yet."

"Ya, me too, and where iz my leg?" mumbled Marlene.

"That greedy bastard wanted it all for himself. He stole your map and went to get your sister's... I tracked him down, but then you showed up. I started the fire as a distraction… Who knew the place was storing explosives? Imagine my despair when I found out that you didn't die. Back slaving for you, if I didn't want all my previous efforts to go to waste. Just bide your time, Korb, bide your time… Your best years so you may be rich when you're old and crippled. Damn legacy! It's too late now..."

He went to the head of the table. I saw he looked quite a bit younger than in his disguise and he was quite well-built. "Tomorrow you will die," he declared, eyes locked on Orlin. "Nothing you say will change that. If you give me the treasure I will let the others live, including the demon next to you, and your grandson. That is the deal I will make with you."

By now I could barely keep my eyes open. Nikki had given up and was asleep with her head on the table. I reached under it and took Anna's hand. She didn't fight it. *Is this a good sign?* I asked myself. *Or is she just drugged?* I decided I'd accept either.

Before the Captain could open his mouth again, Sigrid rose to her feet. The expression on her face was darker than the patch on her eye. She pulled the knife out of the table and, taller than the trees, she stood facing the cook. Even the torch lights quivered as if fear itself had blown over them. Her voice echoed in my groggy head like an avalanche of rocks rumbling down the mountain. I still hear it:

"I've nourished you and made you my confidant. Perfidious snake! *Für alle Hunde in der Hölle*, there is no poison strong enough to stop me from bringing justice to you once and forever."

She stepped over the seat and faced her nemesis, who

was now backing up in disbelief. "Impossible!" he exclaimed. "You ate the soup."

She laughed, "You should've known me better by now, you *Hurensohn*! Nothing will stop me."

She launched at him. But before she stepped once, fast as lightning, he drew the gun and fired.

The bullet hit Sigrid in the leg.

She hesitated, released a moan from the lowest of her throat, but took another step. This time he took his time, aimed carefully and hit her other leg. She fell, side on the table still holding on the knife. Groaning and cursing and spitting and crying she pulled herself back near the Captain. Then she turned to Albert, or if you wish, Korb.

"You think you have won, huh?" she moaned.

"I will win no matter what," he answered. "Right now I still need you. But your turn will come."

"I bet you didn't think of this," she groaned. She turned to the Captain, who had watched the scene holding his stomach, and placed one hand on his back. An endless pain streamed from her eye. "I forgive you, Orlin!" she said and, with a diabolical howl, raised the knife, held it still, though only for a blink, then buried it deep in her husband's back.

CHAPTER 21

A TALE OF A NOSE AND MOUSTACHES

I can fight as a hundred. I can drink as ten. I can love as one. But I will cry as none. Real men cry only in their sleep when they don't know it. Someone once said that. I think it was me.

The next morning, as I reclaimed what I had lost the previous evening—my senses that'd be—I became aware that my cheeks were wet just as if I had been crying in my sleep. The shock of seeing Sigrid stab my grandfather had knocked me out and my head had fallen into the soup plate. So it could've been soup I felt on my face. Except my head wasn't in the plate anymore, but near it. I tried to move, but my hands were attached under the table to my feet. The others were in the same situation; only our heads were sitting on top like puppets whose strings had been cut. My face was wet and sticky. Soup and tears. I know it because Anna told me.

As I opened my eyes, she had a subtle smile on her lips. I could only see her lips, her eyes being hidden behind the bowl that sat between us. I stretched my nose and pushed it upwards. For once I could use it to do good. But, I was to discover that it hadn't been the first time. Two nose-lengths away, she was indeed smiling. The blue of her eyes was the pure blue you find in the untainted sea reflecting the pristine sky, and in her bright polished teeth, the whitest thing I'd ever beheld, I could see my reflection.

"I think your nose saved you from drowning in that soup," she said. "Why were you crying?'

"I wasn't crying," I replied.

"Yes you were. I watched you."

"I was dreaming of you," I said spitefully. "You are so mean and ugly it made me cry."

"That's why I can't get rid of you? You follow me everywhere like a little dog."

"Yes, because I'm traumatized. I have to stare at you hours every day to cure myself."

She laughed—like a thousand angels ringing heavenly bells.

"Oopf, my nose it's itching and I can't scratch it!"

"Let it itch, let it itch…" I sang dreamily.

"Les tittich?" I'm sorry, I don't speak French.

"Me either…"

"You're an idiot!" she laughed again.

"I am sorry for everything I've done," I said. "I am not worthy of someone like you."

"It's true," she smiled. "Too bad you apologize too late."

"But I've apologized before," I said. "Why are you listening this time to me?"

"Because now I don't have a choice," she said. "And no, you've never apologized before. You've acted like you did, but you haven't. Women need words sometimes."

You remember I've told you I have words to fill up the sea? Well it wasn't always the case—over the years, the stock accrued, from none, it seems, to now, as I lived and things happened to me. Furthermore, try to fit this in your small head: sometimes, when you have too many words it is hard to find the right ones when you need them—so you'd be better off carrying your head empty, save yourself a sore throat.

"Oh!" I said. "I'll make it up to you, Anna, I swear."

"But it's too late now," she replied.

"Why?" I asked, most innocently.

She considered me for a second, but she must've seen pure oblivion for she answered, "What is the matter with you? Are you comfortable at this moment?"

"Yes," I answered.

"Really?"

"Yes. I'm looking at you and talking to you, what more could a mortal desire?"

"Would you like to touch me?" she asked.

I sighed from the bottom of my feet, "Once, then die and go to heaven."

"Ahh! You drive me crazy! Just try and touch me, you idiot!"

"I can't," I said still dreaming. "At the moment I'm

touching my feet... Why am I touching my feet?"

"Because you're an idiot, that's why," she retorted. "And unfortunately, you will die in this state."

I closed my eyes to free my brain from her enchantment, and I woke up and remembered, "Orlin," I muttered, "she killed him."

"Yes she did, and now *he* will kill us."

I lifted my head and looked around the table. On my other side, Nikki returned a sad look, but managed a short, bitter smile; Marlene, with her hair looking like it had survived the passage of a tornado, was staring into nothing; as for Sigrid, her front was resting on the table and I could not see her face.

"Do you think Ros Nir will come in time?" Nikki asked.

Before I could answer, a voice which had once been Albert's spoke, "Good," it said, "I see you awoke. I want you to all be present when I pronounce your judgment. Because of this woman you all love so much, your friend and sister, you will never leave this place. It is *she* that has killed you."

I glanced back at Sigrid. She had raised her head, but her eye was empty, as if no soul inhabited her wretched body.

"I bandaged her wounds so she could see you die," continued Albert. "It's her fate. See everyone she cares for die before her. You've done it to yourself woman. You see? Three young souls and your sister. For what? For your pride? Was your pride worth so many lives?"

"Where iz Orlin?" asked Marlene moaning.

"I dragged him in the woods. I need the space for what

I am to do next. To you witch! To you!" he yelled in Sigrid's ear. "You'll be last, but I promise you I'll make it worth your wait!" He then turned to Marlene, "You see what your sister has done?"

Marlene gazed at her then turned her head to Albert and cursed him. "Zhe evil iz you, *salopard*," she said. "You aave destroyed eer life. You should go back to Eell where iz your place."

"Nothing would've happened Miss *Puffmutter*," he growled back, "if she had given up the map at the right time. I spent my youth slaving for her—I, too, have lost something. Only the hope to get what is mine keeps me going, now I've lost that too. And I will make you all pay for it."

"Your people killed eer baby, first time zhey came, you idiot. What mozher would reward eer baby-killer?"

"She shouldn't have fought back," he smirked. "Besides, I don't care. It is finished, we both lost. Now, who shall I start with? Maybe this young lady here?" He pulled Nikki's head up by the hair until she groaned in pain.

"Wait!" I yelled.

"What do you what?" he barked at me. "You can beg, but it won't change anything."

"I can finish the deal," I said.

"What deal?"

"The deal that you had with Orlin."

"Nobody can finish that deal but him. And he is dead."

"I can," I said. "I know where he holds it."

He came behind me, set his hands on the table on each side of me and snarled in my ear, "Listen to me, you bugger. I didn't like you from the moment I saw you; now that you so desperately try to delay my plans, I like you even less, so I will begin with you. I will slit your throat in front of your sweetheart, then slit hers before you have time to die. I think this will make me feel better." And he caught my hair, pulled my head backwards and put the knife on my throat.

I moaned, for I felt the sharp edge of the blade cutting into my skin, "If you kill me your treasure will be lost forever," I said looking up at him.

"You lie!" he screamed.

"See for yourself if I do and then you can kill me, but if I am not, let us go. Look in my right pocket."

I prayed that it was still there for I had forgotten about it. He rummaged through my pants and when he pulled his hand out he was holding a diamond.

Well, my beauties, you all like diamonds, I know. I wish I had some with me for my young hug-a-nurse, for she gives me great comfort. Ready to save the world one hug at the time she is. I wouldn't stay in her way for the same world, but I would trade her for a bottle of gin right on the spot, or for even a half—but only for the time it takes me to empty it, then I'd take her back. Where was I?

Remember the day Orlin showed me the treasure and I ran my hands through the heap of stones in the small chest? Well one of them got stuck in the crease of my hand and I couldn't get rid of it. I just didn't tell you then because I didn't want to ruin the moment for me, that's all. I seemed to be a magnet for such things. There was nothing

I could do. It wanted in my pocket and was insistent about it. It said it was an orphan, had no relatives amongst the thousands it lived with. I have a noble soul when it comes to orphans, or young maidens, so I gave it harbor in my pocket. There were so many of them there in the chest, it couldn't be missed, I thought. Later, I felt guilty of course, terribly guilty, for I had stolen from my grandfather; but remember that not long before that, offering harbor to orphaned things was my wont. And anyway, at that particular moment, it wasn't like I was applying for a clerical job. I had just accepted to be a pirate and eventually, as I was informed, would have to kill a man—I think I've told you all that. Anyway, that is all just to show you that once, in the remote past, I was capable of remorse. Not anymore.

The thought of saving an orphan and maybe having it adopted by Anna cheered me somewhat, for, you should've guessed, she was its final destination. A civilized man, as I considered myself, should get his woman with the power of his spirit and his charms; only a savage would knock her out with a rock. So I wanted to use it as a last resort, after, and only if, manners had failed. So attached I grew to that stone that soon I forgot that I was carrying it in my pants, and thank heaven all my other clothes were dirty, for I would've changed back on the *La Baveuse*.

It turned out to be a lucky steal.

"Did he give you this?" Korb (thus I will call him, unless I forget—but don't count on me to go back, erase it and start anew) asked, watching the stone flash in the light. It was larger than the tip of my index finger and as thick—a well-developed youngster, almost an adult.

"I took it," I said, "from a pile of thousands just like it."

I didn't find it necessary to mention that it was one of the bigger ones, for strength relies in numbers, not size.

"Did he show it to you?" he asked. "Why would he do that?"

"I am his grandson," I said, and for the first time in a long time was proud of myself.

He looked at it more, then smiled and said, "I knew you were a little thief the moment I saw you. Stealing from a grandfather you hardly knew... I like it." He then turned to Sigrid, "You hear that old bag?" he spit at her. "You killed him for nothing. His grandson, the little thief that brought you here, will now betray you. Again!" He laughed and punched her on the back.

She groaned and her eyes arose until they met mine, but I couldn't see anything in them. She looked at me like she didn't know me.

Suddenly he stopped and pulled my head up. "I will kill her in front of you, if you lie" he said wiping the knife against Anna's cheeks.

"Don't tell him anything!" she said holding her head proud, and she cursed at him. It made me feel better at that moment, though I now find a maid with a foul mouth distastefully crude.

I smiled at her and said to him, "I know where it is."

"Where?"

"Not far from here, but I'll have to take you. You won't find it otherwise."

"What is there?"

"Many chests with gold and jewelry. One full of diamonds. You will need our help to move them."

"Do I now? Hmm, maybe…" He let go of my hair.

"Not before you swear that you'll keep the promise you made to Orlin. That you will let us go."

"I will keep my promise about you lot. But for her I won't," he said pointing at Sigrid with the tip of his knife.

I glanced at her. She looked pitiful and defeated. "I don't care about her," I said and this time I meant it.

He played the knife in Sigrid's face. "You unfortunate old hag! The thief doesn't care about you. You will see the gold you thought was yours, in my hands. Then I will use this knife here to gut you like the pig you are. The same that killed your husband. I pity you. Now, let's go boy!"

"The chests are big, I told you. We need help."

I could see in Anna's eyes that she was wondering what I was doing, but as I was wondering that myself, I couldn't answer. I just didn't want to be alone with him.

"We'll take these two pretty girls here," he said, "I hope they're strong enough… for their own sake."

He saddled himself with a large rifle and hung it around his neck, then cut us free.

"Is it far?"

"No," I answered. "Not far."

We left Marlene and Sigrid, heads on the table, facing each other.

Never betray the treasure, the Captain had said. *It will be forever cursed.* Well, I didn't last long. At least I wouldn't be the one owning it.

They followed me in silence. The sun was up in the sky and there was a light breeze pleasantly breathing from the sea. Cheerful birds were caroling in the trees and lustful pests noised around in a frantic search for a mate. No one should die on a day like this, I thought. God should mind and not allow it.

When we arrived at the rocks, the sea was high.

"We can't go by foot on high tide," I yelled to cover the waves. "We have to take a boat from there," and I revealed the small estuary where the boats were hidden.

Arrived at the place, he whistled on seeing them.

"I see Orlin was a true pirate. Look how much stock he has here. Take that one, but check if it has enough fuel."

It did. As I was steering, I prayed that the slab could be moved on high-tide. I couldn't see why not, for it was on rails, but you never know when the cat you're chasing turns out to be a tiger, goes a saying. It wasn't easy maneuvering among the forward reef and they had to help by covering the sides through the more advanced reef, but once we got closer to the Captain's rock the sea reined in its grief.

"Where is it? I can't see it," Albert yelled. (Hell, I shall call him Albert then!)

"It's not made to be seen," I yelled back. "It's this one here."

I pulled the boat near the slab and jumped out. The

water came up to my chest, but every now and then a swell would wash over my head giving me a taste of the sea. I tried to push the slab but I couldn't as I was being constantly washed away by the waves. Anna jumped behind me, anchored herself to the ground and caught me in her arms to hold me still. It felt good, I tell you, and I wished I could've reciprocated.

"I hope you know what you're doing," she said, as I was pushing.

I didn't. Believe me I didn't. But I didn't say anything. At our second effort the slab moved. Slowly I pushed it all the way back. There was already water inside, but it didn't reach far for it was carved into an inclined path. I towed the boat as far as it would go.

"It's over there," I cried.

He motioned for us to go in front. He opened one chest and I could see his eyes spark at the view of the gold as he dipped his hands in the Captain's stores.

"Finally!" he murmured. "A lifetime of waiting…"

He had us load a chest onto the boat, mentioning that we would later bring the *La Baveuse* around closer to the rock. The chest was heavy and Anna got a large cut on her leg but didn't complain. I pushed the boat out and climbed in it; because of the weight it sunk low in the water. Carefully, I navigated the rough waves, but once in the open, the sea was calm. To get to Marlene's boat, which wasn't visible from there, I had to follow the curved coast.

"So what are you going to do with us," asked Nikki once we were in open waters. "Are you going to leave us here?"

He thought before he answered. "I need help to sail the boat. I will take you all with me and drop you off when I get where I want."

Hunger and greed and evil were oozing from every inch of his face. He could barely contain himself with them. They were seeping out of his squinched eyes and his partially open mouth like mist from the forest on a cool morning. He had one hand on the gun and with the other was curling the tips of his moustache in an attempt to hide the perfidiously victorious grin that was edging out from under it.

And, there on that barque, in that moment, I took charge of my destiny for, there on that barque, in that moment, I understood that he would kill us. He would use and then do to us what his father had done to his sailors. He was his father son. And, so there on that barque, I decided to fight. No better occasion to fight than there in that barque. There wouldn't be another, I knew it. So, what if I died? We all do. It's not why or when or where, but the how. I understood it, you see. I've seen countless people closing their eyes and crossing their hands and waiting for death. I've seen few fight. It is not easy, but listen to me junior: act always like you *know* you will die. Abandon the hope that if you keep your head in the sand you will be shown pity, or that justice will find you at the very last hour. Justice doesn't have eyes or feelings; she has the senses of a predator, and can sense your energy, your will; she preys on them. And she can only do that if you're above the ground and moving. Fight like you know you'll die, and maybe you won't. And if you do, cheer up, you may fly to the Heavens; for cowards don't fly, they sink. Listen to me, and maybe when your time comes, you'll be rewarded.

I looked at those girls, they were scared; so was I. But I was the man and the man should die first, if nothing else. He was made for the job. If even one of them makes it out alive, it would still be a victory for me, I could hear myself thinking.

As I coasted along the shore, *La Baveuse* came in sight. Albert stood up and turned his back on us to look at it. I judged that was the moment.

I brought my index to my lips and I motioned the girls to keep quiet, then passed the tiller to Nikki; I got up and slowly, moved towards him. I figured if I could push him over board we would get away.

But fate wanted for one of my feet to get caught in some rope at the bottom of the boat. Malediction! As I was trying to free myself he felt me and turned around. For a moment he looked puzzled, then he saw my eyes and understood. I shot toward him. He tried to turn the gun on me but another step and I grabbed it.

"Jump!" I yelled to the girls.

They jumped.

I was wrestling for the gun, but he was stronger than I. Much stronger. We were only two hundred yards from *La Baveuse* and the same from the shore at this point, but our boat had slowed down as there was no one to run it. As I was fighting him, I faced the shore and saw movement on the beach. A full figured person was limping toward the edge of the water. Limping fast.

Marlene.

She stopped. She bent down. She pulled something from under her dress. Then she was rooting inside her brassiere. She was trying to fit something inside something else. In the meantime, I was being pushed to my knees. Every muscle was tearing, my every cell screamed fighting for survival. I could see murder in his eyes. That moustache looked ridiculous. Marlene lifted something on her shoulder to eye level. Cemented in place she stood on only one leg. Then I suddenly understood: it was her peg leg she held on her shoulder. The metal leg. The gun in my hands was slowly turning on me. I could almost see inside the dark deepness of the barrel. I was overpowered. I felt when he pulled the trigger and, with a supreme effort I pushed the barrel down. The bullet hit me in under the ribcage on the left side. I felt a sting—that's all. An insidious grin ran across his face. All this happened in the time it takes a star to twinkle once, or you to take a breath. Next, I saw smoke on the beach. I heard the report and I saw something flying at incredible speed towards us.

I didn't understand it then, for it flew faster than my brain works, but I tell it to you now. She had fired at us. A missile. It hit the bow at the waterline. We were blown to bits.

Silence.

I think I was dead for a while there. Luckily I don't breathe when I'm dead. Then I was resurrected. And I tried to breathe. And I panicked. I opened my eyes and I saw a cloud of blood billow in front of me. My blood. Something moving behind it caught my attention. I turned my head and for an instant I looked into a bright, dark eye. It slowly slithered past me and through the swirls of my blood, close, so close that I felt the cold skin of its tail rub against my arm. It went seven yards forward and turned around. Moustache Dick. The arrow, my arrow, there through his snout. I watched him, hypnotized. Eye to eye. He floated there for what seemed like eternity. The built pressure was piercing my ears, but I couldn't move.

Then he bolted at me! Terrible speed. I closed my eyes and waited. Waited… Waited for his teeth… Waited for death! Come to me!

Nothing happened. I opened my eyes. He had swum around and we faced again. Taunting. Ten feet and no more separated us. My own blood floated like a veil between my killer and I. "GO ON!!!" I wanted to cry. I felt that I'd been there for all my life. Like I'd spent eons waiting for him. I just wanted to be free.

I had forgotten I was drowning. He swam closer. He got so close that I couldn't see his eyes. I lost all fear. I reached out and timidly touched his snout. It felt stretched and dry. My fingers drifted backwards onto the spear. I wanted to pull it out, but he suddenly flicked back. He hesitated. Then he jerked! Fast as lighting! Incredible speed, I tell you—but this time I kept my eyes open. He missed me by a foot and I watched his great mass fly in front of my eyes. The current spun me around, and, there on the other side, Moustache Dick opened his colossal jaws and closed them on Albert's chest. He had been struggling a few yards away out of my sight. My last memory of him is his terrified face as he was pulled into the deepness. No! No. My last memory of him is the tips of his moustache tailing behind, waving a final goodbye.

The same shark that almost had him a while back. My shark. Moustache Dick.

With nothing else to do, I, then, gave up and closed my eyes.

Chapter 22

Where I wake up in heaven

Now, I ask you: *Was it whisker envy or was Moustache Dick a justiciary shark?* You judge and give the answer to yourself. Me, I asked myself this question for many years. It doesn't bother me no more.

Nor did it bother me while an angel was kissing me. When an angel kisses you, you don't ask questions—you kiss back. And so I did. But then I started coughing and squirting water through my mouth and nose at the same time. *Is there water in heaven?*

The angel moved away and the light hit my eyes. Blinding light. Heaven is bright, I know. Then the angel slapped me. *Is that allowed in heaven?* I asked myself a little confused.

"Gross!" the angel said.

What kind of language is this? Can you talk like that in heaven?

"Turn him on his side," another voice said.

Something lifted and turned me over. Something very

powerful. My eyes opened and fell upon a wide, bold head, smiling dumbly down at me. The smile was blinding. I felt like I had seen that smile before. *What? Am I in heaven or in hell? And more important—was* that *the angel kissing me?* I lifted my head and saw Nikki and Anna busy wrapping my waist. There was a surgical kit next to me on the table.

"So I think that shark kinda liked you," said Nikki.

Liked me or liked Albert more—a question for the ages.

"He saved you," she continued, nodding to the right. "He freed Marlene and Sigrid. Marlene blew up the boat."

"He" was the bold head smiling at me. "He" was Babar, the goliath. I was lying on the table; the same we'd had our last dinner on. I nodded a thank you to Babar. He showed his huge gold teeth. The bandages on his left shoulder were coming apart, but it didn't seem to bother him when he motioned toward the sea and acted out with his hands and his body something that looked like a shark eating someone with a moustache. I would have not understood, except that my memory was coming back. I nodded "yeah" and smiled, then stood up and checked myself. The bullet had gone through my lower left side—somewhere near the spleen—and exited. I have the scar to this day. One of many.

I stepped down and the pain about broke me in half. I breathed deep and gradually straightened my body. *Wait until my friends at home find out I was shot,* I thought, *I'll be the king of the neighborhood.* They never found out.

Anna smiled at me and suddenly my pain seemed sweet. I would've doubled it to keep that smile alive.

"You were brave," she said.

I was. And lucky. But, as I told you, only the brave are lucky.

I denied it with a modesty that made me worthy of any kingdom in the world, then I asked after the others.

"Marlene is still on the beach resetting her leg, Sigrid is there," she answered.

"Did you know Marlene's leg launched missiles?" I asked incredulous, despite the demonstration.

"Of course. We accompanied her often when she practiced in the ranges."

"She practiced in the ranges?"

"They built that thing for her and the missiles she keeps in her brassier all the time were custom made just for her by some crazy dictator."

"Custom fit to her…?" I tried to ask.

"Yeah, she opened a franchise in his country back in the day that was very popular with the members of his government. Kept their interests focused in the right direction—or that's what he said anyway."

I believed it. A franchise of that kind, stick it anywhere and it'd be guaranteed to keep focused the members of any institution, even the half-dead place I'm stuck in now. I'd make sure of it.

I limped to where Sigrid, both her leg wounds dressed, was sitting, her back against a tree. I felt like I was in charge now.

"It's over," I said to her. "He is dead."

She lifted her head and stared at me. Then her thin lips

widened shyly in a fragile smile. A sad smile. A vulnerable being.

"I'm sorry for Orlin," I said.

She looked down and I could swear I saw a tear drop in the sand between her legs. If it did, it rolled up and sank fast though, because the next moment it wasn't there.

"With Babar you go!"

I froze. That was a voice I had never heard. It sounded like it was coming from a young man's throat, but there wasn't another young man for islands. And I was trying to decide if it was I who spoke or my head was playing tricks on me. I turned around and there was Babar looking straight at me. I returned his straight look right back and I saw him opening his mouth and instead of another smile, the words, "With Babar you go!" came out. The surprise froze me up. I had been sure the man was a mute; he had never spoken a word before. He pointed toward the woods and repeated his phrase. His voice was that of a boy and there was stumbling in it, as of someone who hadn't spoken in a long time.

He turned and took to the trees, "I think he wants us to go with him," I said like a genius. I called the girls and held out my hands to Sigrid. She raised her arm and I helped her. She couldn't stay on her legs and was about to fall when the giant caught and lifted her in his arms like a child. Disgruntled, she grumbled a little, but put her arm around his neck.

The girls showed up and propped me on each side and we were about to leave when Marlene called out, "Where we going?" she asked as she joined us.

"I don't know," I said. "With Babar we go."

And we followed him. An army of invalids leaning on each other, some limping, some hobbling, some swearing, all moaning. Fifty yards later Babar, who had gained some distance, stopped and set Sigrid down. We arrived and saw Sigrid crying over a body. This time she was crying, I tell you. We stood silent.

"I'm sorry I didn't get to know him better," I said.

"Ee was a good man," Marlene added.

Sigrid lifted her head and frowned. "Take him to the boat!" she said. "We have to hurry."

We hesitated.

"You don't want to put eem in ground eer?" Marlene asked. "I seenk ee want zhis."

"He is not dead stupid. He is alive!" answered Sigrid laughing and just then we saw that her tears were tears of joy.

Marlene released a cry and, as expected, fainted. This time the girls ignored her, and letting go of me, rushed to the Captain. Unsupported, I fell on my behind, but still managed to drag myself closer. The Captain, my grandfather, lay on his stomach on a bed of leaves. His head sideways, he was unconscious but you could see the leaves near his mouth moving with his breath. His wound was dressed and chewed leaves poked out from under the bandages. Babar had taken and brought him there after Albert had discarded him in the woods for dead. Had saved his life. Later, as I came to know him better, Babar proved to be the best medicine man I ever met. He knew herbs and plants and the ways to use them, and with a leaf could kill an elephant and with another bring him back. Now, from behind us he was nodding and smiling, happy as a child.

"Thank you," Sigrid said to him.

Every one hastened to thank him and touch him and shake his hands... Not long ago he was our enemy, now he had saved our lives. This life works in the strangest ways, I tell you.

Two days later, the boat of wounded docked in Palau at the hospital quarters. The people there thought we had arrived from a war zone, but as it is not in their habit to ask many questions, we answered few. While we were in the hospital, Marlene and the girls gave an interview to the local television and it was aired all over Asia. It proved to be more of an advertisement for the new franchise she was planning to open in Manila, and she used the girls as bait. Good ol' Marlene! As for the wounded, she insisted that a gigantic marine monster had attacked the boat and would've dragged it under but for the crew who fought heroically. Unsuccessfully the host tried to affirm and prove that the wounds we displayed were made by man-made weapons; she stubbornly held to her monster and almost knocked him out with her prop when he alleged that science is the best lie detector. "Science *mon cul*,"[11] she said. "If I tell you zhat my brassiere 'olds the power of destruction of zhis entire building? Iz zhat science to you?" Dumbfounded, the host stopped insisting, and a new legend of a gargantuan monster that attacks ships from bellow and drags them to the abyss was born that day.

A month later, the Captain was released and we were all there to see him out.

What happened next?

Many things. Most important—I became a pirate and a guardian. Albert's death was attributed to me and I found myself worthy of what was inside the Captain's rock. I was given to Ros Nir to be taught the trade. As for my relationship with Anna, I found out, when I was planning to tell you about it, that my vocabulary is too limited to describe even part of what I experienced. And if I tried, I would just be considered crazy and perverted and probably be thrown out of this place. Suffice to say, it was a beautiful dream.

That brings me to my last point, to the story which will never be told.

I have guarded those riches for decades. I have spent them and I've also accrued them. But what the Captain said to me on the day I found out he was my grandfather proved to be right. "A betrayed treasure is a cursed treasure," he said. I was the one who betrayed it and I was the one guarding it. But I think he was only partially right, for no matter what had happened, the treasure was already cursed. When you think at the sorrow and the tears and the blood it had left behind, you'll understand that the heap of gold laying there in that murky cave was born cursed. And I, its guardian for decades, fought powerful forces that came from everywhere and sometimes from nowhere to lift my curse and set me free. I have defeated many enemies, I have lost many loved ones, I have sacrificed my life to it. I've been attacked and I've been betrayed, many I have shattered and destroyed… and now, now I'm here and they… they're not far. I can feel their presence. I know these things. Give me a bottle of liquor and a pinch of tobacco and by God let them come! Let them come!

My mission has ended. To hell with you, I'm ready to live again!

Rose's addendum

I don't know what to make of this. I don't know if I'll ever see a penny for my efforts. Should I beg justice and search amends there is only God I could beseech for on a stormy night, as sudden as his entrance was and as blusterous as he made his presence known, the old man has vanished.

I was on the night shift. As nothing ever happens during the night shift. I took the time to set down on paper the old man's blabber. The rain was beating down the glass of the windows and the wind played unearthly songs around the building's corners and in the folds of the bricks, when I heard a big ruckus coming from the second floor where he was lodged. At first I thought a hallway window must've been blown open, but then I heard voices. Bawling and cursing. Horrible cursing like only he was capable. I set my pen aside and rushed to the place. As I arrived at the head of the second floor's stair I saw, down the hallway, his door wide open. Before I could make another step I heard him cursing again, this time his voice weaker, as it would be if he was struggling, then the sound of broken glass, and silence.

When I arrived the room was empty. He was gone. The window was broken and wide, and there on the carpet, in a pool of blood, lay his broken recorder with the last of his words on it as I have inscribed them.

Make of it what you will.

Acknowledgments

This book wouldn't exist were it not for my wife and Japan.

Anna provided me with the occasion. She then spent countless hours of hard work editing it—only to have to work as hard (or more) forcing me to rewrite; for, I am as stubborn and ornery as an old mule. And, without her help my life would be just a field barren of grass and flowers and trees and everything that makes a field a field. A desert, I mean.

Japan is where the book was conceived and this would have not been possible without the support and kindness of the wonderful people of Higashiyoshino and Kawakami-mura in Nara-ken. I was afraid that I would never be able to express my gratitude and this is just a small attempt. Thank you! I love you!

And I would like to thank you, the reader, for putting up with this cranky pirate. I know it wasn't easy; I myself cursed him to hell a few times. Does he have to be so crabby and rude? He said, "Yes." ...So there you have it!

www.ingramcontent.com/pod-product-compliance
Lightning Source LLC
Chambersburg PA
CBHW031118210626
46816CB00016B/1685